ALMOST PERFECT

Visit us at www.boldstrokesbooks.com

By the Author

Visiting Hours

Bird on a Wire

Across the Dark Horizon

And Then There Was Her

Queen of Humboldt

Swipe Right

Two Knights Tango

Almost Perfect

ALMOST PERFECT

by

Tagan Shepard

2022

ALMOST PERFECT
© 2022 By Tagan Shepard. All Rights Reserved.

ISBN 13: 978-1-63679-322-1

This Trade Paperback Original Is Published By
Bold Strokes Books, Inc.
P.O. Box 249
Valley Falls, NY 12185

First Edition: November 2022

Credits
Editors: Ashley Tillman and Cindy Cresap
Production Design: Susan Ramundo
Cover Design By Jeanine Henning

Acknowledgments

This book represents a massive shift in my career. It was scary and hard and the best decision I've ever made.

Thank you to Luc, Amanda, and Celeste for giving me advice and strength. Thanks to Kris for guiding me in this journey and making me feel safe in the face of change.

Thank you to Sandy and Rad for taking a chance on me. I'm so proud to be a part of the BSB family.

Thank you to Ashley for making me laugh and making me think and nerding out about Buffy with me. What an amazing experience having you edit this book.

Thanks to Kate and Cade for always being the best writing friends anyone could ask for.

Always and forever, to my incredible wife. Cris, you are the stuff dreams are made of. I could never do any of this without you.

Dedication

For all the fans who changed the world

CHAPTER ONE

This is going to be the best day of our lives."

"We're twelve years old, Chelsea, that's not exactly a high bar."

Olivia couldn't help but agree with her little sister's best friend, Lewis. She knew better than to let Chelsea see her smile, though, so she turned back to the stew she'd been stirring and let them work it out.

"It doesn't matter if it's a high bar, it's a bar we're crossing today." Chelsea held her chin high while she spoke, Olivia could tell by the sound of her voice. "Today is gonna be the best, isn't it, Liv?"

"It sure is," she said. When she saw Lewis's expression slip, she decided to play peacemaker. "Not just for you two. For me, too. My bar is a little bit higher than y'all's though."

It wasn't a ringing endorsement of Lewis's smugness, but it was enough for them both to let it go. They went back to packing their most prized possessions into their huge backpacks, making sure nothing wrinkled, rubbed, or chipped anything else. It was easier said than done. Chelsea and Lewis were the kind of kids who carried adult, oversized backpacks to school.

While most of their peers preferred tablets and school-issued laptops, Chelsea and Lewis liked the physicality of paper books and writing with ink pens. Today the extra space their eccentricity required came in handy not for a studying emergency, but because the only thing they loved more than watching *Midtown Avengers* was spending every penny of their allowances on *Midtown Avengers* merchandise. They had action figures, trading cards, and posters, all ready to show off or have signed. Olivia had only just managed to convince them that bringing along their bobbleheads would risk too much damage.

"Liv, can we go now?" Lewis whined. "Please?"

Olivia checked her watch again, wondering how her mother had managed to stretch her coffee date so late into the morning. Her mom's boyfriend, Rick, wasn't the type to linger over conversation and though her mother had taken a long weekend from work to allow her kids time for the convention, Rick should've been into the office at nine.

"Soon, Lewis, I promise. We have to wait for Allison to get home, but we'll be there in time for the doors opening. I promise."

She turned back to the stew pot so the kids didn't see her frown. Hope that's a promise I can keep, she thought.

If there was one thing Olivia had learned in her twenty-seven years of life, it was that her mother may be full of love, but she wasn't exactly full of adult levels of responsibility. Most of the time it didn't bother Olivia. She'd definitely signed up to help out and coparent her little sister, but today she wanted to have that same unbridled enthusiasm she saw in Chelsea and Lewis. Instead, she was simmering chicken stew for her mother and grandfather's lunch, hoping she wouldn't miss out on the con because her mother had forgotten she was taking care of Poppa for the weekend.

Just as her disappointment bubbled to the surface like the stew in front of her, the townhouse's front door crashed open and her mother rushed in, purse sliding off her shoulder in her rush to shut the door behind her.

"Sorry." Allison panted. "I'm here. Sorry."

She skidded across the tile entryway, her sky-high heels catching in a grout line and her thighs, held frozen together by her skin-tight skirt, struggled to keep her upright. Catching herself just in time, she stood back up to her impressive height and huffed a sigh of relief, sending a single brunette curl fluttering in front of her eyes. Olivia watched her with a laugh, checking her own hair in the mirrored surface of the microwave. She'd inherited her mother's rich brown curls and fortunately, her morning hunched over a pot hadn't made them frizz.

"You look beautiful, darling," Allison said, hopping into the kitchen as she wrenched one of her heels off. "You're a knockout."

"Thanks, Mom," Olivia said. She kissed her mother on the cheek and handed her the wooden spoon. "It could use another twenty or thirty minutes. Don't salt it too much. You know Poppa's supposed to cut his sodium intake."

Her mother's hand froze on the way to the salt cellar and she rolled her eyes. "I can take care of my own father, you know."

"I know you can." Olivia shared a smile and a shake of the head with Chelsea. "You two will have a great afternoon together."

"When will you be home?"

"I promised Mrs. Cole I'd have Lewis home by the time her shift ends. Plus they'll need dinner. Maybe sixish?"

"No," Chelsea and Lewis shouted together. Chelsea held her best friend's hand and continued, "The main floor doesn't close until seven and there are panels and workshops and all sorts of stuff."

"There are three days of events." Olivia grabbed her keys. "I promise we'll get to see everything, even if we come home for dinner every night."

Lewis and Chelsea shared a look that turned Olivia's blood cold, but they agreed in unison that this day could end when Olivia said it would. Before they could make any more schemes, she shouted a good-bye to her grandfather and shuffled the kids out to her car.

Riley St. James had only ever been in a limo once before in her life. Her high school boyfriend had rented one for winter formal, thinking she'd be impressed. She had been impressed enough to keep dating him until sophomore homecoming even though she suspected she was a lesbian even then. That limo had smelled like teenage boy and spilled beer.

This limo was far nicer than the one from high school. First of all, it was driven by a gorgeous white woman whose deep brown hair reflected the golden rays of the Western Florida sun perfectly. With a wink, she ushered Riley into the passenger compartment where the biggest gift basket she'd ever seen rested on the bench seat. Riley bit into a pear that leaked juice down her chin as they pulled away from the curb. She was tempted to crack open the bottle of champagne tucked inside the basket, but she was technically working, so she forced herself to wait. If this was the car QueerCon had sent to retrieve her from the airport, her hotel room would certainly be worth savoring.

The drive to the convention center took a half hour thanks to heavy lunchtime traffic, but Riley sat back and enjoyed every moment of it. The Tampa skyline had nothing on Miami, but at least they were different skyscrapers twinkling against the pure blue sky. The tinted windows meant passersby filling the sidewalks gaped, unable to see that the person inside was far from a celebrity. Riley sat back in the plush leather seats and soaked it all in. The wining-and-dining would surely wither away once the actors and showrunners started arriving, but for now she was a star.

"Riley St. James, such a pleasure to meet you."

A pale blonde in her early twenties with a hoop nose ring and clipboard clutched against her chest pulled the limo's door open, letting in a blast of summer heat. Riley climbed from the limo.

"I'm Heather." The woman held out her hand. As Riley shook it, Heather continued, "Welcome to QueerCon. We're so honored to have you."

"Thanks," Riley said. "It's great to be here."

"Can't tell you how happy we are to have an influencer of your caliber here for our inaugural con."

Riley winced at the term "influencer" but fought the instinct to correct her. Heather seemed sweet.

"Why don't we get inside? You have a base tan, but this," Heather indicated her pale cheek. "Does not do well in the sun."

"I had the same problem when I moved to Miami. I grew up in Upstate New York and I burned like a lobster my first few summers."

Her driver gave another wink and Riley's cheeks burned. She averted her gaze as soon as politeness would allow. When Heather marched into the hotel lobby, Riley was right on her heels.

"How long have you been in Miami?" Heather asked as they wove their way through the milling crowd.

Once or twice, Riley caught a gasp and her own name whispered in a strange voice. She tried to act casual as she focused on Heather, hoping everyone thought she was too distracted to hear her own name, not that she was snobbish.

"Almost ten years," Riley said, the words surprising her. "I hadn't realized it was that long."

"It's a cool place to live. Not like Virginia. That's where I'm from, and not the beach side, the mountain side. Right this way." Heather led her through a door that held a "Con Personnel Only" sign and the babble of the crowd dimmed as it closed. They were in a less flashy area of the hotel, maybe an employee corridor, for a few minutes before emerging into a smaller lobby surrounded by meeting rooms. Each of the rooms were set up with comfortable furniture and tables full of snacks. There were fewer people here and most of them wore the bright green T-shirts of the con staff.

"These are the VIP Green Rooms." Heather turned to her with a sheepish smile. "We couldn't get one of the bigger convention centers that has a smaller ballroom for the purpose. We had to settle with the meeting rooms since it's our first year."

"It's cool," Riley said. She caught sight of someone she thought might be Dot-Marie Jones, but she was shuffled through a door at the far end of the hall before she could be sure. "It's my first year, too. I've never been to a convention."

"What? Seriously? None of them?"

"Nope." Riley stuffed her hands into her pockets and hoped she looked casual.

"Sorry, I'm just shocked. I mean, you're so popular. I'd thought you'd want to meet all your fans."

"I did, but I guess I wasn't important enough for the other cons. None of them would spring for the hotel room or airfare or anything and an internet journalist doesn't make that much money." Too late she realized Heather might've been offended by the thought she'd tried other organizations first. "It's not like I'm a real celebrity. I mean I'm not an actor or anything."

"Well, you'll find we're not like the other cons," Heather said with a distinct air of pride. "We focus on every layer of queer entertainment and the folks who report on it are huge for us."

Riley knew it was Heather's job to butter her up, but she couldn't help feel a little special. Heather ushered her into one of the rooms and showed her around. Apart from the QueerCon staff, she was introduced to an actress who'd played a bit part on a really good web series and two writers for *Wynonna Earp*. Heather left her to settle in and, after a quick stop at the snack table, Riley made straight for the writers. Apart from the chance to make a contact or two, it spared her from talking to the actress who, while eager, hadn't wowed Riley with her acting skills.

It took a while for the writers to warm up, but after downing a Mountain Dew each, Riley finally got them to talk about life in a writers' room. As she suspected, both had glowing praise for their showrunner and the open, creative vibe she'd created on set. Far too soon, they both left for their first panel and Riley forced herself not ask them to look over her scripts. She was sure they'd spend all weekend inundated with requests to help people break into the industry and she didn't want to be the first person to pester them. Besides, she had scheduled a one-on-one with a prominent agent for Sunday. If she could sign with him this weekend, she'd be the one all the up-and-comers would cozy up to next year.

Instead, she yanked her phone out of her pocket, shuffling through screens in her usual order. Her first stop was Twitter, where she discovered a slight uptick in followers since the morning. That was a good sign. She'd probably crack 80,000 followers by the time her first panel ended at this rate. Sure, she didn't have the numbers some of the A-listers here could brag about, but it was a respectable enough number. She'd already added the number to the query letter she intended to send out with her spec scripts as she shopped for agents.

"If I can ever get up the nerve," she said to herself as she switched over to Instagram.

She noticed a drop of three followers on TikTok, but couldn't blame them. She still hadn't mastered the platform. Her Facebook numbers were holding steady, but sooner or later folks would figure out she was using a bot to keep her posts coming. Riley dropped her phone onto the table screen-up so she could keep an eye on notifications, then ripped a cookie in half and tried to use the methodical movement of her jaw to calm her nerves.

"Hey, Riley." Heather returned looking only slightly more flustered than when she'd left. "Sorry I was gone so long. Settling in?"

"Totally. Snacks are great, but I'd kill for a cappuccino."

"No espresso maker back here, I'm afraid. There's a coffee bar on the main floor if you want to grab something after your first panel." She checked her watch and then her clipboard. "In fact, we have to get you over to that, but you have a two-hour break before the second. Why don't you check out the main floor in between? Besides coffee, you'll find all the vendors down there and booths for all the shows with cast and crew in attendance. You'll probably run into a lot of fans. Might be a good way to get your QueerCon experience rolling."

With one last look over her shoulder at the actress, who was now heavily engrossed in the phone screen inches from her nose, Riley followed Heather to her first ever convention panel.

CHAPTER TWO

Chelsea and Lewis ran so quickly and so close that their badges clacked into each other with every other step. Olivia hurried to keep up with them, just as excited but better able to hide her glee. She had fifteen years on her little sister and those extra years had taught her that unbridled joy was too often a target for cruel peers. Once they passed through the bank of open doors leading to QueerCon's main floor, she abandoned all her reticence.

Olivia had never seen so many people that made her feel at home in her own skin. Everyone was so happy the place looked like one big smile. People were hurrying between booths, pointing at displays and clutching purchases like they were all the One Ring. Half the crowd was in cosplay, and Olivia noticed at least a dozen women cosplaying Flame Fingers, her favorite character from her favorite show.

Lewis skidded to a halt as the main floor lay out before him.

"We're here," he whispered.

Chelsea pulled their joined hands to her chest, nearly yanking Lewis off his feet. "Yes, we are. We're really here." She turned back to flash that delighted smile at Olivia.

"You two need a minute before we go in?" Olivia asked.

Lewis whipped around to stare incredulously at her. "And waste a minute of time we could spend at the *Midtown Avengers* booth? Have you gone completely bonkers?"

"Careful there, kid. I'm your ride home."

"Threatening to leave me at the most wonderful place on the planet isn't going work. I'm already planning how Chelsea and I can shake you to hide out overnight."

Olivia laughed, but when Chelsea poked him in the ribs, she started to wonder if it was a joke after all. She decided drastic measures were necessary. Gripping each of them by the shoulder, she walked in the middle to keep them from plotting as they marched into the crowd.

The main floor would've been intimidating even if it wasn't Olivia's first time at an event like this. The crushing crowd was clearly antsy and kept bumping into all three of them. Some of the bulkier cosplay outfits made the claustrophobic atmosphere even worse. But nothing could dampen the kids' excitement.

"We should be in cosplay. Why didn't we think of that?" Lewis asked.

"I don't know if I could pull it off," Chelsea said, staring at a Harrow the Ninth cosplayer in full black body suit, bone corset, and meticulous face paint.

"I could," Lewis declared. Then he'd deflated and said, "If I could make a costume."

"You totally could." Olivia patted his shoulder. "You can do anything."

He shrugged in reply, but she was sure she caught the hint of a smile.

"Where to first?" Olivia asked.

"Let's take this slow," Chelsea said, pushing her shoulders back with her usual confidence.

The ballroom was set up with countless small booths, arranged in neat rows and separated from each other with short walls or racks of merchandise.

The first row of booths were mostly artists selling their fan art. Olivia recognized a few folks by their Twitter and Instagram handles. She wasn't quite brave enough to think of herself as one of them, but she envied their chance to show off and sell their work. Maybe next year Olivia would work up the nerve to rent a booth for her own fan art. It wasn't like any of the artists were being ignored. A few of the tables were better attended than others, but for the most part the crowd spread their love around. Olivia gave herself a second to wonder what it would be like to watch someone fall in love with one of her drawings, but there was far too much to see for them to linger too long anywhere.

The kids led Olivia into the second row. Most of the big publishers of queer fiction had booths here. Individual authors, including many who were self-published, were scattered between the bigger booths. She made a mental note to come back and browse the books for sale, but she wanted to wait until she had the chance to meet her favorite authors. Hopefully, some of the bigger names would trickle in as the weekend went on.

After the publishers were booths selling comic books, collectibles, and memorabilia. There were a few things that caught Olivia's eye, but her walls were too full to accommodate anything more. Chelsea didn't seem to have the same concerns, because she sprinted in that direction, Lewis at her heels. Olivia followed at a more leisurely pace, taking in as much as she could.

Looking around at the crowd, Olivia tried to remember the last time she'd been among a group of people like this. With shared passions and relaxed joy. As she strolled through the aisle in her sister's wake, she took a deep, contented sigh.

"Cool, isn't it?"

Turning toward the voice, Olivia saw a woman about her age with a cute blond pixie cut. She was waiting in the short line for an independent filmmaker's booth, her arms full of bulging shopping bags.

"Which part?" Olivia laughed.

"Being around so many gay people," the woman said. Her eyes roamed the crowd. "I don't think I've ever been around so many gay people in my whole life."

Olivia had stopped going to the overly commercialized Pride parade years ago and had been too nervous to go to gay bars since the Pulse nightclub shooting. She had a few queer friends, of course, but most of her world was firmly, unswervingly straight.

"If I have," she said, "It's been a long time."

The woman nodded and shrugged, drawing in a lungful of air. "I feel like I can take a deep breath in this crowd, you know? Feel normal for a day or two."

Olivia gave it a try, sucking in a deep breath. She let it out with a joyful puff of laughter. "You know what? You're totally right. It is really cool."

Olivia continued into the crowd, testing out her newfound deep breathing. With each step—each asymmetric haircut and same-sex couple holding hands—she felt more relaxed. More herself.

Maybe Chelsea was right, she thought. Maybe this would be the best day of their lives.

Riley's first panel couldn't have gone any better. She had been paired with three other online journalists, two from queer websites and one who ran an incredibly popular YouTube channel. They'd discussed the various ways they all engaged with fans and whether their content was dictated by engagement.

They'd all lied their asses off, of course. The writers insisted their editors would never let outside pressure drive their stories, but it was clear to see the ways they catered to both advertisers and studios. The YouTuber had dodged, talking about his latest videos and teasing future installments any time a tough question came his way. Riley had insisted she didn't need to cater to her fans because they shared the same obsessions. It had been the crowd's obvious favorite response.

She spent ten minutes sitting on the edge of the stage, chatting with the audience before she slipped away. Her sluggish brain still needed a cappuccino and she thought she'd earned a chance to scope out the event. So she left the panel rooms behind and followed her handler toward the big attraction.

The main floor wasn't far. The rumble of noise Riley had taken for traffic was in fact the roar of a thousand excited voices contained in one massive ballroom. Heather gave her a brief rundown of the layout and left Riley to explore.

She moved through the first few rows quickly, not stopping until she saw a table selling *Buffy the Vampire Slayer* collectibles in the fourth row. She'd been a fan for ages so she browsed but didn't buy. Passing out of the vendors, Riley found herself in a much busier section. The people here were all crowded around booths larger and more professionally decorated than the vendor tables. Lifesize cutouts and posters covered with bright slashes of color provided backdrops and sound effects and theme music competed with the roar of voices. These were the booths for the biggest queer shows currently on TV, streaming, and filling the web. Studios paid a premium to get the most eyeballs from the biggest fans and QueerCon was clearly a destination for a lot of them. Riley didn't see any of the actors, but she couldn't get close enough to any of the studio booths to really see well.

The brightest and flashiest of the bunch was, of course, the booth for *Midtown Avengers*. Riley rolled her eyes as the theme music played through poorly adjusted speakers. Poppy and obnoxiously repetitive, the theme song alone was enough to make her cringe.

The poster art for *Midtown Avengers*, or Middies as the fans called both the show and themselves, was an homage to the comic book that had started the story. The Avengers themselves had been guest stars in a brief story arc for another Marvel Comics character. By the end of the run, people were clamoring for more, but Marvel Studios wasn't interested. They sold the rights to a tiny studio out of Canada, the home of most American queer entertainment, and the rest was history.

"Excuse me, aren't you Riley St. James?" a timid, muffled voice asked from over Riley's shoulder.

She applied the widest smile she could manage for strangers and turned to find Captain Marvel grinning at her.

"Sure am," Riley said, considering a handshake but opting for finger guns instead. "Aren't you Carol Danvers?"

Captain Marvel laughed, and it was a snorting, frenetic sound nothing like Brie Larson's. This Captain Marvel was also six inches shorter than Brie and Black, with skin the rich color of tiger's eye. The strangeness of her laugh made Riley smile and put her at ease.

"Carol yes, but not Danvers."

"Nice to meet you, Carol."

Riley held out her hand at last, but Carol pulled her into a rib-cracking hug instead. She pulled back at the small sound of surprise her hug shook out of Riley, her eyes full of mingled regret and excitement.

"I'm sorry. Geez. I shouldn't have done that. I'm really sorry."

"It's totally fine, Carol. I'm excited to be here, too."

"It's the greatest, isn't it?" Carol looked around, her earth-brown eyes glowing as they skittered from booth to booth, face to face. "It's my seventh Con. Well, my first QueerCon of course, but I've been to all the others."

Before Riley could stop her, she started listing off all the conventions she'd been to and where they'd been held. Not just the general conventions either, but some for specific shows. She was clearly in her element, but her jubilance didn't make Riley feel out of place. Rather, it made her feel like part of an experience she couldn't have anywhere else.

Carol's Captain Marvel suit had a rainbow star in the center of her chest rather than the original gold. It was far from the only rainbow adornment Riley could see. Nearly everyone had a flag, pin, scarf, or wheelchair spoke guards proclaiming their sexuality. The badges everyone wore, including the one Heather had handed Riley back in the Green Room, included colorful pronoun pins. Queer couples held hands everywhere she looked. A nearby male-female couple included one partner sporting the pink, purple, and blue of the bisexual pride flag. Even living in Miami, Riley had never seen so much obvious queerness in one place.

"Sorry. I'm talking your ear off. I'm such a nerd." Carol sputtered to a stop.

"First of all, you're no more a nerd than I am, and second, you have to stop apologizing. You're the first fan I've met. It's the coolest."

"You'll meet a ton more while you're here." Carol met Riley's eyes with a weak smile. "Do you think I could get a selfie?"

"Totally."

Riley snatched her phone and took several shots of them together making funny faces. Before Carol could hurry off, Riley made her promise to share the pics on social media and tag her. Carol promised she would and Riley made her way across the hall, away from the garish booth for *Midtown Avengers* and, she hoped, toward the coffee bar Heather had promised.

CHAPTER THREE

The kids had shown remarkable patience, but Olivia could see it was wearing thin. After making their obligatory tour of the rest of the main floor, they turned to each other and gave synchronized nods. Then they turned back to the crowd and bolted toward the back wall of the ballroom, heading for their whole reason for coming to QueerCon.

The *Midtown Avengers* booth was their one and only destination for the morning. They'd memorized the panel schedule and none of them had any events until after lunch. It was a good thing they'd cleared their schedules because the booth was easily the most popular of the room. There wasn't exactly a line to wait in, more like a scrum that oozed forward as each fan reluctantly moved on. Olivia gathered them into the back of it and found, to her surprise, they were moving forward at a good clip. Still, after twenty minutes of waiting, the novelty had worn off and she was so thirsty she couldn't stand it.

"Hey, Chels? Lewis? Would you two be okay if I stepped out of line to grab a drink?"

"We can't let you back in," Lewis said importantly. "That would be cutting."

"It's cool," a woman in Flame Fingers cosplay said from over Olivia's shoulder. "I don't mind."

"Oh, no. Thank you, but I'll wait for them by the snack bar." She turned back to her sister. "Can you behave here alone?"

"Of course I can," Chelsea said. "I'm not a kid. And how come you didn't ask Lewis?"

"'Cause I'm better behaved than you. Obviously," Lewis said.

"Sure," Olivia said, certain her plan had worked. Those two were the best of friends, but they were also as competitive as siblings. If Chelsea thought Olivia trusted Lewis and not her, she'd go out of her way to be a picture of maturity. Lewis would see how she was acting and try to be even better behaved just to prove Olivia right. "Thanks, you two."

As she walked away, Olivia saw Chelsea raise her hand to smack Lewis's shoulder over his comment. Then she lowered it and crossed her hands in front of her, straightening her posture for good measure. Lewis, who had already braced for impact, screwed up his eyebrows at her restraint and crossed his own hands in front of him. A cheer went up from the group already at the table and Olivia watched the two kids vibrate with repressed excitement, but they didn't move, only smiled at each other and clutched at the hems of their Middies shirts.

The line at the snack bar was much shorter than the Middies' booth line and moved much faster than the coffee bar line right next to it. She got her sparkling water in record time and bought a pair of water bottles for the kids, shoving them into her bag. Leaning against the wall next to the coffee bar, she could just see through the crowd to where her sister waited patiently in line, so she settled back and pulled out her phone. While she sipped her water, she scrolled through her news feed, stopping on every picture of QueerCon that came up.

"All the bright, shiny displays in here and you're looking at your phone?" The voice was deliciously husky and came with a teasing edge of flirting. That alone was enough to make Olivia look up, and the sight that greeted her made her instantly happy she had. The woman standing in front of her, a half-smile lifting the left side of her face, was possibly the most alluring person she'd ever seen.

Her blond hair was so short on the sides Olivia could see the change from her richly tanned temples to the pale white beneath. The rest was pulled up into a tidy quiff. The style lengthened her face, accentuating her tall forehead and rounded jaw. Her cheeks and the point of her nose were round as well, bordered by deep smile lines and a shallow dimple on one side. It was a perfectly androgynous face, just the type Olivia preferred.

Her handsome face wasn't what caught her attention, though. The feature that made her nearly choke on her drink, were the woman's eyes. To call them blue would be an injustice. They were a deep, vivid blue that looked like they went on forever. They sparkled with the hint of laughter, but there was a rigidity to them that begged Olivia to meet this woman and know her from the inside out and back again. They were also very familiar eyes.

After a long moment, the blonde's smile deepened and she turned to look over her shoulder. "Is there someone cool behind me?" Looking back, her face fell in mock horror, the twinkle never leaving her eyes. "Oh, my God, is there mustard on my chin?"

"No. It's just—you're Riley St. James."

"I've heard of her," Riley said, stepping forward to let a large group press through the door behind her. The movement had the added benefit of moving her another step closer to Olivia. Close enough to bring a hint of her cologne, a musky, rich scent as androgynous as the woman herself. "Never seen her in the wild though."

"You can't miss her," Olivia said, warming to the banter. "She's blond, perfect tan, gray skinny jeans, a pale blue shirt that really sets off her eyes."

"Huh, I have a shirt like that. And those pants."

"Then I have a secret to tell you," Olivia leaned close enough to hear Riley swallow hard and watch the edge of her smile falter. "Riley St. James got into your pants."

Riley gave a chuckle that rumbled through her chest like thunder and sent Olivia's heart rate up twenty points. "I have a secret, too," she said. "I don't think I can keep this going. I'm so bad at this flirting thing."

"Spoiler alert, you really aren't," Olivia said.

A moment stretched between them and Olivia held perfectly still, afraid to blink and break the spell. It had been years since she'd met anyone who made her fingers tingle and her mouth water like that. She wanted to hold onto the feeling as long as she could.

In the end, Olivia broke the moment first. Even though she knew Riley was way out of her league, there was a look in those eyes that was halfway between hunter and terrified prey. She took a step back and held out her hand. "Olivia Duran. I'm a really big fan. I read everything you write."

"Not my diary I hope." Riley shook her hand. Her palm was soft and her shake firm.

"Do people even keep diaries anymore?"

"My therapist says journaling is a very useful tool."

"Oh, God. I'm so sorry. I'm such a jerk. I didn't mean that."

"I'm teasing," Riley said. "I mean, yes, my therapist said that, but I'm not offended."

The laughter and the glint in Riley's eyes didn't keep the creeping flush of embarrassment from Olivia's neck and cheeks. "I shouldn't have said that. It was really stupid."

"It's okay, Olivia," she said and Olivia liked the sound of her own name on Riley's lips. She caressed the syllables, the tip of her tongue flicking against her teeth for the l and her lips wrapping around the i's. "But if you really want to make up for it, you can let me buy you a drink at the opening night party?"

There was a hopeful, almost pleading lilt to the question that seemed so at odds with Riley's confidence. For a heartbeat Olivia was desperate to say yes, but she knew she couldn't. "I'm not going to the party. I have to have my little sister and her bestie home by six."

"That's too bad." Riley looked like she might turn to leave, but then she looked at the toes of her shoes and said, "There's plenty of time for me to buy you lunch, though."

"Are you—never mind."

Riley looked up, the pleading had reached her eyes. "What?"

Olivia considered playing coy, but it didn't matter either way, so she decided to tell the truth. "I thought for a minute you were asking me on a date, but you're so far out of my league the Waverider couldn't even help."

Truth had definitely been the right choice because Riley's entire aspect changed. She straightened her back and the crooked smile was back and just as devastating as ever. She leaned in, resting her forearm against the wall beside Olivia's shoulder and said, "Does Captain Lance know you stole her ship? 'Cause I am asking you on a date."

Olivia was pinned to the wall by those sapphire eyes inches from her own. She couldn't speak or move, only stare into the swirling blue depths. They weren't gemstones, they weren't nearly that cold or solid. They were the depths of the ocean, sinking below the waves into the deep chasm of her pupils.

Just as she opened her lips to say yes, a cannon ball slammed into her.

"Oh, my gosh, Liv." Chelsea squealed. "You should've seen it. They have posters and they're giving them away for free."

"Give her some air, geez," Lewis said.

Catching her breath as Chelsea looked up with a toothy grin, Olivia noticed Riley take a few steps back. At least she didn't leave. Chelsea's face was so animated, Olivia couldn't help forgive her terrible timing. She caught Riley's eye as Chelsea and Lewis prattled on about everything they'd seen and heard and done at the *Midtown Avengers* booth.

"As you can see, I have two lunch dates already."

Chelsea, her story spent and her excitement returning to its normal twelve-year-old level, turned to stare at Riley. "She's that blogger you think is hot."

The heat returned to Olivia's cheeks and she grabbed Chelsea's shoulder tight enough to earn a squeak of displeasure. "She's not a blogger, she's a journalist."

"I'm both." Riley's smile only faltered for a moment. She held out her hand and said, "Riley St. James."

"Chelsea Duran-Spencer." Chelsea shook the offered hand. "This is Lewis, my best friend."

Lewis shrugged after shaking Riley's hand. "Never heard of you."

"You're not exactly her target audience," Chelsea said, making them both waggle their eyebrows.

"Okay," Olivia said, pushing Chelsea toward the other troublemaker so she could face Riley. "I'll just get these two out of here before they really embarrass me."

She turned, following her sister who, without realizing what she'd interrupted, was hopping off toward the snack bar. She forced herself not to look back. Not to see Riley's relief for the bullet she'd dodged. Before she could take a full step, that soft palm touched her again, this time on her bare forearm, making the whole right side of her body tingle.

"What about tomorrow?" Riley asked. "Have lunch with me tomorrow?"

Not trusting her ability to speak in coherent sentences, Olivia applied her widest smile and nodded. Riley's response was equally nonverbal, just a puff of laughter that sounded like she'd been holding her breath. When she let go of Olivia's forearm, she shoved her hand into her back pocket and backed away, nearly colliding with the doorframe.

"DM me?" Riley asked.

"Okay, sure."

At an insistent call from Chelsea, Olivia finally tore her eyes away from Riley and headed back into the crowd.

CHAPTER FOUR

When Heather collected her, Riley was still catching her breath from the conversation with Olivia. It was perhaps the first time in her life she'd successfully asked a woman on a date. It was perhaps the first time in her life when she'd successfully talked to a woman. She had never been one of those masc women who flirted well.

"Not until today, apparently," she said under her breath.

"What was that?" Heather asked, her eager face turning to Riley.

"Nothing. Just talking to myself."

"I do that all the time." They turned down a corridor lined with conference attendees. "Are you nervous? This is your first time on a show-specific panel, right?"

"Yeah, but I'm not nervous." More like annoyed.

"Good. No need to be. You'll be the hit of this one." Heather tapped a nail covered in chipped black nail polish against her clipboard. "*Midtown Avengers* Through the Media Lens. You won't be the only one on the panel who recaps Middies episodes, but you're the most popular by far."

"Cool," Riley said, trying to inject some enthusiasm into her words.

Middies had made her famous on a different level than her past episode recapping, but her big secret was she hated the show. Her recaps were more than an overview of the plot lines of each episode. They were soaked in sarcasm that gave her many jokes a sharp edge.

Her fans took the tone as teasing—like someone making fun of their favorite sibling. Like most sibling teasing, however, there was a note of honesty in Riley's venom.

The truth was Riley had disliked the show when it first came out. She was the only full-time recapper on Gayntertainment's staff, so she had no choice but to cover it. Over the last four seasons, she had grown to hate it. She just didn't see the appeal. Superheroes were overdone and Middies specifically felt like a rip-off of both the Marvel Universe movies and *Legends of Tomorrow*.

And honestly, if you're ripping off a network show in the age of Netflix and Hulu are you really doing anything right?

The farther along the corridor they traveled, the thicker the crowds became until Riley was finally able to see the crush was really just one, densely populated line. There were enough Flame Finger and Mind Bender cosplayers for her to guess what the line was for.

"Yep," Heather said, noticing her attention. "These are folks waiting for your panel. Isn't that cool? It'll be standing room only."

"Cool," Riley said again, realizing she sounded like an inarticulate idiot, but what else was there to say? She just had to grit her teeth and smile through this for her career's sake.

Riley held her forced smile in place as she greeted a few of the fans at the front of the line while Heather unlocked the door. It seemed like about half knew who she was and the other half couldn't care less. She liked the odds. As they headed into the room, she caught a flash of dark brown curls, but didn't have time to check and see if it was Olivia before Heather ushered her into the room.

The other panelists were already in place, leaving Riley to play catch-up on introductions. The panel was moderated by a YouTuber who hosted a popular series on queer entertainment and gushed nonstop about Middies on their show. They were just as exuberant in person as they were on their channel and Riley forced herself not to roll her eyes. The panel was filled out by another journalist, an acquaintance of Riley's who worked for BuzzFeed, the preeminent Middies fan fic author, and a blogger in her fifties who seemed to be teetering on the edge of hysteria.

"Isn't this so amazing?" the blogger gushed as Riley sat down next to her. "We're on stage, talking about Middies. It's incredible."

"Sure is," Riley said, wishing she'd arrived earlier so she could've taken any other seat. "Have you ever done one of these before?"

"Oh, yeah, I went to ClexaCon last year and we had the same panel there. Minus you, of course. So happy you could make it to QueerCon. I love your recaps."

"Thanks, that's very kind of you." Riley changed the subject so she wouldn't have to admit she'd never read the woman's blog. "I was hoping one of the actors would be on the panel. We would've pulled a much bigger crowd."

"That would be an absolute dream. Have you met any of them?"

"Not in person, but I did a phone interview with Matthew Barnes earlier this year."

To her horror, the blogger turned her chair so they were facing each other, so close their knees were almost touching. "He's my absolute favorite. I'm just so pleased the studio hired an actor with cerebral palsy to play the character. It infuriates me when able-bodied actors are hired to play disabled characters. Don't you agree?"

The rest of their conversation followed in much the same manner, with the blogger, whose name Riley struggled to remember, stating her opinions and insisting Riley agreed with her. She did agree with nearly everything, but the way she dominated the conversation and demanded Riley's attention didn't ingratiate her. She didn't even let up when the doors opened and the audience filed in. At least they provided a welcome distraction.

The crowd waiting in line had seemed significant when Riley had passed, but as they took their seats, she saw just how big the group was. The first two rows had been reserved for attendees who'd purchased VIP tickets, but the chairs behind were gone in seconds. Riley was relieved to see that Olivia and her crew got pretty good seats, though. They'd been close to the front of the line, but Riley doubted she'd be able to see them once the lights were dimmed in the audience. Still, while she herded them into seats, Olivia made a point of making eye contact with Riley more than once.

Watching Olivia, Riley wondered again how she'd managed to maintain a flirty conversation for so long. Olivia was a knockout. She looked to be a few years younger than Riley's thirty-two, but that probably had a lot to do with the way her thousand-watt smile lit her features. Her hair was shoulder length, tightly curled and the same rich, golden brown of her eyes. Her wide mouth and thin lips were the key feature in her round face.

Then there was her body. Riley stared unabashedly at her slim form. She had the long lines of a runner tucked into a loose, flowing skirt and a gauzy muslin top the color of sunshine. Long lines were an understatement. The first thing Riley had noticed about Olivia was her height. At least six inches taller than Riley, who relished the height difference. Despite her obviously feminine qualities her makeup was minimal and the only jewelry she wore was a leather cuff on her left wrist. Somehow it suited her better than gold. Everything about her looked simple, unrehearsed. Exactly what Riley craved.

"Do you think they'll ask about The Proposal?" the blogger asked in a hush, dragging Riley's attention away from the low sweep of Olivia's top as she leaned over to make sure Chelsea and Lewis were situated.

"God, I hope not," Riley said without thinking. A barely suppressed gasp from the blogger made her scramble for an excuse. "I mean not right off the bat. We have three days here. What else will we talk about if we start with the best part?"

The answer more than satisfied the blogger. She tittered her agreement and turned to the panelist on her other side, freeing Riley to go back to staring at Olivia. The moment she looked back, however, she was busted. Olivia stared right at her, one eyebrow sliding up when Riley's gaze landed on her. Riley shrugged and was rewarded with a wink from Olivia.

That wink stole every last scrap of Riley's heart. She was officially crushing on this woman, and she'd never survive if they didn't get that date tomorrow. All she had to do was nail this panel and then try to catch Olivia before she could run off. Asking Olivia to slide into her DMs felt tenuous. Riley really wanted to get her phone number to be sure this one didn't get away.

"Okay, everyone. Find your seats if you were lucky enough to get one, we're about to get started," the moderator called.

There was a generalized scrambling of feet and papers interspersed with a few hoots and even a whistle from the back of the room. The crowd laughed and then a charged silence descended as the lights dimmed so the stage was the focal point of the room. The ring of light didn't extend to Olivia's seat and Riley decided it was a good thing. She'd need all her focus to keep the fake smile in place.

"Welcome, one and all, to our panel—*Midtown Avengers* Through a Media Lens. We'll be exploring the different ways fans and the press interact with our beloved show and how Middies has embraced that interaction on every level." The moderator held the mic away while they waited for the cheering to die back down. Riley relaxed a little as she realized how friendly the crowd was. "You probably know everyone up here," they continued. "But let's go through the motions, shall we? We'll have a little fun with the intros, too." After another round of applause, the moderator said, "I'll ask everyone on the panel to introduce themselves and then tell us their favorite part of The Proposal."

Hoots and whistles covered Riley's groan. Of all the things she hated about Middies, the thing she hated most was how they'd jumped the shark to end the last season. Middies' last finale featured the return of a crowd favorite guest star who proposed to the lesbian character.

Flame Fingers was a masc Vietnamese woman with a dry wit and a fetish for Doc Martens. Mind Bender had arrived in season two like a tiny blond Yorkie to corral the flailing Avengers and had seduced Flame Fingers in the process. It was such a predictable storyline of the girl-next-door rule follower forcing the angsty bad girl to care about something. Then Mind Bender broke her heart by leaving at the end of her contract. Fans were furious and the show had been scrambling to regain the trust of their sapphic audience. The Proposal was their way of doing that, but the blatant manipulation infuriated Riley.

"Why don't we start at the far end? Riley?"

"Uh, well," Riley struggled to find some way to force her irritation down and lie convincingly. "I'm Riley St. James. I'm a journalist, blogger, and Middies recapper."

Pausing for the audience's roar of approval, she grasped at the only available straw.

"I'd have to say my favorite part of The Proposal was the line. Y'all know the one. Mind Bender's big romantic moment. Say it with me." The whole crowd chanted along with her, "I love you, you big, wild superhero."

As the last syllable died, Riley gave her first genuine smile of the afternoon. She might hate being on this panel, but at least she had the crowd in the palm of her hand.

CHAPTER FIVE

Olivia pulled the plug on the sink and let the slurping noise of sudsy water draining away cover Chelsea and Lewis bickering. They sprawled out across the rug on either side of a worn game board, arguing over the rules of Risk for the millionth time. Olivia watched them through the pass-through, snatching the dish towel off its peg.

"I get to fortify my position before you place your new armies, Chelsea," Lewis said.

"Then do it, geez, you take so long." Chelsea drew out each word, mocking Lewis as usual.

"It's called strategizing."

"It's called delaying and it won't work. You're going to lose Africa. Deal with it."

"Not if I properly fortify my armies which I am allowed to do."

"Fine." Chelsea dragged out the word and rolled over to face the ceiling, tossing her infantry piece into the air and catching it just over her nose. "You're still going to lose."

They continued to argue, both over the game and which Middies episode to watch while they played, while Olivia cleaned. When they were driving home, the three of them had decided on a lineup of favorite episodes to rewatch, but the kids had been too keyed up to sit still. Two episodes into their watch list, they decided to split their focus between their favorite show and their favorite competitive pastime.

Olivia had stacked the last of the clean bowls in the cabinet and Lewis had lost Africa in a humiliating two-pronged attack on Madagascar by the time the front door opened and Allison rushed in.

"Sorry I'm late, dears." Allison kissed Chelsea and then Lewis on the forehead. "Traffic was a disaster. Did everyone eat?"

"Yep. I'm going to collect Poppa's tray in a minute, but he's falling asleep so I don't want to disturb him," Olivia said.

A grumble from down the hall belied her comment.

"I'll be there soon, Poppa," Allison called.

She did not, however, make any movement toward the hallway to Olivia's grandpa's room. They both knew Olivia was right. Even on the best of days, he struggled to stay awake long past dinner, and today's excitement surely tired him out. If they gave him enough time, he'd be asleep and well-rested to supervise another busy day tomorrow.

Allison turned to the kids. "Isn't it time for you to get home, Lewis?"

"Probably," he said, settling an artillery piece onto Greenland, then turning his attention to Mind Bender demolishing a bad guy onscreen.

She gave him a moment to get up. When he didn't, she said, "So why don't you do that?"

Lewis sighed in his long-suffering way and hauled himself to his feet. Olivia caught the slight eye roll he directed toward Chelsea, but he was very polite when he said, "Thank you, Mrs. Duran-Spencer. Thanks for letting me tag along, Olivia."

"You're welcome, Lewis. Thanks for keeping Chelsea in line today," Olivia said.

"Bye, Poppa," Lewis shouted before jogging through the door, slamming it behind him. Another weak grumble filtered down the hall in response.

Allison settled onto a barstool with a groan, kicking off her heels. She looked tired, but in that happy way Olivia knew all too well. She poured a glass of water and handed it across the counter to her mom.

"How was the date?"

"Fine," Allison said, but her cheeks went dusty rose.

The blush settled it, she was smitten with the new guy and Olivia couldn't really blame her. Two dates in one day and flowers every Friday. He was laying it on pretty thick. Hopefully, he wouldn't break her heart like the last one and the one before that.

"How was the convention?"

"Fine," Olivia said, knowing she was equally incapable of hiding her happiness.

"She's got a date with a celebrity tomorrow," Chelsea shouted from the floor where she was sweeping game pieces into a bag.

"You what?" Allison asked, nearly coming off her stool. Her smile was so wide Olivia had to look away.

"Don't get too excited, she's not that big a celebrity."

"A lady this time," Allison said. "Excellent. An actress? Writer? Come on, who?"

"Riley St. James," Chelsea shouted. She turned the TV off and abandoned the remaining game pieces.

"That blogger you've been crushing on?"

"She's not a blogger." Chelsea fell onto the stool next to Allison. "She's a journalist."

Allison wrapped an arm around Chelsea, who only gave a token protest before settling into the hug. She shot a wink at Olivia. "I'm more excited about the crush than her job title. So she's not a total jerk in real life?" Allison asked.

"I don't know. We haven't been on our date yet."

"How did all this happen exactly?" To her annoyance, Allison directed the question not at Olivia, but at Chelsea.

"She just started talking to her. Want an ice pop?" Chelsea asked.

"Sure. Olivia, can you get us ice pops?" Allison asked. "Which her started talking to which her?"

"I can get them." Chelsea hopped off her stool. "I don't know. Lewis and I walked up and they were being gross."

"What do you mean being gross?" Allison asked.

"Flirting." Chelsea made the same face she made about steamed broccoli as she grabbed two ice pops. "They were standing too close and giggling at nothing."

"Flirting isn't gross," Allison said. Chelsea dropped a cherry ice pop in front of her and she turned a pouty face on Olivia. "I wanted grape."

"Yes, it is," Chelsea said. "No one wants to see their sister do that."

Allison grinned at Olivia, who dutifully delivered the grape pop. "So you were flirting with Riley St. James?"

"No," Chelsea again spoke before Olivia could answer. She said around her ice pop, "Riley St. James was flirting with her."

"You sure they weren't flirting with each other?" Allison snapped her twin pop in half, handing one stick to Olivia and keeping the other for herself. "And why weren't you with her the whole time?"

"Well, Mom, they wanted to play with knives. Rusty ones," Olivia said before Chelsea could continue to narrate her life. "It seemed like a good idea so I left them to do it."

Allison stuck her purple stained tongue out and turned back to Chelsea. "Why weren't you with her?"

"We were waiting in line at the Middies booth and didn't want to leave. We could see each other the whole time."

"Except when she was making out with her celebrity girlfriend?"

"Eww. Mom." Chelsea shook her head and mumbled, "Gross."

"If you two are finished," Olivia said, trying to keep a straight face as she watched her little sister and mother tease her. "I'll go get Poppa's tray and then go to bed."

Allison came around the counter at last and pulled Olivia into a hug. She smelled like her powdery, floral perfume and nice clothes. Olivia hugged back with all her might.

"I'll take care of Poppa," Allison said and she pulled back far enough to look into Olivia's eyes. "You shower and get a good night's rest. I'll take Chelsea and Lewis tomorrow so you can linger over your date."

"Mom, you don't care about queer entertainment," Olivia said, giving her mother an out even while her heart fluttered with anticipation.

"No, but I care about my queer daughter and my other daughter's queer best friend. I'll take them to that sandwich place downtown while you go on your date." She shared a warm smile with Chelsea. "Now both of you go to bed."

Chelsea jumped down and threw her popsicle sticks away before shuffling down the hall. Olivia wanted to sprint upstairs to her room and Riley's latest article. According to her Twitter notification, it was a recap of her first day at QueerCon, and Olivia wanted to laugh at her first impressions. Still, it didn't feel right to leave Allison with cleaning up and settling Poppa.

"You sure?" Olivia asked.

"You don't think I can take care of myself, do you?" Allison put her fists on her hips and held back her laughter.

"Of course you can't."

"Ungrateful daughter," Allison said. "You're right, of course, but you're still ungrateful."

"Good night, Mommy." Olivia kissed Allison's forehead and scampered up the stairs to her room and Riley's article.

CHAPTER SIX

By the second day of QueerCon, Riley was finding it hard to maintain her fake smile. Fans approached her all morning and it was a thrill to see how many people loved her work. If only they wanted to talk about anything other than Middies. Even her biggest fans seemed to forget she did anything else with her time besides recap Middies episodes.

It would have been annoying enough to have to talk about a show she disliked, but she'd been hoping this con would be a good way to talk her way into a TV writers' room. She had spec scripts ready to go and her bona fides as a minor queer celebrity were on full display. Only problem was she couldn't get away from Middies long enough to introduce herself to anyone important.

She'd given too good an answer on the Middies panel day one. It had been the only answer, of course. Anyone would've given it if they'd had first crack at the question, but the line was so popular with this group that they all wanted to talk to her about it.

"The way she appeared out of nowhere, right when you thought the season was over," a Mind Bender cosplayer said. "Just walked right into Flame Fingers's room, grabbed her, and kissed her. Then she dropped to one knee and said..."

This was the way they always did it now. They wanted Riley to say the line just like she had at the panel. She groaned through it because what other choice did she have?

"I love you, you big, wild superhero."

The cosplayer giggled and jumped up and down, clapping. "It's so romantic."

"Totally. Speaking of," Riley said, shifting to something that elicited real enthusiasm from her. "Did you see my article on the fight for the Juliantina movie? *Amar a muerte* fans made a real movement there. Like Fight for Wynonna big."

"Yeah, I heard about that," she said, her smile faltering for a heartbeat before she hitched it back up. "You know what'd be perfect? If Jodie Gray got a role in it. Not as Mind Bender, of course, that wouldn't work. I'd love to see her play a villain though, wouldn't you?"

"Sure. That'd be cool." An alert on Riley's phone saved her from continuing the conversation. "Sorry. I have to go. Time for Maria Guerrero Chávez's workshop."

"Oh, are you doing a piece on *Three Broken Lines*?"

"I've already done several. I write recaps of their episodes, too." Riley was finding it increasingly hard to keep the bitterness out of her voice. "The workshop is on television script writing."

She'd hoped the fan would ask her about her interest, but it was clear no one at this con would care if she got her dream job as a television writer unless it was on *Midtown Avengers*.

The workshop was well attended, and most were there for practical knowledge. With the fan element toned down, Riley was able to focus on Chávez's expert advice. She took so many pages of notes her hand cramped halfway through and she had to scramble to keep up. Chávez was responsive to the crowd and answered all Riley's questions before she had a chance to ask them. After a brain-wringing hour, she left with a smile on her face and incredible insight on how to start her dream career.

As she made her way into the corridor she caught sight of Olivia, alone today and wearing a hint more makeup. She looked up and caught sight of Riley, who had tried a little harder with her own outfit today, and a sweep of pink flooded into her cheeks.

"Maybe this con is worth it after all," Riley mumbled to herself.

It was quite a battle to get through the crowd, and the megawatt smile Olivia leveled on her as she arrived didn't help.

Stumbling to a halt, Riley dazzled with her wit by saying, "Hey."

Olivia's smile widened and she leaned in close. "Hey yourself."

The twinkle in Olivia's eye had Riley's head spinning and she had to fight hard to do more than grin and blink. She finally managed to say, "You look great."

Olivia reached out and pinched the sharp corner of Riley's button-up collar. "You too." She rubbed her thumb over the fabric, her wrist close enough that Riley caught a burst of her fruity perfume. After a quiet moment, she seemed to realize what she was doing and snatched her hand back, the dusting of pink on her cheeks blazing back to life. "Um, want to get some lunch?"

"Definitely." Riley dragged her eyes away from the sweep of Olivia's lips with difficulty and nodded toward the door. "After you."

Wanting to slip away from the QueerCon crowd, they walked a few blocks to a little café nestled between a park and the river. A warm breeze was at their backs the whole walk and they were able to grab the last table on the patio. It wasn't a great view, but the sky was a perfect, cloudless blue and the red-and-white-striped umbrella kept the sun out of their eyes.

"I thought you might feel at home with Cuban food," Olivia said, indicating the restaurant around them. "You live in Miami, right?"

"I do. It's great, thank you."

Riley found herself even more tongue-tied than she usually was around beautiful women. It had everything to do with the way Olivia wouldn't hold eye contact for more than a few seconds at a time and blushed each time Riley looked over at her. This woman was a curious mix of confidence and shyness. The quirk made her want to learn more about Olivia—to find out what other quirks she had.

"Tell me about yourself," Riley said, half-hiding behind her menu.

"What do you want to know?"

"Everything."

Olivia laughed, her shoulders relaxing visibly. "In TV shows the character always responds with 'how much time do you have' or something witty like that."

"What's your witty response?"

"Well, I won't ask how much time you have 'cause I'm not nearly that interesting. More like what'll we talk about after the two minutes it'll take to tell you my life story."

"I'm sure we'll come up with something," Riley said, her voice dropping an octave without conscious thought.

Olivia's eyebrow shot up at the suggestive purr and she was about to respond when the waiter arrived to take their order. "Sorry," Olivia said to both the waiter and Riley. "I haven't even looked at the menu yet."

He hurried off to his many other tables and they applied themselves to their menus. Riley couldn't make the words come into focus. All she could think about was the way Olivia's eyebrow had arched and the warmth of her knee so close under the tiny bistro table. Her nerves returned and, when the waiter tried a second time, she still had no idea what she wanted apart from him to leave so she could talk to Olivia.

Picking something at random, she handed over her menu and returned her full attention to Olivia. There was a shine to her hair that hadn't been as evident the day before and the curls seemed more tamed today. Her dress revealed acres of richly tanned skin without being scandalous. Riley followed the line of her shoulder with eager eyes and only realized when she'd made her way across Olivia's round jaw up to her chestnut eyes that she'd been caught staring. There was a twinkle in those eyes that said she wasn't at all upset about Riley's interest.

"So, uh…" Riley's tongue was heavy in her mouth, making the formation of words a chore she was barely up to. "What do you do?"

The tip of Olivia's tongue slid along the bottom of her teeth, making Riley shiver in the heat, and she said, "I have a very glamorous job. I work in the entertainment industry."

"Do you?" Riley wracked her brains, desperate to remember if she'd ever seen Olivia on screen. She was certain she'd have remembered a face like that. "Actress?"

"As if," Olivia said, taking a long sip of her water and toying with the paper straw. "I'm a little more on the periphery of the industry. I work for the cruise lines."

"Oh yeah? Tampa's a big port for cruises."

"Not as big as Miami, but yeah, we have a lot through here." Olivia looked down at the table and the lightness of her tone shifted. "I'm not really part of the cruises though. I'm just a parking lot attendant at the Port of Tampa."

"That sounds..."

"Boring."

"I was going to say interesting," Riley said. "You get to see every cruise that leaves Tampa. And I bet everyone you meet is in a great mood. I mean they're either about to go on vacation or they're coming back from vacation, right?"

Olivia stared at her openmouthed. "You're joking, right?"

"No. Should I be?"

"You've never worked in customer service, have you?"

"Um, not exactly."

Olivia reached across the table, covering Riley's fidgeting hand with her own, and put on a mock serious expression. "Then I hate to be the one to have to tell you this, but people? They're pretty big jerks. Especially to people in the service industry."

Their waiter appeared, setting down their iced teas and looking like he'd run a mile since they'd seen him last. After thanking him, Riley asked, "She's right, isn't she?"

There was a clatter of cutlery falling to concrete nearby and a shrill shriek from the person who'd dropped it. The table turned an accusing glare on the waiter as though he'd been responsible for the accident though he was on the other side of the patio. He sighed. "Uh, yeah." He hurried off.

"I guess I'm a little sheltered," Riley said.

"That's okay." Olivia settled her chin on the palm of her hand and said, "I'd much rather be on a date with someone who doesn't realize how bad it is to be a server than someone who's rude to the server."

The waiter returned with their lunch and Riley recognized how hungry she was. It turned out she'd ordered a Cuban sandwich in her haze and it smelled divine, the mingled aromas of rich pork and the tang of mustard and pickles made her mouth water.

For a time, they ate in silence, stealing glances at each other and grinning when one or the other was caught. Riley had never been on a date like this. She felt completely at ease and more nervous than she'd ever been in turns. Olivia was as alluring as she was easygoing and the combination, for a woman like Riley who rarely dated and even more rarely enjoyed a date, was devastating. When it all got to be too much, she tried focusing on the day and the city around her, finding it almost as intoxicating as the company.

Tampa was much less ostentatious than Miami. The waterfront was beautiful and lush with grass and palms rather than the sea of concrete and sand Riley was used to. Being so close to the park, there was a freshness to the air, as though the scent of flowers was just out of reach of her nose. Boats lazed by on the river, their sails bulging in what felt like a gentle breeze on land.

As beautiful as the city was, Riley's attention kept returning to the café and the woman across from her. Olivia piled ropa vieja onto tostones with obvious relish, the sun kissing her cheek as the breeze shifted the flaps of their umbrella, plunging her in and out of shadow. Her smile seemed a permanent fixture, leaving a lightness in her eyes. The chatter of the other patrons died away to a gentle hum. All the cares and uncertainty Riley normally carried on her shoulders melted away in the perfection of this one moment.

"How'd you get into journalism?" Olivia asked after satisfying the first rush of hunger.

"I guess it was *Glee*." Riley pushed a fried plantain around her plate. "Probably every queer entertainment reporter our age will say that, but it's true. Season one came on while I was in college and I had a blog."

"Didn't everyone back then?"

"Yeah," Riley said with a laugh. "I started recapping *Glee* on my blog, pushing hard for Brittana early on. People found it and thought my recaps were funny."

"You do have a great dry wit."

"Thanks. I try." Riley was full, but she didn't want the date to end so she toyed with her food. "It was really cool, too. To have a network care about us. To tell our stories. Don't get me wrong—they screwed it up a lot, which ended up being good for me. Easier to make jokes. But still, they were telling our stories."

"I remember watching it with my high school girlfriend. She had just transitioned and it was hard for her at home and at school. No matter what was going on, we always sat down together to watch *Glee* and forget it all for an hour."

"That was a long time ago for her to transition. I imagine it was hard," Riley said.

"The good outweighed the bad. Being able to live as herself was huge."

"But the two of you didn't make it?"

"She went to college in California, I went to school in Georgia. We couldn't make the long-distance work. She's married now with three kids and the white picket fence and everything," Olivia said.

"Which school did you go to?"

"Savannah College of Art and Design."

"Wow." Riley nearly dropped her fork. "SCAD's a great school. What'd you study?"

"Animation and illustration. I wanted to draw comics."

"You don't anymore?"

"I do, but life got in the way." A buzzing interrupted her explanation and Olivia fished her phone out of her bag. "Speaking of which, we should be getting back to QueerCon, don't you think?"

"I'd rather stay here with you." Riley was rewarded with a wink across the table. "But I don't want to get Heather in trouble for losing me."

As they walked back to the con, Riley again noticed their height difference. Olivia strode beside her with an easy, long gait. She was a good six inches taller than Riley, who knew the difference would only be accentuated if Olivia wore heels. Something about the way she walked told Riley she wore them often.

In an attempt to force her mind away from those enticing mental images, she asked, "So, tell me, what's the thing you're most passionate about?" It was a silly first date question and one she loved to ask. There was no wrong answer except not having an answer. Riley didn't have the personality that allowed for a milquetoast partner. She threw herself into everything in life and she didn't mesh well with women who didn't do the same.

For the first time all afternoon, Olivia looked nervous. She didn't look at Riley, but rather at her messenger bag, slung across her chest. She toyed with the frayed strap as she opened her mouth, then closed it again. Turning to Riley with a weak smile, she said, "I don't really have time at the moment. I've got to focus on my family."

"Oh," Riley said. The answer intrigued her since it was clearly not the one she'd wanted to give, but it was a first date, so she allowed Olivia her secret. "Are there seven more siblings at home? I don't know if I could handle that many Chelseas."

"What if the others are like me?"

Riley let herself be bold. "Seven of you sounds pretty amazing to me."

Olivia looked away and tucked a loose strand of hair behind her ear, which Riley took to be a good sign. After waiting for traffic at the next crosswalk, Olivia said, "My mom's had a tough time. She raised me alone, then she married Chelsea's dad and he died in Iraq. Grandpa got sick a few years ago and moved in with us, but he's particular and mom doesn't really handle him well. She's a bit flighty."

They arrived back in front of the hotel and the sidewalks were thick with people milling about, grabbing fresh air and sunlight between panels. Riley took Olivia's hand and guided her toward a clear spot by a potted palm. She liked the feel of Olivia's hand in hers, so she held on.

Rubbing her thumb over Olivia's knuckles, Riley lowered her voice and said, "Sounds like you take care of everyone around you. Is there anyone who takes care of you?"

Olivia moved a step closer, bringing the warmth of her body and the scent of her perfume with her. "The position is currently available. Would you like to submit an application?"

Riley's gaze was frozen to Olivia's lips. How they arched up at the corners and glistened, rose pink in the bright sun. She leaned forward, inch by inch, her mind spinning on what those lips felt like. What they tasted like.

"Riley. There you are." Heather bounded up with her trusty clipboard clutched in one hand and her other waving. "I've been looking all over."

"Sorry, I uh…" Riley stepped back from Olivia. "Went out to lunch."

"Hi there." Heather held out her hand to Olivia. "I'm Heather. How are you enjoying QueerCon?"

"It's great."

"Sorry to interrupt, but Riley's next panel is starting in ten minutes, and we have to rush to get her through the crowd."

"It's fine." Olivia turned to Riley. "I'll see you around?"

"Sure. Yeah," Riley said, dragging her steps behind Heather.

They'd nearly made it to the door when Riley gathered her courage and whipped around, jogging back to where Olivia still stood next to the potted palm.

"Can I, um…" Riley swallowed hard and avoided Olivia's eye. "Get your number?"

She held out her phone, but Olivia didn't immediately take it. After a long moment, her stomach started to feel as heavy as her arm. Heat rose in her cheeks at the thought Olivia might be shooting her down.

Just when she decided the sidewalk should swallow her up and put her out of her misery, the phone slipped from her hands and Olivia's thumbs flew across the screen. Riley barely had time to blink before she handed it back.

"So is it okay if I text you later?" Riley asked quietly.

Olivia stepped back into her space, forcing Riley to look up into her warm brown eyes. "You better."

Then Olivia was gone, melting into the crowd surging through the hotel's entrance. Heather's touch was gentle but insistent and Riley fell into step behind her, the soles of her shoes barely making contact with the ground.

"I didn't realize what I was interrupting." Heather winked. "Sorry about that."

"Your timing was perfect, actually," Riley said, slipping her phone back into her pocket and coming back to herself slowly. "I'm not great with dates, so the shorter the better."

"Riley St. James not good with dates? Really?"

"Really." She rubbed the back of her neck. "Especially if I like the girl."

And she really, really liked this girl.

Chapter Seven

Olivia had to hustle from her lunch date to the Tampa Port. She had agreed to pick up a half shift for a friend, but she didn't want to rush her date with Riley. Fortunately, the Port parking lot wasn't far from the QueerCon hotel, so she didn't have to fight downtown traffic. She made it just in time and clocked in before changing into her uniform, a drastic measure she rarely resorted to. The rest of her evening would be full of silence and calm, so a little excitement to start the shift wasn't unwelcome.

The Port was empty, one wave of ships having left Friday and the next not due in until early the next morning. The only tickets she'd have to cash out would be tourists who couldn't find somewhere cheaper to stow their cars. The light workload didn't bother Olivia, especially not today.

One of the few memories Olivia had from her dad was sitting at the Port and watching the massive cruise ships pull away, people on both ship and shore waving and shouting as the horn blasted through peaceful afternoons. Olivia would wave her tiny hand frantically at the distant people milling around onboard, their clothes a blaze of tropical colors, excitement radiating from their faces.

She was in fifth grade when she came home from school to find her mother lying on the living room floor, weeping with a crumpled note in her hand. When Allison explained her father had left, Olivia thought he'd finally gone on the cruise they'd always dreamt of. She waited for him to come back and tell her all about it. She even went to the Port to meet him getting off the boat, but he wasn't there. It was only exhausted seniors and bleary-eyed couples with sunburns. It took her months to accept he hadn't gone on a cruise.

Olivia shook herself and reached for her bag, remembering for one pleasant moment toying with the strap when Riley had asked her about a passion. Her sketch pad fit nicely on the small desk in her booth if she moved her stamps and credit card machine to the back corners. Flipping to a blank page, she closed her eyes and called into her mind Flame Fingers's tall, thin frame. The image she landed on was from the final battle from last season, the one Flame Fingers barely survived before heading home to find Mind Bender waiting in her bedroom. Waiting with a ring in her pocket and a proposal on her lips. Olivia smiled, letting the TV show in her head spool forward to that romantic final scene.

I love you, you big, wild superhero.

Mind Bender's lips moved in her mind, but the voice she heard was Riley's from the QueerCon panel. Riley's voice. Coming from Riley's full lips, with their exaggerated bow. The spot on the bottom right where she chewed when she'd asked Olivia for her phone number. The way her upper lip twitched up to the shadow of a smile when Olivia flirted with her.

Forcing her mind back to Flame Fingers in the battle, Olivia started to sketch. She made a wire form sketch of her whole body in the traditional comic book pose of a woman running with her hair flowing behind her, her fists in front of her. It was a pose Olivia had drawn a million times before, starting when she was little and she'd draw her favorite characters from *The Candy Box Kids* and *Kim Possible*. Those early years taught her to sketch quickly and hold images in her mind to fill in the details later. It was also her first foray into the passion she hadn't been quite brave enough to tell Riley about: fan art.

Olivia was blissfully ignoring her surroundings, sketching the layers of flame lifting from Flame Fingers's swinging fists, when the door beside her wrenched open. Olivia's squeal of surprise drowned out the matching one from the booth's abused hinges.

"Hey there, sis," Chelsea said, plopping onto the worn carpet at the back of the booth. Her backpack rattled as she tossed it down. "What's up?"

Using an eraser to attack the errant line connecting Flame Fingers's knuckles to her knee, Olivia said, "Nice one, Chels. You're lucky I didn't ruin this."

"I thought you were giving that to Jodie Gray today?"

Olivia removed the last trace of the stray line and checked the entrance and exit lanes of the lot before refocusing on her drawing. "This is a new one." She tapped her toe against her bag. "The Mind Bender one's still in there."

"So you chickened out?"

"No, I didn't chicken out," Olivia said. "I didn't make it to the main floor today and I definitely didn't see any of the actors."

"'Cause you had a date?"

"'Cause I had lunch plans."

Olivia's phone vibrated with an incoming text and she dropped her pencil so fast it clattered to the floor. She didn't even check to see where it had gone.

Riley texted, *Hey there*

Hi, Olivia texted.

It's Riley. A moment later she sent another, *Riley St. James*

Olivia's smile was so wide it made her cheeks ache. *I know who it is LOL*

"Sure," Chelsea chimed in from her nest on the floor. "Not a date at all."

"Shut up and do your homework."

Chelsea stuck out her tongue and Olivia stuck hers out right back. The honk of a car horn snapped Olivia's attention back to her work. She issued a timed ticket to the tourists who'd been sent by a nearby hotel whose lot was full, then turned her attention back to her phone.

Riley pushed the hotel room door open with her foot, hauling a bag full of QueerCon swag in one hand and her messenger bag in the other. She let the door slam closed behind her and dropped the bags in the center of the room. Her room was a suite, so the dragging walk to her bed was a long one, and she finished it by flopping, face first, onto the squashy king bed. She groaned as the fresh cotton smell of the comforter and the welcoming softness of the pillows enveloped her.

Her phone buzzed and she barked at it, leaving her head buried between twin mounds of goose down. It buzzed again and she swatted at her hoodie pocket, trying to make the sound stop. After the third ring it went silent and Riley sighed, letting her shoulders relax and her body fall deeper into the mattress.

She was on the verge of dozing off when her phone buzzed again. She groaned, knowing there was only one person in her life who would be this insistent. Riley wrestled the phone from her pocket, turning her head just enough so she could talk.

"What do you want, Dani?"

A burst of club music and the rattle of glasses assaulted her ear and Riley jerked the phone away. Her best friend's voice came to her from far away, jumbled in with the still audible noise of a good time.

"What a kind greeting. Gosh, I'm so glad I called to check up on you."

"Are you at a bar?"

"It's Saturday night, of course I'm at a bar. Why aren't you?"

"I can't leave. The blankets have accepted me as one of their own," Riley said, rolling over with a muted groan. "Leaving now would break their little fluffy hearts."

"You're in bed already?"

"I literally just walked in the door, Dani. Give me a break, yeah?"

The only response was a muffled sound like fabric rustling and a throaty laugh Riley instantly recognized as Dani's. Another voice, this one an octave higher and with the distinct slur of alcohol, mumbled in the background. Riley had been through this before. Dani had never been able to say no to an interested woman, even one so obnoxious as to interrupt a stranger's phone call, so Riley settled in and waited.

Dani was very much like Riley, only a foot taller and filled out with impressive muscle rather than the extra weight Riley carried. They both presented as androgynous and they both attracted the aggressive femme of the queer female species. When Dani was at a club, women in miniskirts appeared as though they'd sprung fully formed from the sticky concrete dance floor.

While Dani flirted, Riley let her mind wander to the aggressive femme she'd gone on a lunch date with. Olivia wasn't as persistent as Dani's current conquest sounded, and that suited Riley fine. As much as she wished she was as suave as Dani, she was generally hopeless around women. When she'd seen Olivia, however, she knew she'd hate herself forever if she didn't say something. The gift of watching her smile when she recognized Riley was enough. The way her eyes sparkled when she returned Riley's banter, jab for jab.

"Yo, Grandma?" Dani's voice cut through her daydream. "You fall asleep on me?"

"Almost." Riley forced herself to sit up. "You know how much I love listening to you chat up women."

"Not my fault the ladies can't get enough of me."

Riley wedged the phone between her ear and shoulder as she wrestled her tablet out of her bag. It had been a while since her last text with Olivia, but she could at least go over everything they'd said while Dani chatted.

"If they're so obsessed with you, why are you on the phone with me?" Riley asked.

"Thought I'd do you a favor. Listen close, you might learn something."

"Yeah, like how to get a straight girl to slap you."

"That was one time and I apologized," Dani said. "Speaking of obsessed, having fun with that gaggle of Middies super fans?"

"You should've heard the questions I got at my last panel," Riley said, pulling up her messages app and smiling at the sight of Olivia's name. "It's like there's nothing else going on in the world except one lesbian superhero proposing to another."

"It doesn't exactly happen every day. You gotta admit it's pretty badass for the studio to center a queer story like that."

"I'd like it more if it wasn't such obvious pandering," Riley said.

"So what if it is pandering? Don't we deserve to be pandered to for once? They do it for the straight cis white guys enough."

"Or they could just tell authentic stories about us instead."

"Authentic stories about a queer woman whose fists burst into flames so she can throw fireballs?" Dani asked.

"Authentic stories of queer women falling in love."

Dani burst into a fit of laughter and Riley took the opportunity to switch to speaker phone. Having recovered, Dani said, "Remember when she was just coming into her powers and she was on that date? She set her own pants on fire with a half-naked woman in her bed."

Riley let her laugh it out, absorbed in scrolling through her texts with Olivia. When Dani was finished, Riley said, "That scene was funny, but it was a long time ago. Now all anyone wants to talk about is The Proposal. And they talk about it like that—you can hear them capitalize the words when they say it."

"Oh, no, poor Riley St. James. You have to talk about hot chicks making out on TV with a bunch of love-obsessed queer women."

"There are other shows they could be obsessed with is all I'm saying. I wrote awesome *Wynonna Earp* recaps. And my *Three Broken Lines* recaps were hilarious. Why couldn't they love me for that? I'd kill to be tied to one of those shows forever."

"What does it matter as long as they love you, bonehead?"

Riley wiggled into the blankets, but her discomfort wasn't physical. "I mean whatever."

"Don't you 'whatever' me, rock star. You're awesome and don't fucking forget it."

Riley couldn't help smiling. "Thanks, Dani."

"So did you score with any of 'em yet?"

Riley was about to respond sarcastically when a notification chimed from her tablet with a new text.

Olivia texted, *Do I get to see you again before the end of con?*

"What was that?" Dani asked, then answered her own question. "Are you texting with someone while you're talking to me?"

"Of course not," Riley said in a monotone, her eyes fixed on the tablet screen. "You always have my complete focus."

"Holy shit, you're trying to nail one of 'em after all. Nice work, Riles."

"I'm not trying to nail anyone, you uncouth ass."

Riley texted back, *Absolutely you will*

"Bullshit. She come up to you in Mind Bender cosplay? That tight leather bodysuit thing? Give me details."

"God no. You know I'd never hit on anyone in cosplay."

"You need to loosen up. I'd hit on anyone in a leather bodysuit, no matter what she was trying to look like."

"She was not in a leather bodysuit," Riley said, running back to her bag to grab her schedule for the final day of con. "But she's gorgeous and I did hit on her."

"Stop lying to me. I know you'd never hit on anyone. How'd she approach you? Does she read your stuff?"

"Hey, I can hit on a woman," Riley stammered. "I've done it before."

"Name once."

"Yesterday," Riley said.

Olivia texted, *Tomorrow?*

"I didn't see it, doesn't count. Name one other time," Dani said.

"Shut up."

"Thought so."

When Riley didn't respond, Olivia texted, *Lunch?*

"Stop texting," Dani said. "I hear the notifications. You aren't paying attention to me."

"Would you rather I pay attention to you or make a date for tomorrow?"

"Tough call," Dani said. "I'm naturally selfish so I want the attention, but you need to get laid."

Riley texted back, *I have an interview with an agent right after lunch—probably shouldn't risk it*

"I do not need to get laid," she said to Dani.

You're writing an article about an agent? Olivia asked.

No. Trying to get signed by one

OMG that's awesome. Good luck!

Thanks, Riley texted.

"When was the last time?" Dani asked. Another rustling interrupted her words. This time they ended with the slightly nauseating sounds of kissing. "I gotta go. Good luck."

Dani hung up without another word and Riley tossed her phone away. Dani had been her best friend for a long time, probably too long. Still, as much as she liked the thought, she wasn't the type of woman to go to bed with someone she'd just met. Even if the thought of it made her stomach churn pleasantly.

Olivia texted, *How about I find you on the floor and let you buy me a coffee?*

I can work with that

Great, Olivia texted. *Gotta get back to work—see you tomorrow ;)*

Riley slapped her tablet closed, then rolled over and stared at the popcorn ceiling. She thought of the wink at the end of Olivia's last message and warmth spread from her chest all the way to the tips of her toes.

CHAPTER EIGHT

The line wasn't moving at all, but Olivia was fine with that state of affairs. She clutched her bag too hard to her chest. Every now and then a wave of panic would overtake her and she would squeeze a little harder, then she would worry about wrinkling the drawing and she would panic again, this time purposefully releasing the pressure on her bag.

"Stop freaking out," Chelsea said. "It'll be fine."

Olivia was about to reply that yes, of course it would be fine, she was just nervous, when Lewis's head whipped around so fast his bangs fanned out in front of him like the fringe of an angry animal.

"Of course it won't be fine," he said. "I'm about to meet Blinker. In the flesh. There's no way I'll keep my cool."

Olivia's nerves fled in the face of the kids' banter. She pressed her fingertips to her lips to keep the smile at bay. "You aren't meeting Blinker, Lewis."

"I know. I know. You don't have to lecture." He exchanged an eye roll with Chelsea, who switched from teasing to defending her best friend in a flash. "Blinker isn't a real person. I'm meeting Matthew Barnes."

The line moved forward two steps and Olivia caught sight of a small, condescending grin from the woman in front of them in line. She was cosplaying Mind Bender and the leather body suit she wore hugged all the right places.

"Matthew Barnes is almost as amazing as Blinker," Lewis said.

The cosplayer turned to him, her smile wider if still a little condescending. "He is pretty great, isn't he?"

"Pretty great?" Lewis said, pushing out one hip to rest a fist on. "He's a god. The way he played that scene where he confronted his fear of being alone. There were tears in his eyes. Real tears. You can't fake acting like that."

"And his action scenes?" Chelsea said. "He's like a gymnast and a ninja wrapped in one."

"I imagine using forearm crutches since his teens really helped develop all that upper body strength. Probably helps with the stunts," the cosplayer said. She turned her smile away from the kids and leveled it squarely on Olivia. "But I've never been into muscles. Or men."

The line moved forward again, forcing the cosplayer to turn away. Olivia took the reprieve to study her. Not-so-subtle flirting aside, she wasn't the type who'd normally catch Olivia's eye. The way she held herself was a bit too femme for Olivia's taste. She preferred the androgynous type, and this woman swayed her hips far too much for Olivia's liking. Still, the attention was flattering, and she hadn't freaked out about giving Jodie Gray her fan art for at least three minutes.

"My name's Beth," the cosplayer said, holding out her hand.

"Olivia," she said, shaking her hand. It was the weakest shake she'd ever experienced. "This is Chelsea and Lewis."

"Nice to meet you," she said, not bothering to glance at the kids. "Who are you here to see?"

"Jodie Gray," Olivia said, toying with the flap of her bag.

"Mind Bender fan, huh?" Beth's smile was cocky as she indicated her outfit.

Olivia attempted to return her smile but failed to get any real weight behind it. "Yeah. I guess so."

"You might find you like me better than the real thing." She shuffled backward with the flow of the crowd so she could continue to flirt.

"I seriously doubt it," Chelsea said with a sneer that Beth returned in kind. Turning back to Olivia, she asked, "So how was your date yesterday?"

Before Olivia could respond, Beth folded her arms over her ample chest and said, "Couldn't have been that good of a date or else she'd be here with Olivia, wouldn't she?"

"She is," Lewis said, crossing his arms to match after pointing over Olivia's shoulder.

If she hadn't been distracted by her nerves and Beth's attitude, Olivia might have noticed how pleasant the room had become. There was a warmth behind her, close enough to touch, and the intoxicating aroma of coffee and Riley's musky perfume. She turned and found herself face-to-face with Riley.

For the last day of QueerCon Riley had gone all out in a Wonder Woman graphic tee and worn, dark washed jeans. The V-neck exposed just enough of her collarbone to be enticing and the jeans hugged her hips in all the right ways. Olivia bit her cheek to hold back a groan and squeezed hard at the strap of her bag to keep from reaching out and caressing Riley's arm with both hands.

"Hey there," Riley said.

"Hey yourself."

Olivia watched Riley's eyes perform the same dance over her body and, when she saw Riley's throat bob as she swallowed, Olivia knew the care she'd taken in selecting her outfit for the day had been well-spent. She wouldn't normally have worn a dress to an active, crowded event like this, but the sundress with little yellow flowers had a plunging neckline and a hem that only reached to mid-thigh. It showed a lot of skin and Riley seemed intent on cataloging every visible inch. As she stared, Riley leaned forward enough that she rattled the stanchion holding the nylon rope separating her from the autograph line.

Reaching out a hand to steady the stanchion, Riley finally looked away, blushing so hard Olivia had to look away herself to maintain any semblance of self-control.

"Sorry about that," Riley said.

"No cutting," Beth said and then turned her back decidedly on the four of them.

Chelsea and Lewis immediately burst into laughter and Beth's back stiffened. Olivia shushed them, but couldn't help a laugh herself when she saw the delight in Riley's confused expression.

"I wouldn't dream of it," Riley said to Beth's back, then she turned her attention to the kids. "Ready to meet Jodie?"

"Olivia's doing Jodie," Chelsea said. "We're going to see Matthew Barnes."

"He's perfection," Lewis said.

"He definitely is. Have you met him before?"

"No. Have you?"

"I wish. I've talked to him on the phone and he's super nice. Not just to reporters, either. They say he's great on set. Nice to the crew and everyone."

"Of course he is," Lewis said. "'Cause he's perfect."

"Pretty close," Riley said, but she was looking up at Olivia when she said it.

Never one to miss a chance to embarrass her sister, Chelsea said to Olivia, "She obviously doesn't know you snore."

"She definitely doesn't know that," Olivia said. When the crowd moved forward, putting Riley next to her instead of the kids, she whispered, "Yet."

Riley was taking a sip of her coffee, so Olivia's teasing was rewarded with a sputtering choke and a flurry of coughing. She couldn't help herself and used the excuse of the coughing fit to pat Riley gently between the shoulder blades before letting her hand wander down to the small of Riley's back. Each muscle her fingertips passed tensed with her touch and Riley's eyes widened into big round pools of dark pupil and shimmering blue.

"Ugh. Get a room," Lewis said, turning away from them.

"I got something for you two," Riley said. She was careful to keep her eyes away from Olivia.

"For us?" Lewis asked, his voice squeaking with surprise.

"She's trying to get in with my sister by sucking up to us," Chelsea told him.

"Will it work?" he asked.

"Depends on what it is," Chelsea said

"It's not that great," Riley said, "Just something I scored as a sorta-not-really-VIP." She held out an open palm, stacked high with tokens the size of half-dollars. Each one was a quarter-inch thick and glimmering gold. The kids gasped in unison and Olivia couldn't help staring at the tokens greedily. When neither of the kids reached out, Riley held them closer. "Go on. They're all for you two."

Lewis's hand actually shook as he reached for the treasure. He plucked the token from the top and examined it, his eyes going as wide as the gold coin in his palm. He flipped it over and squealed, "Blinker."

Chelsea grabbed the rest of the stack, jumping up and down and squealing each character's name as she examined the tokens. "Flame Fingers. Mind Bender. Teflon Kid. They're all here."

"The set was part of my swag bag," Riley said as they swapped the tokens back and forth, examining each little detail. "I thought y'all might like them."

The kids didn't respond, they were too absorbed in their new prize. Olivia watched them gush over the character carvings on the tokens and the show logo on the reverse. She couldn't remember the last time she'd seen her sister so happy, but she knew it'd been even longer for Lewis.

She leaned close to Riley, taking in her warmth and enticing scent. Putting her lips close to Riley's ear, she whispered, "I think you've thoroughly won them over."

The moment Olivia's breath touched her skin, Riley shivered, sending a gush of pride from her scalp to her fingertips. If there was one thing Olivia loved, it was throwing a gorgeous masc of center woman off her game.

Riley turned to her with unfocused eyes. "Just them?"

"Oh, you won me over a long time ago," Olivia said, sliding forward with the line, Riley keeping pace with her like a puppy on a leash. "The only question is what you intend to do with your victory."

"I—oof."

Too intent on staring at Olivia, Riley hadn't noticed how the line changed direction. She walked straight into a stanchion, nearly toppling over it. Olivia caught her laughter by biting her bottom lip, but Chelsea and Lewis weren't as successful at holding theirs back. They did try to compose themselves, slapping hands over their mouths when people turned to look, but sputtering laughter broke through the barrier.

For a moment, Olivia was worried Riley would be angry. She was only embarrassed. When she straightened, her face was bright red. She turned her horrified gaze on Olivia, then her attention was drawn by the laughing kids. She stared at them for a long moment, then looked down at her knees still wrapped around the stanchion. Her laughter started low and slow but picked up momentum and soon she was laughing almost as hard as Chelsea.

Turning back to Olivia, she smacked her open palm across her red face and mumbled through her fingers, "Smooth, St. James. Very smooth."

Olivia stepped forward, gently peeling her fingers away so she could look into those pale-blue eyes. Sliding her own fingers between Riley's she said, "I've never been a fan of smooth."

Riley stared at their interlocked fingers, then looked up into Olivia's eyes. "Lucky me."

"Hey, Liv," Chelsea shouted from a few feet away. "The line goes this way."

Olivia didn't bother to look away when she said, "Be right there."

She watched Riley look at the layout of the autograph line and discover that, now that they were close to the tables, she couldn't follow. The line snaked farther away, leaving a large open space for the crowd to form at each table. When Riley looked back to her, there was a new determination in her gaze.

"I was wondering if you have plans for the after party tonight?" she asked in a rush.

"I, um. I'm not going. Tickets are pretty pricey."

"I wouldn't be going either, but they gave me a VIP pass," Riley said. Her hand felt hot and maybe a little sweaty in Olivia's palm. "It—Well, it includes a plus-one."

"Are you asking me a question, Riley St. James?"

"You're not going to make this easy, are you?"

"Never."

"Olivia, will you be my date to the after party tonight?"

Olivia brought a long fingernail to her lip, tapping it against her teeth as though she was considering. "I'll be your date to the party, but only if you agree to be my date to dinner beforehand."

Riley put on one of those devastating smiles, a dimple appearing on her right cheek. "It's a date."

"Liv," Lewis shouted.

"I should go," Riley said.

"Yeah, me too."

"You aren't leaving."

Olivia smiled and said, "Neither are you."

"I'm not going to meet a hot actress. You are."

"Yeah, well," Olivia leaned down close to Riley's ear. "She isn't nearly as hot as you."

She could feel Riley's whole body shiver, so she pulled away, careful to ensure her cheek rubbed against Riley's as she left. Then she swept down the line, mumbling apologies as she caught up with the kids. She didn't let herself turn around to watch Riley go since she'd ignored her responsibilities to her sister long enough.

A few minutes later they were shuffled into the cordoned-off space ending in the actor's individual tables. A QueerCon staffer directed them to the different tables for each of the Middies actors. Fortunately, Jodie's table was right next to Matthew's, so she could keep an eye on Chelsea and Lewis. Unfortunately, she ended up in line right behind Beth, still surly in her Mind Bender cosplay.

After a few awkward moments in line together, Beth turned and there was something startlingly close to remorse in her demeanor when she said, "Sorry for being a bitch back there. And for snapping at your sister. Wow, when I say it like that, it sounds bad, doesn't it?"

Olivia gave her a genuine smile in return. "It's okay."

"It isn't really, but thanks for saying so. I'm not really good with people."

"We're all a little weird. That's why we're here, right? To find people who are weird like us."

"Yeah, I guess so."

Beth's remorse evaporated and she looked more relaxed. There was a moment when Olivia thought she was actually going to try flirting again, but she was spared another awkward rejection by a shout from the staffer at Jodie's table. Just like that, it was Beth's turn to meet Jodie Gray. As disconcerting as the moment with Beth had been, Olivia now knew real fear as she recognized she was next.

Olivia reached into her bag, her fingers trembling on the folder inside. She didn't allow herself another moment of doubt. She carefully pulled the folder out and held it close to her chest as she watched Beth take a selfie with Jodie. Then Beth was dragging her steps away and the table was clear. The staffer in the neon shirt waved Olivia forward and she was standing in front of her favorite actress in the world.

"Hi, I'm Jodie" Jodie Gray held out a hand covered in at least a dozen rings.

Olivia shook her hand, the noise of the room finally flooding back into her ears. "I'm Olivia."

"Nice to meet you, Olivia." Jodie signed a headshot with a purple marker. "Did you travel far to the conference?"

"No, I live here in town. How about you?"

Olivia's insides curdled with embarrassment. Where did Jodie Gray live? Wouldn't a real fan know the answer? They weren't filming now, were they? Chelsea and Lewis would know all of the answers to those questions. She shot a glance over at Matthew's table. The kids weren't at the front yet, and they were staring at her open-mouthed.

"I came from Vancouver so my flight was really long." She drew out the last word as she drew out her trademark four-leaf clover on the end of the "y" in her last name. "But I love coming to these events and QueerCon has been one of my favorites, for sure."

"This is my first con."

"Seriously? That's great. How's it been for you?"

All Olivia could think of was Riley. The butterflies in her stomach at the first meeting. The panel when Riley quoted the Mind Bender line. Their lunch date. Just a few moments ago in line.

"Incredible," Olivia said.

Jodie held out the signed photo and said, "Can't ask for much more. Want a selfie?"

Olivia took the photo and held out her folder awkwardly, saying, "No, thanks, but I made this and I wanted to give it to you."

Jodie opened the folder and stared silently for a long time.

Olivia distracted herself by carefully slipping the signed photo into her bag. As she clipped it shut, she said, "It's just some fan art. It's kinda my thing. I mean, it's not great or anything."

"Olivia." Jodie's voice sounded strange, making her look up. Wonder lit Jodie's heavily lined eyes. "This is absolutely amazing. You drew this?"

"Yeah. You like it?"

"Like it? I love it. You're incredibly talented. Carrie, come here for a minute."

Carrie Nguyen, whose line was by far the longest since Flame Fingers was the most popular character with the queer audience, sat on Jodie's other side. She made apologies to the fan in front of her before slipping over to their table and looking at Olivia's drawing. Her jaw dropped like a cartoon character's.

"Girl, that's so good. You did this?" When Olivia nodded, Carrie continued, "You've got talent. No joke, this is better than the stuff our art department does, but you didn't hear it from me."

"Thank you," Olivia managed to stammer before Carrie hustled back to her table. All the fans in that line were craning their necks, trying to see what the fuss was about.

"Can I post this on my socials?" Jodie asked.

"Of course." Olivia's voice squeaked. Jodie had a huge social media presence. Over half a million followers on Twitter alone.

"Give me your links so I can tag you."

Olivia wrote down her Twitter and Instagram handle on a sticky note. "Thanks for doing that."

"I always tag artists when I post their work. Especially when I love it this much."

Jodie bounced out of her chair and pulled Olivia into a tight hug that rattled with her many bracelets and rings. Olivia was so star-struck and happy she walked out of the autograph line without waiting for the kids.

CHAPTER NINE

Your script is good," the agent said without looking up at Riley. "But why *The Railyard*? I've seen a lot of *Midtown Avengers* scripts this weekend."

"Too many, I'm guessing?" Riley was trying for chummy, but she worried it came out bitter. "I wanted to make sure I stood out."

"Let me give you some advice." He straightened the pages in his hands. "Studios don't want writers who stand out. They want writers who can work to a deadline and stick to the established tone. Have you watched *The Railyard*?"

Riley bristled and she could tell she was blushing, but she knew the drill. She didn't want to be the nobody who argued with a big agent. She sat straighter in her folding chair and said, "I write to deadline all the time. As a freelancer, I sell articles all the time to major outlets and I'm a contract columnist with a popular queer entertainment website."

"Gayntertainment, yeah." He said the name of the site, which boasted nearly a million weekly views, with contempt. "Clever. But being a blogger is not the same as being a screenwriter."

That was the moment Riley knew this interview was a bust. It took all her willpower to stay in her seat, and not ruin her dignity by marching out of the room.

"I write articles, not a blog." She tried to keep her tone upbeat. "But I've been doing master classes and reading everything I can get my hands on. I understand the medium and I understand the process. I can be a real asset in a writers' room."

"I'm sure you can." He stood and held out his hand. Riley shook it reluctantly. "I'll be in touch."

She waited until she wound her way out of the room, dotted with two-seater tables where other aspiring artists were having similar luck, before she said, "Fat chance."

Sure, Riley had never scored a one-on-one with an agent before, but she was pretty sure that guy was never calling her. Even if it had gone better, she would've known nothing would come from this from the sheer number of interviews happening in that room. There were at least ten agents, all meeting with three or four people an hour. She'd thought this interview was exclusive, but it turned out to be a cattle call. It almost felt better that no one who went in that room was likely to get a call back.

"Almost," she mumbled.

Riley switched off her phone's airplane mode and a flurry of notifications popped up. It took a moment for her to remember she'd scheduled a tweet for one o'clock. Stepping to the side of the hall, she checked the traffic on it.

"Not viral, but not bad."

She had a few hundred likes, but that was usual given her number of followers. Hopefully the QueerCon hashtag would get her a few more eyeballs than usual, and maybe it would blow up later.

"I really liked your tweet," a voice said.

Riley thought she was alone, so the voice so close startled her.

"Sorry. I'm sorry," a woman with a messy bun and ridiculously enthusiastic smile said. "Didn't mean to scare you."

"No worries," Riley said. "Hi, I'm Riley."

When Riley stuck out her hand, the woman just stared at it in awe. Several long, slightly awkward seconds passed before she collected herself enough to shake Riley's hand.

"Kelly. Hi. I'm Kelly."

"Nice to meet you, Kelly. I dig your shirt."

Kelly dropped Riley's hand and yanked on the hem of her *Candy Box Kids* shirt. Riley couldn't tell if it was vintage or one of those shirts that came pre-worn to look vintage. Something about how Kelly blushed made her suspect it was the real deal.

"Did you watch *The Candy Box Kids*?" Kelly asked, then looked away. "Of course, you did. You talked about it in an article last year. That it was one of your favorite cartoons ever."

"Good memory. It sure was, right up until the new *She-Ra*. *CBK* was the only cartoon with queer coded characters when I was a kid. I was totally obsessed."

"Me too." Kelly had an adorable way of squealing at the end of her sentences and her unabashed enthusiasm put Riley at ease. "Steve's mom and her 'best friend' were so cool to see. I really connected with them. I was probably the only one watching who didn't care about the kids at all. I just wanted them to go to Steve's house after school so I'd get a glimpse of his moms."

"You definitely weren't the only one. I wanted that, too. I'd get so bummed if they went to Rachel's house instead."

"Same."

Riley's disappointment from the failed interview lessened as she settled into the conversation. "Did you watch *Arcane*?"

"Yeah." Kelly scrunched her face like she was embarrassed. "I wasn't a huge fan. Vi's hot, but the show's a little too gritty for me. Maybe if they actually get together in season two, I'll change my mind."

Riley didn't mention she loved the show. Sure, the relationship between Vi and Caitlyn hadn't developed into anything explicitly romantic yet, but no one could deny it would soon. Plus, Riley lived for gritty.

"I'm sure you're hurrying off somewhere," Kelly said. "I just wanted to say hi and thanks for your articles and recaps and everything."

"Thank you for reading. If it wasn't for my fans, I'd have to get a job writing about baseball or something. I hate sports."

Kelly laughed and seemed to relax now that she'd gotten the appreciation out of the way. This was the part of con Riley hadn't expected and couldn't get enough of. People had been coming up to her nonstop, telling her they were fans. It was so easy to forget about the other side of the screen when she posted articles online. Especially when she was writing about Middies just to pay the bills.

"I wanted to come to your last panel, but the *Batwoman* panel was at the same time and I couldn't miss Meagan Tandy." Kelly fanned her face as she smiled. "You understand, right?"

"Of course. Now I wish I'd skipped my own panel to see her."

When they laughed together, a few folks walking by looked over at them. Riley realized that, apart from her brief moments with Olivia, this was one of the few fun times she'd had all weekend.

"I wanted to ask you," Kelly said. "I know folks have probably been bombarding you with Middies questions the whole time you've been here."

Oh, great. It was fun while it lasted.

"But I wanted to ask you about *The Railyard*."

Riley's fake smile slid off her face. She blinked twice and then said, "Really?"

"Is that okay? I'm sorry. I know you're huge on Middies." Kelly was back to blushing and twisting the hem of her shirt. "But I think that scene at the end of *The Railyard* this season was…"

"So much better." Riley practically yelled.

Kelly giggled. "Well, yeah, it was, right?"

"Look, I love the Middies engagement," Riley lied. "But give me a zombie apocalypse over superheroes any day."

"*Batwoman* aside, I have to agree. That line in *The Railyard* finale when Erin is trying to get Carmen to run away with her?"

Riley recited this line happily, "I want better for us, not just good enough. I want us to thrive, no matter what life throws at us."

"And then Carmen launches herself into Erin's arms." Kelly squealed.

"You know what I love about *The Railyard*? They had the chance to bury their gays like so many other shows, but they didn't."

"Exactly." Kelly stepped closer. "They chose joy, but it totally worked, even with zombies and death and everything."

Riley was so excited, she wanted to drag Kelly back into that room and force her to repeat that for the arrogant agent. She'd chosen joy for her spec script and that's what people wanted, whether he knew it or not. Maybe it was good he wasn't interested. She didn't want an agent who couldn't see her vision.

"It keeps them from being a carbon copy of other zombie shows and it'll keep them high up in the ratings," Riley said.

Kelly's face was alight and Riley couldn't help comparing it to the way Olivia lit up when she talked about the Middies. If only Olivia got like this about something good, not some dime-a-dozen superhero show.

"Do you think they really have a chance to thrive?" Kelly asked.

"Gosh, I hope so. They deserve it, don't they? This last season was tough on them."

This was why Riley had accepted the invitation to QueerCon. The chance to geek out with fans about the good shows. If only they'd had *The Railyard* actresses here this weekend. But *The Railyard* didn't have nearly as big a following. Zombies could be a hard sell for people who craved happily ever afters. Middies brought lighthearted laughs and that would always sell better.

"I should probably let you go," Kelly said, her excitement ebbing.

Riley looked around, surprised to see they were alone in the lobby. She hadn't realized they'd been speaking so long, and frantically checked her watch.

"I'm keeping you from something. I'm sorry," Kelly said.

"No, I've got time." The butterflies were back with a vengeance and Riley thought she might burst. "I've got a date tonight and I'm a little nervous."

"That's awesome. I'm sure you don't need to be nervous. You're Riley St. James, after all. Any woman would be lucky to have a date with you."

Riley's ego got a bit of a boost at the faint hint of disappointment in Kelly's voice. "It's not that cool to be Riley St. James, but I am pretty excited for the date."

"Then I'll let you go get ready. Thanks for the chat and it was really nice meeting you."

Kelly headed off to the hotel exit and Riley made a beeline for the elevators. Refreshing as it was to geek out about lesbians on TV, she needed a shower and a good old-fashioned bathroom mirror pep talk before dinner with Olivia.

CHAPTER TEN

The eyeliner pencil quivered beneath Olivia's lid. She rarely wore more than lip gloss and a little mascara to highlight her eyes, but this party required going all-out. It felt like she'd already been at the mirror for an hour, and she just wanted to be done. She wanted to be sitting at a dinner table across from Riley.

Letting out her breath, she slid the pencil along the rim of her lower lid. Miraculously, she drew a straight line. Switching to the other eye, she forced herself not to think about just who she was going on a date with and the pencil didn't tremble. She set the eye liner down, then started working on her cheeks, letting her mind wander with the less delicate task.

When they were together, teasing and flirting, it was easy to forget who Riley was. In fact, most of the time it was Riley who was off balance. The power shift was thrilling for Olivia, but when she was at home and had time to think about who she'd been teasing, her stomach did somersaults.

Apart from her popular social media platforms, Riley had been a freelance entertainment journalist since before she left college. She'd published on all the big-name online platforms and there were rumors she'd sold a story to *Rolling Stone*. There was hardly a queer woman in the world who didn't know Riley St. James and that was before she began modeling for TomboyX. She was out of Olivia's league by several orders of magnitude.

Swiping mascara across her lashes, she considered how easy it was to talk to Riley, despite her celebrity. She didn't act like Olivia thought a celebrity would. She didn't make every conversation about herself or pretend like she was doing Olivia a favor by going out with her. Plenty of her exes, who had no claim to fame, had done that. No, Riley was sweet and down-to-earth and she was kind to Chelsea and Lewis. As long as Olivia could force herself to stay away from those underwear ads, tonight could be an amazing date with an amazing woman.

Olivia had just set down her mascara when the front door burst open. Peeking around the powder room door, she checked the time on the living room clock. Allison had cut it close, but she was here now. Olivia forced down her nerves and surveyed lip colors.

"Olivia, sweetie," Allison said, gripping the doorframe with one hand and her long necklace in the other. "I'm late. I'm terrible. Please forgive me."

Choosing a dusty rose lipstick, Olivia laughed at her mom. "Of course I forgive you and you're not terrible. How was your date?"

"Fine, but it doesn't matter because I've ruined yours."

"No, you haven't. I don't have to leave for ten minutes."

"Olivia, come quick." Chelsea rushed into the room looking just as distraught as Allison. "Poppa fell."

"What?" The lipstick clattered into the sink as Olivia turned to her sister. "What happened?"

"He was going to the bathroom and he fell."

"I've told him not to go without me to help him," Olivia said as she rushed down the hall.

Fortunately, she hadn't put on her heels yet, but the mid-calf, off-the-shoulder dress in emerald green satin clung too tightly to her hips and legs to allow her to run. She stumbled down the hall, Chelsea close behind, and her mother last, nearly toppling over Chelsea to look into the room.

Poppa was sprawled across the bed, half on the mattress with his bad back perched on the edge. He wasn't groaning as Olivia had feared, but he was trying feebly to roll over. Rushing to his side, Olivia put her hand on his chest, feeling the fluttering of his heart like a scared bird beneath the thin fabric of his undershirt.

"Poppa? Are you okay?" When he tried again to sit up, she held him down gently. "I don't want you moving until I'm sure you aren't hurt. Did you hit your head?"

"He didn't." Chelsea sniffled. She was standing back in the doorway like she was afraid to come in. "I was walking by when I heard him call out. He lost his balance and fell back onto the bed."

"I'm fine, Liv," Poppa said in his wheezing, grumpy tone. "Just help an old man sit up. I've still got to pee."

Olivia helped lever him up, supporting his neck and helping him bend at the waist. He'd been a carpenter his whole life and physically fit well into his seventies, but he'd lost his core strength after a bout with pneumonia.

"Better, Poppa?" Olivia asked when he was sitting up, catching his breath.

"No, it's not better. I have to pee."

Allison laughed from the door, her arms wrapped around Chelsea's shoulders. "He's fine alright. Want me to take him?"

"He wants to take himself," Poppa said. He looked sheepishly at Olivia. "Help me stand up, will you?"

"I'll help you stand up all the way to the bathroom," Olivia said.

He hadn't just lost his balance, Olivia could tell by the way he walked. Even with her helping, he was shaky on his legs. She allowed him to stand on his own while using the bathroom, but she made sure he kept the door open just in case. Once his hands were washed and he was back in bed, she went to work checking his blood pressure and his glucose.

"Your blood sugar's a little low. Why don't we get you some juice?"

"I'll take a beer instead."

Chelsea got a glass of orange juice while Olivia and Allison set up a few chairs around the bed. He grumbled the whole time, but since it was Chelsea who held the straw for him, he didn't have a choice but to drink. The color came back into his face almost immediately.

Allison stared at her hands. "It's possible that I didn't make him finish lunch."

Olivia snapped her head around and glared. "Mom, you know he needs to eat his meals. How many times have I told you?"

"I know the old grump needs to be bullied." She turned her annoyance on her father. "But he only listens to you."

"That's because I don't take no for an answer."

"I can hear you two. I haven't died quite yet," Poppa said.

Chelsea snuggled up beside Poppa, laying her cheek on his bony shoulder. The only thing he responded to better than Olivia's nagging was Chelsea's cuddles. He sighed and wrapped an arm around her, even going so far as to apologize.

"It's okay, Poppa. We're just glad you're all right," Olivia said, plucking her phone from the floor where she'd dropped it.

"What're you doing?" Allison asked.

"Texting Riley," she said with as much good-will as she could muster. "There's no way I'm making it to our date."

Chelsea sat up so Poppa's arm fell off her shoulder. "You have to go."

"Of course you're going on your date," Allison said.

"I don't have a choice. The restaurant's all the way across town. I'll never make it."

"Please go, Liv." Poppa's mournful voice made her look up as soon as she pressed send. "This is all my fault. I promise I'll be a good boy and eat all my dinner."

"Oh, Poppa." She dropped her phone on the mattress and took his hand in both hers. "You are more important to me than any date."

"But this is Riley St. James," he said.

"How do you know who she is?"

"You think I can't hear you talking 'cause I'm an old man? I know how much you like that girl."

Her phone buzzed, but Olivia was too busy reassuring Poppa to pay attention. She did, however, notice when Chelsea picked it up and started typing.

"How did you figure out my passcode again? I just changed it."

"I didn't," Chelsea said without looking up from the screen. "I added my thumbprint to your phone."

"Chelsea." Allison's voice was stern. "How did you learn to do that?"

"I used your phone to Google a video ages ago."

"Can you get into my phone too?" Allison asked. Chelsea didn't answer, but her smile spoke volumes. "Chelsea Louise Duran-Spencer, you will take your thumbprint off my phone immediately."

"Excuse me," Olivia said. "What is happening with my phone?"

"Riley responded to your text about missing dinner," Chelsea said.

"What'd she say?"

"She said she understands and she wants to know when she can see you again."

"She wants to see me again?" Olivia asked.

Chelsea looked up with a disgusted scowl. "Of course she does."

"And what did you say?"

Chelsea clicked off the screen and held out the phone. "I told her you can still make it to the party."

"You told her what?"

Olivia snatched the phone back as it beeped with a new message. Riley's text read, *Great. I'll be waiting outside with the tickets.*

"Don't argue." To her surprise, it wasn't Chelsea who said it, but Poppa. "You're already dressed. You may as well go, right?"

Chelsea's smile was smug as she leaned back into Poppa's shoulder. Olivia was about to protest when Allison cut her off.

"It'd be a shame to waste all that time and makeup, after all."

"Oh, no." Olivia touched her cheek. "Is it too much?"

"Not at all, sweetie." Allison leaned forward and touched her freshly curled hair. "It's the perfect amount. I never get to see you dressed up."

Olivia turned to her sister and grandpa, who both nodded in agreement. The dead weight of disappointment in her belly bubbled into excitement. Without another word, she leapt from the chair and shuffled back to her room for her purse and shoes.

Chapter Eleven

Riley's wingtips clicked on the concrete pool deck as she bounced on the balls of her feet. She smoothed the thighs of her dark-washed jeans and straightened the lapel of her suit jacket. She'd decided against a tie tonight, hoping the casual lavender V-neck would telegraph an ease she didn't feel. Hearing footsteps approaching, she spun, holding her breath in anticipation of seeing Olivia, but she let it out slowly. A woman in a leather miniskirt walked beside her girlfriend, the two of them exchanging enough flirty glances that Riley doubted they'd be at the party long.

Deciding a solid amount of pacing was in order to settle her nerves, Riley strode to the end of the velvet rope and back again, slapping her phone against her open palm.

"Relax, St. James," she whispered, doing her best to channel Dani's friendly ribbing. "This girl likes you for some reason. Tonight will be great."

The staffer scanning tickets shot her a wink, making Riley realize just how loudly she'd spoken her personal pep talk. She turned to retrace her steps away from her embarrassment, but was distracted by another pair of approaching partygoers. This couple was just as flirty with each other as the last, but one looked up in time to notice Riley.

"How's it going, Riley?"

It took her a moment to recognize Heather without her staffer T-shirt and clipboard. Heather pulled Riley into a crushing hug then introduced her girlfriend, a woman so tall she made Riley feel like a teenager.

"You clean up awful nice," Riley said.

"Same." She looked around with concern. "You okay? Why aren't you in at the party?"

"Waiting on my date," Riley said, nervously swallowing the last word.

Heather leaned back into her girlfriend's arm. "Must be quite the girl to make the great Riley St. James nervous. You've been very popular this weekend."

"Have I?"

Heather shook her head. "She is quite the girl then. You haven't noticed the way everyone's been drooling over you since that Middies panel with the quote."

Riley rolled her eyes, but hopefully Heather didn't notice. "If you say so."

"Have a good night, Riley. If I don't see you again, it's been a pleasure showing you around this weekend."

They shook hands and, as Heather disappeared into the party, Riley realized she would genuinely miss her company. She'd made Riley's first con experience so easy and those easy moments were a relief when Olivia set her head spinning and stomach flipping. While she wanted to spend every possible moment with Olivia, Riley had been relieved dinner was canceled. Unlike their lunch date, when there seemed to be unlimited hours available to them, this date marked the end of con and she couldn't help worry they wouldn't see each other again. The thought set Riley's feet in motion again.

She didn't want this to be the last time she saw Olivia. Maybe they could figure something out. Miami and Tampa were only a few hours apart, after all.

"Hey."

Olivia's voice cut through Riley's nerves. She turned in slow-motion, equally desperate for and frightened of that first glance.

"Hey." Riley stuttered over the single syllable.

The addition of heels to their existing height difference meant Riley turned around to find herself at eye level with Olivia's lips.

"Sorry I'm late," Olivia said with a breath of laughter that told Riley she'd been caught staring.

"No problem." Riley found her voice and a sliver of confidence. "You look…"

No word seemed adequate to the moment. Olivia's emerald dress fit her like a second skin and her soaring heels shaped her legs with devastating precision. Her eyes sparkled with mischief as usual, but the way her lipstick highlighted her smile took Riley's breath away.

Olivia stepped close and ran a fingernail down the lapel on Riley's jacket from neck line all the way to the button over her navel. "I could get used to seeing you dressed up," Olivia said.

"Maybe you could see it more often." The words were out of Riley's mouth before she could stop them. "I mean, maybe we could see each other again. After tonight. Dressed up."

"I like the sound of that." Olivia leaned close and Riley's mind emptied. "How about we go to this party first?"

"Sure. Yeah. That sounds good. Party."

"Oh, wait." Riley's heart sank, sure she was ready to disappear back into the night. Instead, Olivia asked, "How did your interview go? With the agent?"

"Oh." Riley swallowed hard. Olivia was looking at her the way she had that first time they met. The stars in her eyes like she, Olivia, was the lucky one to be having this conversation. Riley couldn't bring herself to ruin that glow. "Great. Really great. He said he'd call soon."

"That's wonderful." Olivia squeezed her hand and said, "I knew you'd get it. After all, you're Riley St. James."

Guilt flooded through Riley for a heartbeat, but Olivia didn't give her a chance to dwell on it. She moved surprisingly fast in heels so high. Pulling Riley's hand, she led the way into the roar of the crowd.

The QueerCon After Party was held at the hotel's rooftop bar and pool. Hundreds of people were milling around the multiple bars and dancing to the techno beat on the dance floor. Olivia navigated them through fancy-dressed partygoers until they were in the beating heart of the crowd. The music vibrated up through the concrete and shook the last of Riley's nerves from her bones.

"Want a drink?" she shouted into Olivia's ear, though she still wasn't sure she could be heard over the music.

"Later. Dance with me first?"

Riley was all too happy to oblige. Her confidence surged the moment she set foot on the dance floor. Her dancing skills far outstripped her conversational skills, and she was thrilled to talk with her body for a while. Happily, Olivia was clearly in her element as well. They slid through the song together, their bodies rarely touching but electricity keeping them constantly connected.

As the songs ticked by and Riley felt more at ease, she moved closer, letting a hand flit to Olivia's hip and then away again. Olivia moved closer in response, never reaching out but inviting Riley's touch. Begging for a connection. Sweat collected around Riley's collar and in the close-cropped hair above her ears.

The song changed to a smooth hip-hop beat and Riley danced across the polished wooden floor. Olivia watched her, a half-smile curving her lips. Riley moved in, sliding up to Olivia's side and behind her. Olivia grabbed a handful of her curls, pulling them up to expose the long, bronzed column of her neck. She looked over her shoulder, locking eyes with Riley, her gaze inviting Riley closer still.

Riley rested trembling hands lightly on Olivia's hips. Olivia rolled her body into Riley's with the chorus, settling their overheated skin against each other, layers of sweat-dampened cloth trapped between. Riley rolled with her, her steps flaring with the music, but her focus firmly settled on the thousands of places their bodies touched. They moved together well, fitting touch to music, intimacy to song. Riley leaned close to Olivia's exposed neck, drinking in the feel of her, the smell of her.

When her lips were close to Olivia's skin but not quite touching, she whispered a question. It was innocuous, a gentle inquiry if Olivia was having fun, but the words didn't matter. The caress of her breath against Olivia's skin was her goal. Just as she hoped, Olivia responded to the kiss of Riley's breath. She could feel Olivia's sharp inhalation. Could sense the shiver run through her. Olivia's step faltered for a moment and, in that moment, Riley knew she wasn't the only one excited by this date.

Just as the shiver ended, so did the song, leaving them with a crashing silence only broken by the hollow echo of their own panting breath.

"Ready for that drink?" Olivia asked, her skin glistening with sweat.

Riley couldn't manage more than a nod. A thousand eyes were on Olivia as they passed through the crowd, but Olivia didn't seem to notice any of them. Riley couldn't help the swell of pride in her chest. All these beautiful people around them, and Olivia wanted to be with her.

The burst of pride deflated somewhat when they stopped at the back of a mile-long line for the bar.

"How's your grandpa?" Riley asked, annoyed with herself that she hadn't thought to inquire earlier.

"Oh, he's fine. I'm really sorry about dinner."

"Not at all. Family comes first."

They inched forward. Olivia asked, "What about yours?"

"My family? There's not much of it. My parents live back in Upstate New York."

"Brothers and sisters?"

"Nope. Just the three of us and we don't see each other much," Riley said.

"I'm so sorry to hear that. I can't imagine not being close to my family."

"If I had a sister like Chelsea, I'd want to hang out with her all the time, too."

"If you had a sister like Chelsea, you'd have to hang out with her all the time. I can't get rid of her," Olivia said.

"Sounds like a good problem to have."

Olivia stepped close and ran a fingernail along the shell of Riley's ear. "It can be tough to get privacy."

"Yeah." Riley swallowed hard and fell face first into the swirling depths of Olivia's brown eyes. "I bet it is."

A slow, sensual smile spread across Olivia's lips and Riley was about to say something stupid and ruin the moment when she felt a tap on her shoulder. Heather's grinning face swam into focus as

Riley climbed her way back into the world. The sound of the music smashed into her just as Heather spoke.

"Sorry, what?"

"I said you can go to the bar in the VIP section." Heather pointed to a raised balcony behind the pool. "It'll be quicker and more private."

Riley ignored the way Heather winked and cut a glance at Olivia. "Oh, I didn't realize we were allowed up there."

"Just show them the tickets on your phone." Heather pointed to the staffer standing at the velvet rope. "There are some tables up there, too. You might even be able to talk without shouting."

Heather melted back into the crowd, and they happily abandoned the long line for the seclusion of the VIP section and snagged a table along the railing. The view of downtown Tampa was spectacular, but Riley only gave it a cursory glance. Olivia had all of her attention.

Riley had chosen beer, wanting to sip something slowly and make it last all night rather than getting drunk and missing out on this last chance to get to know her date. Olivia had decided on the night's theme drink, a fruity, bright red cocktail they called "Wayhaught" but she took one sip and set it aside.

Sliding along the curved bench seat until her whole body was pressed against Riley's, Olivia leaned in close, her breath tickling Riley's ear. "I've wanted to kiss you all night. Will you let me?"

Riley answered with her body, pressing close to Olivia and trailing her lips up the length of her throat until their lips brushed once, twice, and then locked. Olivia melted into the kiss, allowing Riley to lead but following with enthusiasm. Riley was slow and soft at first, reveling in the warmth of Olivia's lips and the mingling flavor of her lipstick and the cherry syrup of her drink. Her mind spun pleasantly as the kiss progressed, bringing the exhilaration and centrifugal pull of driving into a curve at reckless speed. She waited until she felt the tremor of desire settle into Olivia's skin before she deepened the kiss.

Olivia's lips parted and she accepted Riley's tongue with a sharp intake of breath. Riley groaned at the first taste, tilting her head to fit more closely to Olivia. She dove into the kiss, losing herself in this woman and not wanting to be found. Olivia responded to every brush of lips and tongue as though they'd been kissing all their lives. The way their bodies had synced on the dance floor was nothing to how their mouths danced in unison. Olivia slid a hand up Riley's arm and under her suit jacket, gripping her shoulder.

Riley broke the kiss, gasping for air and purchase as the world righted itself around them. Looking into Olivia's eyes, cloudy and unfocused and inches away, she felt the wild need for more. To hold Olivia closer than she could here on this windy rooftop. To see her and be seen in return. She yearned to know if their bodies would find that shared rhythm in everything they did together and she knew, by the way Olivia stared at her lips with obvious hunger, that Olivia wanted the same.

"Olivia? It is you."

Riley's mind turned slowly after the kiss, and it took her a long time to register what she was seeing when she looked across the table. Jodie Gray, dazzling in a simple scoop cut silver dress, stood across from them, smiling at Olivia as though they were old friends.

"Hi," Olivia said. It came out as a croak. She cleared her throat and tried again. "Hi, Jodie, how are you?"

"I'm fabulous. Have you met Matthew Barnes and Carrie Nguyen?" she asked, indicating the group with her.

"Not officially." Olivia stood and held out her hand, leaving a ghost of her warmth behind on Riley's thigh. "It's such an honor to meet you all."

Matthew shifted his weight to one forearm crutch in order to shake Olivia's hand. He squinted at her through the thick lens of his round eyeglasses. Combined with the day's growth of beard and the wide set of his shoulders he looked like the quintessential example of the hipster Hollywood type—effortlessly handsome and perpetually at ease.

"You're the artist, aren't you?" he asked.

"Of course she is." Carrie shook Olivia's hand more enthusiastically. "We sorta met earlier. Jodie ripped me away from my station to see your piece. The more I look at it, the more I love it. You're super talented."

"What piece?" Riley asked, feeling awkward as the only one sitting.

"Oh, I did some fan art and gave it to Jodie in the autograph line today." Olivia slid back onto the bench beside her. "I'm surprised you remember," she said to Jodie.

"How could I forget? Have you seen my post on Instagram? It has three thousand likes. You're huge online right now."

"Am I?" There was a note of fear seasoning the surprise in Olivia's voice. Riley put a hand on her thigh and Olivia clung to it.

"You didn't know?" Jodie's voice had the lilt of teasing to it.

"I haven't really been online today."

Jodie whipped a phone coated in plastic jewels and sequins from her clutch. After a moment of tapping around, she handed it to Olivia with a triumphant, motherly pride. Riley looked over her shoulder at the screen, noting the number of likes had gone up to nearly four thousand. But more than the interactions, Riley was mesmerized by the image.

Riley had seen a lot of fan art in her day. Most everyone in the fandoms were big enough fans to either like or create original artwork based on their favorite shows. The quality of work she saw varied widely, with some stuff that made her cringe and some artists talented enough to have their own booths on the QueerCon main floor. This was better than anything Riley had ever seen.

"Olivia." She couldn't come up with a word to describe what she felt, so she tried to communicate her admiration with her eyes. "You're incredible."

The smile she got in return set her heart pounding almost as much as the kiss had. Olivia mumbled, "You're not so bad yourself, hotshot."

"Hey, that's my line," Carrie said, grinning at Jodie. Apart from the quote Riley had given during the first panel of Con, this was the most popular line from Middies, akin to Han and Leia's moment from Star Wars. "Are you taking commissions?"

"Commissions? Um, I hadn't really thought about it," Olivia said.

"You should. But put me on the list before Carrie. What are your rates?" Matthew asked.

"My rates?"

"How much do you charge for a piece?" he clarified.

"I don't know. I've never sold anything."

"You better come up with an idea," Matthew said. "There are at least a dozen people on Jodie's Insta asking for commissions, but I'm first."

The three actors huddled around Olivia, talking about rates they've seen other artists charge and quizzing her on how long it took her to make the drawing she'd given Jodie. Riley took the opportunity to pull up Jodie's Instagram on her own phone and, sure enough, fans and actors alike were crowding the comments, promising to follow Olivia's pages and get their own "Olivia Original" as they dubbed her work.

With more time to study the piece, Riley was newly amazed by the quality of the work. Her obvious talent could land Olivia a great job in animation or the comic book industry. It was a shame she was wasting it on fan art.

Matthew cut away from the main conversation. "I just realized you're Riley. You interviewed me for Buzzfeed last year."

"I sure did." Riley shook his hand. "You were a great interview. Thanks for your time."

"My time? You're the star here. You made me sound cool enough to belong with these two." He pointed at the actresses still locked in conversation with Olivia.

"Wait." Carrie cut in. "You wrote the Buzzfeed thing? That was awesome."

"Thank you," Riley said. "But an interview is only as good as the subject and Matthew is a great subject."

"Nice sucking up, but I work with him every day, remember? He's boring." She drew the last word out, sounding an awful lot like Chelsea picking at Lewis.

Riley fell into conversation with Matthew, picking up on the same conversational chemistry that had made the interview so good. Soon she'd even convinced him to consider a longer format piece, which was lucky because she'd already pitched the idea to a contact at *Vanity Fair*. The real coup came, however, when a writer friend of his joined their conversation. The writer had worked with Matthew on his last show and was currently on *The Railyard*. Riley admitted screenwriting was her goal.

"You should get Riley in with Ashton," Matt said. Turning to Riley he explained, "Ashton Case, the showrunner on *The Railyard*."

"Oh, I definitely know who Ashton Case is," Riley said. "Is she looking for a new writer?"

"We're always looking for fresh talent. I'm happy to introduce you. What's your email?"

Holding her excitement in, Riley produced a card for her new friend and spent a little time gushing about the show. By the time the guys wandered off in search of another round, Riley had forgotten all about the disastrous agent interview.

A small crowd formed around Riley and Olivia's table and their drinks sat forgotten, sweating in the Florida night. The group had grown beyond the Middies actors to include friends and coworkers from other projects. Before long the group had separated into two smaller camps, one talking to Olivia about commissions, the other quizzing Riley on her past articles and future interview subjects. Even as they carried on as their own centers of gravity, Riley and Olivia never lost contact with each other. Riley's hand had found a permanent home on Olivia's thigh, the warmth of her skin an anchor in the chaos. Olivia, meanwhile, had draped her arm around Riley's shoulders. She drew circles on Riley's neck and occasionally threaded into her hair.

After an hour of chatting with some of the most famous actors at QueerCon, Riley's gaze traveled down to the rest of the party, most of which was enthralled by the happenings in the VIP section. The focus made her realize she was at the center of her first true celebrity moment. Looking over at Olivia, she was met with a sparkling, awed gaze.

She leaned in and spoke into Riley's ear. "Can you believe this? Carleen Richards said she liked my work. The Carleen Richards."

"It's pretty wild. I think I set up an interview with Maisie Richardson-Sellers."

"Seriously? That's incredible."

Though her eyes were filled with pride and excitement, Olivia wasn't able to say more as another celebrity, this time a wildly popular female director, asked her a question about her work. Riley was immediately pulled back into conversation herself. Someone had heard about her possible article for *Rolling Stone*, and she admitted she had pitched an idea but hadn't confirmed interviews yet. Within a few minutes she had names and contact information for managers and personal PR reps from just about everyone at the table.

As quickly as the swarm had surrounded them, they were gone. Blinking into the sudden stillness, Riley turned to see Olivia shoving business cards and coasters covered in email addresses into her purse. She'd collected so many they barely fit. Unfortunately, it wasn't only their table emptying. The DJ announced the final song of the night and exhausted partygoers stumbled toward the bank of elevators.

"That was nuts," Riley said. Her shock was barely enough to keep her disappointment at bay.

"No kidding." Olivia's eyelids were noticeably drooping. "I wish we'd had more time to talk, though."

Riley slid out of the booth and held a hand out to Olivia. "Can I make it up to you?"

"I'm the one who should make it up to you," Olivia said, falling into step so close her hip rubbed against Riley with every step. "We missed dinner because of me."

Riley held back, letting a final group of partiers fill the open elevator and leave them alone in front of closed doors. She turned to Olivia and mustered as much courage as she could find. "Then how about you come to dinner with me one weekend?"

One of Olivia's eyebrows lifted until it was hidden behind a loose curl over her forehead. "Dinner with you?"

"If you're not interested it's okay."

"No. I'm absolutely interested." Olivia stepped forward, looking down into Riley's eyes.

"Miami and Tampa aren't that far apart," Riley said.

Riley was stuck in the moment, aching to lean forward but trapped by mahogany eyes. An elevator chimed behind them, drawing Riley from her daze. Olivia looked uncharacteristically hesitant, her eyes darting to the metal doors sliding open and then to the floor. Riley pulled Olivia into the car with her and stabbed her thumb deliberately into the button that would take them to the lobby. She felt Olivia release her held breath and wondered whether it was a sigh of relief or disappointment Riley wasn't taking them to her room.

"Where are you parked?" Riley asked as the gears ground into motion. "I'll walk you."

"I used the valet," Olivia said, her cheeks a lovely shade of pink in the fluorescent overhead light. "I didn't want to be even later searching for a spot."

"Can I wait with you while they get your car?"

Olivia's smile lit the small space on fire, showing a row of white teeth. "I'd like that."

The air was warmer on ground level than it had been on the breezy rooftop. The valet dashed off when Olivia handed over her ticket, leaving them alone near the same potted palm where they'd lingered after their lunch date. Olivia held Riley's hand tight.

"When's your flight home?" Olivia asked.

"Early. I should probably pack tonight."

"Got any plans tomorrow?"

"I'll be trying to get my cat to forgive me," Riley said. "His mom works from home so he's not used to being left alone."

"Clingy boyfriend." Olivia smiled. "I've had a few of those."

"It's a new experience for me. I'm usually the clingiest, most spoiled one in the relationship."

"Spoiled, huh?"

"I have a tendency to get what I want."

Olivia hummed. "So do I."

A sharp breeze whipped a lock of hair from Olivia's forehead and set it dancing by her smooth cheek. Riley watched it sway for a moment, but the sight of Olivia's lips, lush and still carrying a hint of her lipstick despite the long night, drew her eye. Her tongue peeked out between them, running a course across her bottom lip before Olivia caught the lip in her teeth. Riley thought of her early flight and her empty apartment in Miami. She knew she couldn't go back there without tasting Olivia's lips one more time.

Reaching out to cup Olivia's cheek, Riley pulled her close. Olivia dipped willingly and their lips met as they had before, with the brush of skin on skin before locking in place. Riley tried to be sweet and gentle, but the scent of Olivia's skin and the taste of her tongue drove all restraint from her. She held Olivia close, exploring her mouth with reckless abandon as Olivia met her with equal if not greater passion. She devoured Olivia. Each taste only increasing her hunger until she was completely lost in this perfect, passionate kiss.

The valet revved the engine as he pulled to the curb and Riley took the hint, pulling unwillingly away from the gentle caress of Olivia's mouth. She was pleased to open her eyes to a breathless, hazy-eyed Olivia staring back at her. The desire painted on her bronzed face made it so much harder for Riley to take two steps back and shove her hands deep into her pockets.

"Good night, Olivia. Drive safe."

CHAPTER TWELVE

O livia tried to ease the front door open silently, but the top hinge she'd been meaning to grease for the last month squealed her arrival. Peering through the dark living room toward the low glow of light from the kitchen, she saw she needn't have been so careful.

"What're you doing awake?" she asked.

Allison finished tapping at her phone screen before looking up. "Rick is waiting up for his daughter after a date."

Olivia checked her watch. "She's only seventeen, what's she doing out at one o'clock?"

"Exactly what Rick is waiting to find out. Want a cup of tea? It's chamomile."

Olivia stuck out her tongue and shook her head but lowered herself gratefully into the barstool beside Allison. "You're both waiting up for your daughters to come home. How very parental."

"I wasn't waiting for you to come home." Allison sipped her tea. "I thought this would be an overnight for you."

"Mom, it's only our second date."

"Oh, don't be silly." Allison grabbed the paper tag and dunked her tea bag around in her mug. "I went home with your father on the first date."

"Mom!"

"Shh, you'll wake your sister."

"Then don't say stuff like that."

"Oh, Olivia, if you know, you just know. All those rules are ridiculous. I see that look in your eye when you talk about Riley."

Peeling off her shoes so she could avoid her mother's eye, she couldn't keep from smiling. "Maybe, but I still don't want to know that about you and my dad."

Allison rolled her eyes before pushing off her stool. For the first time Olivia noticed how tired she looked. She was wearing her favorite, well-worn robe and a pair of house slippers whose bright red had faded to pink many years before. There had been a time when Allison had worn this outfit, with a rotating stream of dingy sweats beneath, more often than anything else. That had been right after Chelsea's father's death when Olivia put her own life on hold to help her mother. She remembered all too well how Allison had joylessly gone through the motions of life after her father had left. Olivia had been determined to pull her mother back into herself before Chelsea saw too much of that emptiness. The memories of those long, terrible days floated at the corners of her mind, threatening to burst the happy bubble she'd built through dancing with Riley.

Allison rinsed her mug. "When are you going to see each other again?"

"Soon, I think," Olivia said.

"You sound surprised. Didn't you plan to date after QueerCon was over?"

"Honestly?" Olivia picked at a loose piece of Formica on the counter. "No. I thought she was just looking for a hookup."

"Is that what you wanted?"

Olivia thought back to their lunch date, when she had teasingly remarked that the position of someone to take care of her was open for applications. Riley hadn't responded, so Olivia assumed she'd wanted something short term. It hadn't been ideal, but she would take anything Riley was willing to give. The idea of Riley wanting more, however, sent little tendrils of happiness tingling across Olivia's skin.

"Definitely not. I just thought—I mean, she's famous and popular and she could have anyone there."

"And she wanted you. Not just for the weekend, either." Allison came back around the counter and took Olivia by both shoulders, forcing her to look up. "One day you'll realize how wonderful you are. You shouldn't be surprised a famous journalist wants to date you."

"I guess." Olivia had been prepared for the sparks between them during that kiss, but she'd been truly shocked when Riley hadn't invited her back to her hotel room. "She flies home early tomorrow. We'll probably meet up soon. She said that's what she wanted."

"Well, don't let it go too long before you make plans." Allison dropped a kiss on Olivia's forehead. "Long-distance relationships need a lot of planning."

She flipped off the hallway light as she went to bed, leaving Olivia sitting in the warm glow from the stove hood light. When she thought Riley was only looking for a hookup, she'd been even more forward than she usually was. Olivia had always been comfortable with her sexuality and expressing, in words and actions, exactly what she wanted from a potential partner. Now that a real relationship with Riley was a possibility, she considered slowing things down. Cooling off a little rather than give Riley the wrong idea about her intentions. The only problem was her heart and her body had no interest in being coy and Riley clearly didn't mind Olivia taking the lead. In fact, the way Riley responded to her assertiveness made it perfectly clear how comfortable she was ceding power in the relationship.

But initiating a kiss and texting the same day were two different things. Still, she dug her phone from her bag, staring at the blank screen and trying to decide how Riley would respond if she reached out.

Olivia decided to just text her good night. Riley couldn't be too upset about that.

Firing off the text before she could lose her nerve, she collected her shoes and purse and shuffled toward her room. Thank goodness she was working the afternoon shift tomorrow. She'd never be able to drag herself out of bed for an early workday. As she arrived at her bedroom door, her phone chimed with an incoming message.

Good night. Thank you for a magical evening

❖

Riley was met with the shrill, croaking meow of her feline roommate the moment she pushed through the front door of her apartment. With one hand gripping the handle of her suitcase and the other the broken strap of her laptop bag, she had to kick the door shut behind her. The moment the lock clicked into place, Nicodemus's jet-black face popped out from underneath the sofa, swiftly followed by the rest of his considerable bulk.

Riley made it three steps from the door in the time it took Nicodemus to bolt across the room and launch himself onto her suitcase. His weight tipped her precarious balance and she stumbled forward, tripping over the corner of the rug and dropping her laptop bag. Only her low center of gravity kept her from falling on her face and she'd never been so happy to be only five foot six inches tall.

"This is great, Nic." She hauled the bag up now that she had two hands. He'd settled into a curled position for all the world like he was lying in his cat bed. "Don't mind me. Just exhausted after hours at the airport. I'll just carry you to the couch, shall I?"

He purred in response, the rumbling of his contentment nearly drowning out her groan as she lowered the bag to the floor next to the couch. She collapsed on the couch, sighing with relief as she propped her feet on the throw pillows. Nicodemus immediately jumped up to join her, knocking the rest of the breath out of her when he landed on her diaphragm.

"I missed you, too, buddy," she said as he kneaded his front paws into her ribs.

After sufficiently tenderizing her, he threw his head at her left breast and rolled over to expose acres of fluffy white belly.

"Oh, no, I'm not falling for that one. It's a trap."

Instead, she scratched behind his ear and his purring deepened to a euphoric baritone. He wrapped his paws around her wrist and licked her hand as she scratched, his eyes firmly shut. While Nicodemus bathed one hand and she thoroughly scratched his ears, cheeks, and chin, Riley retrieved her phone from her back pocket. Fortunately, she'd been able to charge it at the Tampa airport because she'd been texting almost nonstop since the previous night.

After leaving Olivia at her car, Riley had decided a very long, very cold shower was necessary. The chill of the water had done little to cool the fire Olivia's kisses had lit inside her, but she managed to distract herself with packing. As she'd climbed into bed a text from Olivia had arrived and they'd talked into the early hours.

She'd ignored her wake-up call, opting to catch an extra hour of sleep and rely on her phone's alarm instead. Barely making it to the airport in time, she'd been relieved to find takeoff had been delayed, allowing her time for a bagel and very large latte. Olivia's first text of the morning—one bemoaning their late night and her difficulty dragging herself into work—arrived as boarding began. Texts flew back and forth between them until Riley was forced to turn off her phone for the short flight, but she'd promised to let Olivia know when she'd arrived safely at home.

Nicodemus had fallen asleep, drooling on her hoodie, by the time Riley gave up on a reply. She knew Olivia was at work, so she might not be able to answer right away, but she couldn't help feeling disappointed. Needing to feel some connection, she pulled up Olivia's Instagram page and started scrolling through a series of selfies that made her stomach flutter. Olivia's eyes were just as vibrant, just as teasing and provocative through the camera lens as they had been in person. Over the weekend, the selfies had given way to shots of QueerCon and the newest entry was the photo of her fan art Jodie had tagged her in. Just looking at the page Riley tracked new followers joining in to heap on praise.

Objectively, Riley had to admit it was excellent work. She'd perfectly captured Mind Bender's intense concentration and the unmistakable glimmer in her eye as she confessed her love to Flame Fingers, present in the work only as the shoulder over which the viewer witnessed the scene. The staging meant anyone looking at the piece would feel like Flame Fingers—like they were the object of this woman's affection.

"This would be perfect if it were from literally any other show," she told Nicodemus.

He gave a whistling snore in response.

Riley turned back to her phone in time to see Olivia's artwork blink out in favor of a black screen announcing a call from Dani.

"What's up, rock star?" Dani said over the roar of music. "You back in our fair city?"

"Yeah, I'm home." Riley switched to speaker phone so she could go back to scratching Nicodemus's chin. "What are you doing clubbing? It's Sunday afternoon."

"Clubbing?" The music quieted to a low hum. "I'm cleaning my place. I always rock out while I disinfect."

"I'm sorry for your neighbor."

"Old Mrs. Sanders takes it in stride," Dani said.

"I don't think carrying her trash out once a week makes up for club music at two p.m."

"Maybe she likes my club music."

"Then why do you need to take out her trash?" Riley asked.

"She's a sweet old lady, she deserves a neighbor who does nice things for her." There was a long pause on the line, then Dani said with her usual bravado, "Besides, she's got a recently-divorced daughter. I can probably hit that if I suck up to her mom."

"You're a real peach, Dani." Riley focused back on Olivia's Instagram page.

"It's true. Nic and I had an awesome time hanging out while you were gone."

Riley rubbed Nicodemus's cheek and he purred with his eyes still closed. "Oh yeah? I figured you left him alone and starving while you went out to get laid."

"No way I'd ever do that to my fluffy godson. Besides, he's way more fun than beautiful women. We watched wrestling together."

"Oh yeah?"

"Yeah." Dani took on a lecturing tone as she said, "Cats are violent creatures by nature. I let him watch sweaty dudes be violent so he could get it out of his system. You should spoil your cat more or he'll start to like me better."

"Wrestling, huh? Then how come my Netflix history shows an epic bingeing of *The Great British Baking Show*?"

"Don't ask me. I had to sleep sometime. He must've stolen the remote."

"Sure, Dani. I totally believe you," Riley said. "Maybe Nicodemus could bake me some cookies sometime."

"Probably will if you're nice. Enough about me. Tell me about the rest of con," Dani said.

"Same as the beginning. Everyone was obsessed with Middies and all they wanted to talk about was my recaps."

"But that's why you were there. It's what you do."

"It's not all I do. They could've talked to me about a dozen other projects I have that aren't about that stupid show." Nicodemus must've been annoyed by her talking, because he jumped down and strolled over to his empty food bowl. "Good news is I talked a couple actors into interviews. I have some cool ideas."

"Nice work, Riles."

"It won't be that annoying Q&A style, either. A real interview that can get me noticed."

"You're already noticed. This'll blast you into the stratosphere where you belong."

Riley finally peeled herself off the couch in response to Nicodemus's aggressive tapping at his empty food bowl. "Damn right."

"Tell me about the girl," Dani said.

"What girl?"

"Shut up. I know there's a girl. You blew off my call last night and I can practically hear your heart eyes through the phone."

"I don't have heart eyes." Riley pointedly closed her tablet.

"You're a terrible liar."

Nicodemus tapped her leg with his paw but Riley ignored him.

"I'm a really good liar actually."

"Your voice squeaked as you lied about being a good liar. So just tell me about her," Dani said.

Nicodemus tapped her leg again, this time adding a croaking meow to his complaint. "Her name's Olivia." Riley struggled to find words to describe her. "She's funny and snarky. The minute I get nervous and start to pull away, she jumps in and takes charge."

"Hot?"

"God yes."

Dani said, "And you talked to her, huh? So you can grow some ovaries when I let you go out alone."

"I am capable of talking to women."

"Sure you are. You've just been single for a decade because you like being lonely."

"I'm not lonely and I'm still single. We only went on two dates. It's not like we're girlfriends or anything."

"Bullshit," Dani said. "You're smitten. Why are you holding back?"

Nicodemus, clearly annoyed by Riley's inaction, tapped her leg again, this time with his claws out. She dumped the food into his bowl as she said, "I'm just not sure."

"Why not?"

"She's a fan."

"Of yours?" Dani asked.

"Yeah, but not a creepy stalker. I mean she's a fan of the shows. Middies mostly, but, like all of them."

Dani's music cut out and her voice came through the line clearer, highlighting her deadpan delivery. "So you met a lesbian who's a fan of seeing lesbians on TV. Weird."

"Come on. You know what I mean."

"I don't actually. I love seeing myself on TV. I love seeing happy lesbians. It reminds me I'm normal," Dani said.

Now that Nicodemus was happily munching away on his kibble, Riley realized she was hungry. She stared into her mostly empty fridge. "Yeah, but do you make fan art about it?"

"Fan art? Wait. The girl you met—is she LivDraws95?"

"How do you know that?" Riley asked.

"I saw her drawing. The one she made of Jodie Gray. She's super talented."

The only thing in Riley's fridge was a bottle of yellow mustard and a six-pack of Corona. She decided it was a beer for lunch kind of day and popped the lid off. "She totally is. She should be in art school, not making Middies fan art."

"You can be a real condescending ass sometimes, Riley. You started out with Buffy fanfic."

"Yeah, and now I do real journalism." Riley said.

"You recap a TV show. You're not about to win a Pulitzer. Maybe your girl has aspirations for more, maybe she's happy doing what she's doing. She's about to make solid money off it. Her goals don't have to be the same as yours, but if you want this to work you need to respect her."

"I do respect her. I just think she's better than fan art. Besides, I told you it isn't that serious yet." Riley's annoyance was tempered when she looked at her phone and saw a notification pop up. Olivia had texted her back with several emojis, including a kissing one. Her tone was much more subdued when she said, "It's too early for the 'making it work' talk. Let me actually get to know her before you pick out a spot for my bachelorette party."

"Oh, I've had that spot picked out for years."

Another text arrived, this one with too many words for Riley to focus on while she was talking to Dani. "Hey, I gotta go. She's texting me."

"Are you kidding me right now? You've been on two dates and you're ditching me for her?"

Another notification popped up.

"Good-bye, Dani."

"She must do that thing where she flicks her tongue over your teeth when she pulls away from a kiss," Dani said.

A bolt of electricity shot through Riley as she remembered Olivia doing exactly that during their last kiss. It was the primary reason for the cold shower Riley had taken. "Bye." She hung up.

Taking her beer and a bag of pretzels back to the sofa, she flopped down to read Olivia's messages. Each word brought a new tingle of happiness until she was completely engulfed in thoughts of Olivia. Nicodemus leaped back onto her chest as she typed her response. She was so distracted by Olivia she didn't even notice him pushing the air out of her lungs with his bulk.

CHAPTER THIRTEEN

Chelsea and Lewis's squabbling faded into the background as Olivia sketched. Her eyes occasionally flicked back to the television screen where an old episode of *Supergirl* played with the volume low. She'd watched the episode before even though the show wasn't one of her favorites.

Despite a bevy of beautiful women, she'd had to sit through seven dull episodes of season one before the eighth finally caught her interest. It was fine for a while, then they started queerbaiting in later seasons and she stopped watching. More than anything, the whole thing annoyed her. They already had queer side characters. The writers could have respected them and the fans instead of teasing them with two straight characters they clearly didn't intend to be queer. She was only watching now because a fan had commissioned a piece.

This method of fan art—watching a show and quickly sketching the scene—had been Olivia's first foray into art as a child. Television had always been an immersive media for her. She'd watched Saturday morning cartoons as a child and spent the rest of the day picturing the characters in her mind, taking them on adventures she could direct with her imagination. It didn't take long for her to decide to draw those scenes out.

Her first attempts were crayon creations that frustrated more than excited her. She couldn't get anything right. She couldn't force the characters out of her mind onto the page. They came out looking nothing like what she wanted. Eventually she took her paper and a new set of colored pencils to the rug in front of the TV and drew while she watched. These sketches were better, but the characters wouldn't sit still long enough for her to get them down on paper.

Olivia was nothing if not determined, however, and she had kept at it. Years later, when she started art school and had to make lightning-quick sketches, she had been the only one in her class who could capture a complete form before the model moved to a new pose. She'd been too embarrassed at the time to tell her professor she'd developed the skill while drawing *The Powerpuff Girls*.

"Can we turn this muck off?" Lewis asked from his curled position in the worn recliner. "I'm trying to finish my homework."

"Isn't school over in a week?" Olivia paused the show on a scene of Alex and Maggie kissing. Netflix had already asked her twice if she was still watching anyway. "How do you still have homework?"

"Mrs. Cline offered extra credit," Chelsea said without looking up from her notebook.

"Do either of you need extra credit?"

Lewis glared at her. "We both need it."

Chelsea was more forthright. "We're the top two in the class right now. If I do better than Lewis on this extra credit, I win."

"Which she won't." Lewis shifted his glare to Chelsea. "I'm going to do better and then I'll be top."

"Either way, we'll be top two." Chelsea went back to her work, her eyebrows pinching together. "But it's about honor at this point."

Olivia gripped her pencil between her teeth to keep from laughing. It must be the influence from Lewis that made Chelsea so determined in her school work because it certainly wasn't genetic. Olivia had only truly applied herself to her art classes and Allison had barely finished high school, marrying Olivia's dad a week after graduation. Both of them were thrilled Chelsea hadn't followed in their mediocre footsteps and even more excited to have Lewis around every day.

"Have any plans for the summer?" Olivia asked.

"I will, starting tomorrow," Lewis said distractedly. "Summer reading lists for the gifted program are handed out tomorrow."

Lewis and Chelsea bumped fists and squealed something about a field trip to the bookstore. Olivia made a note to save a little extra from her paycheck to help Lewis buy his books. The library was out because Lewis insisted on annotating nearly every book he read. His parents didn't have much money and they weren't the type to spend what extra they had on books. No doubt they would gladly shell out the extra funds if it was football pads or baseball cleats. When it came to indulging their gay son with his intellectual pursuits, however, their priorities shifted. They didn't hit him, Olivia was sure of that, but the emotional pain he suffered from their rejection was just as damaging.

"Let me guess," Olivia said with an indulgent smile. "You'll be reading your seventh-grade list and the eighth-grade one, too."

"And the ninth," Chelsea said. "A kid on the bus is getting it for us."

"How will you find the time?"

"I've already made a schedule for us." Lewis pulled up a color-coded spreadsheet on his computer. "We've got this."

"As long as you've left time in there to watch Middies."

"Don't be ridiculous, Olivia. What do you think the pink blocks are for?"

Olivia's phone chirped, and the kids went silent, rolling their eyes at her wide grin. She pretended not to notice as she set aside her pencil in favor of her phone.

Riley: *Hey there*

Olivia: *Hey yourself*

Riley: *What're you up to?*

Olivia: *Thinking about kissing girls*

Riley: *Huh?? Girls plural?*

Olivia: *Definitely not girls plural.*

Olivia: *Watching* Supergirl. *Working on a commission—I'm binging for inspiration*

Riley: *Okay. LOL. If you're busy I can write back later*

Olivia turned off the TV and set her sketchbook aside, settling back into the couch.

Olivia: *I can always make time for you*

Riley: *Glad to hear it*

Just as she was typing out a long, slightly flirty text, the front door opened and Allison came in, shaking off a few raindrops clinging to her coat.

"It's a mess out there." When she didn't receive a response, she continued, "Work was a mess. Traffic was even worse. Honestly, I don't know how people in Florida are so bad at driving in the rain."

Chelsea and Lewis kept to their homework, but they at least managed a grunt of acknowledgement. Olivia was too busy typing to reply. It was fun to flirt with Riley in person, when she could see the blushing, stammering response, but text flirting was much less satisfying and much more prone to misunderstanding.

"Hello?" Allison's face appeared above her phone screen. "Earth to Olivia?"

"Hey, Allison. How was work?" Olivia asked. Lewis giggled into his hand. "What? What'd I say?"

"It isn't what you said, sweetie. It's what you didn't hear," Allison said.

"Sorry," Olivia said. Her attention was drawn back to her phone when a new message from Riley appeared.

Allison leaned over and kissed her forehead. "Why don't you go call her instead? Agonizing over each text is going to give you wrinkles."

"I'm not agonizing over each text." Olivia forced herself to relax the crinkle between her eyebrows.

"Just ask her if she wants to talk, sweetie." Allison had disappeared into the kitchen, but she tossed one pump then the other back through the doorway.

After a moment's hesitation, Olivia decided to give the idea a try. It took Riley forever to reply, making Olivia worry she'd overstepped. When Riley's agreement finally came through, Olivia rushed off to her room without any explanation. She heard Allison's soft chuckle just as she pushed the door shut with one hip.

Her phone rang as she flopped onto her bed, sending a throw pillow and a dingy stuffed dog toppling off the mattress. She took a moment to grin at the photo that came up with the call notification, a candid shot of Riley she'd snapped at their lunch date.

"Hey there," Riley said, echoing her texted greeting. Olivia hadn't realized how much she missed that smooth as honey tone in Riley's voice. "How's the commission going?"

"Really well. I'm not the biggest fan of the show, but I watched the early seasons so I had a good idea of what I wanted to do from the start."

"Cool."

"How about you?" Olivia asked.

"How about me what?"

She sounded so tense and awkward, Olivia couldn't help but smile. "How's work? Starting any new projects? You had a lot of folks crowding you at that party. I hope those phone numbers weren't for personal connections."

"No. No, of course they weren't. I would never." Riley's stammering explanation cut off when Olivia giggled. "You're messing with me, aren't you?"

"Of course. It's a lot of fun," Olivia said.

"I'm glad I can entertain you."

"Oh, I have no doubt you'll excel at entertaining me."

Riley swallowed so hard Olivia could hear it through the phone. "To answer your question, I'm working on a new project but it's super early. I'm hoping to fly out to LA soon and interview Matthew Barnes on set."

"Seriously?" Olivia sat up so fast she knocked another pair of pillows off her bed. "That's awesome."

"It should be a great article. I already pitched it to a major magazine, and I think they're interested."

Olivia didn't mention she'd heard about the deal with *Rolling Stone*. It seemed too much like something a fan girl would say and she definitely didn't want Riley thinking of her as a fan.

"It's a while off, though. I won't be heading anywhere any time soon." Riley took a deep breath and continued in a rush, "In fact, I was wondering if you wanted to come down to Miami one weekend." Before Olivia could reply, Riley hurried on, "No pressure. Only if you want to. And we won't share a bedroom or anything. I have two. No pressure."

"Yeah." Olivia stretched languidly at the thought of spending a weekend alone with Riley. "You mentioned the no pressure thing."

"I just want to see you again."

"I'd like that, too." Olivia ran a hand through her hair, adding a purr to her voice as she said, "Yes, I'd like to come to Miami one weekend and not share a bedroom."

"What, um, what about this weekend? It's short notice and you can totally say no."

"Can I totally say yes?"

"Yeah. You can do that." The tension had left Riley's voice and she sounded relaxed again. There was even a hint of excitement like she'd had when she talked about her upcoming interview. The excitement was infectious, and Olivia started planning the next few days in her head.

"Then yes. I'll leave right after breakfast on Saturday."

CHAPTER FOURTEEN

Riley was up at dawn on Saturday morning, cleaning her apartment with such zeal that Nicodemus retreated beneath the sofa. He soon discovered even that tried-and-true hiding spot wasn't safe when Riley pivoted the sofa to vacuum beneath it. He streaked across the carpet into the guest room. When he saw new sheets on the bed and towels laid out on the desk where Riley's keyboard normally sat, he expressed his chagrin with a long, plaintive howl and curled up in the darkest corner of the closet.

Nicodemus wasn't totally alone in his complaints. The vacuuming was an easy task, but the speed of it reminded Riley how tiny her apartment was. The size never bothered her before because she didn't share the space with anyone other than Nicodemus. Now she recognized that, while her bedroom at the back of the apartment was spacious and airy, the rest of the space left a lot to be desired.

The single bathroom was cramped, and the terra cotta tile made it feel even smaller than it was. Riley used the second bedroom as an office, so her large wooden desk occupied most of the floor space and the daybed was just an uncomfortable couch with high wooden railings on three sides. The mounds of throw pillows, collected over the years in an attempt to soften the bed, didn't make it any more comfortable to sleep in.

Then there was the living room, which was actually a combination living room, dining room, and galley kitchen. Riley was used to cramped quarters, so it didn't bother her that the bistro dining table with mismatched chairs sat in a corner too close to the sofa. Her bookshelf, overloaded with more TV show box sets than books, was a cluttered mess and didn't exactly make her look like an intellectual. Now that she studied the space, it looked more like a college kid's first apartment than the home of a thirty-two-year-old.

Before she had any more time to lament her imperfect living arrangements, Riley's doorbell rang. She straightened her royal blue button-up shirt and smoothed down her khakis as she hurried to the door. She took a deep breath, held it with her eyes closed to the count of five, and shook out her tight shoulders before opening her door.

It was a good thing she'd taken a deep breath before opening the door, because the sight of Olivia forced every molecule of oxygen from her lungs. It had only been two weeks since they'd seen each other, but clearly she'd forgotten just how stunning Olivia was.

Olivia wore bright white cropped pants and wedge sandals that accentuated their several-inch height difference. Her top billowed in the slight breeze created by the opening door, the salmon fabric held up by a thin cord tied at the base of her neck. Riley allowed herself three seconds to wonder about the absence of bra straps on her smooth, bare shoulders before forcing herself to smile.

"Hi," Olivia said, her voice as throaty and inviting as Riley remembered.

"Hi," she said.

After managing that syllable, Riley was able to make her lungs function again. She took a deep breath which included a waft of familiar fruity perfume and the clean scent of fresh cotton. It amazed her that Olivia looked so put together after a four-hour drive. As usual for a Florida summer, the heat and humidity were battling for supremacy, but Olivia looked like a woman who'd just stepped out her front door.

"Can I come in?" Olivia said, leaning forward into Riley's space and bring more of that enticing perfume with her. "The hallway's great but I wouldn't mind seeing inside."

"What? Oh, yeah." Riley stepped aside, holding the door open so Olivia could bring her duffel bag in with her. "Sorry. I don't know what my deal is."

She closed the door, trying to push down her embarrassment and nerves. When she turned around to find Olivia inches from her and closing fast, the embarrassment leaked out of her.

"I think it's really cute how nervous you get." Olivia trailed a long finger down Riley's jaw. "And you smell amazing."

"Thanks," Riley said. She couldn't look away from Olivia's lips. "It's new cologne."

Olivia leaned in even closer, the air between them thick and warm. Her lips brushed against Riley's as she whispered, "I like it."

Riley had thought of nothing besides Olivia and her lips. The way they pressed into hers. The way they opened willingly, hungrily. Riley had dreamt of them. Riley pulled Olivia in, tilting her head at just the right angle to keep their lips barely separated but bring their bodies and faces tight together. She waited until she felt Olivia straining forward, begging with her body, before she joined the kiss.

Olivia's lips were everything she remembered. Sweet and soft and eager. Riley slipped a hand into the mass of curls at the base of Olivia's neck and pulled her closer still. Riley pressed forward with her tongue and Olivia welcomed her, meeting each new caress. She groaned into Riley's mouth, sending a vibration through their shared touch and setting off a series of fireworks in her chest.

Sliding out of the kiss as smoothly as her pounding heart and screaming lungs would allow, Riley opened her eyes to find a rare sight. Since almost the moment they'd met, Olivia had left her unsettled. Now, watching Olivia's chest heave and her eyes flutter open, Riley recognized she might have the same power. Olivia looked like a woman who was trying to uncurl her toes. There was something delicious about being the one to so clearly effect a woman as self-assured as Olivia.

The feeling was short lived. Olivia collected herself far more quickly than Riley had been able to thus far. She let a smile curl onto her lips then spun and marched into the apartment.

"Wow." Olivia stopped in front of the single living room window. "What an amazing view."

"It's not bad." Riley tried to play it down but didn't succeed.

The truth was the view from her place more than made up for the cramped space or the limited décor. From both the living room and the primary bedroom, the windows looked out onto the beach and the gleaming Atlantic Ocean. There were a few blocks of high-rises between the apartment and the sand, but it helped that Riley's place was on the twentieth floor.

Olivia turned to look at her, leaning back against the windowsill. "It's so Miami. I can't imagine what you pay for this place."

"I'm lucky on that one." Riley leaned against the opposite side of the window. She wasn't quite ready to be too far from Olivia yet. "My great-aunt snagged this place when she retired down here. It's rent-controlled."

"Where is she?"

"Nursing home. She had a stroke a few years back. I took over the lease 'cause no one could convince her she wasn't going to be able to move back. When I visit her I have to lie and say I'm sleeping in the guest room and that the place is still hers."

"She sounds a lot like Poppa," Olivia said.

"How is he doing? No ill effects from his fall I hope."

"None, thanks for asking. He's too stubborn to ever truly hurt himself."

"Hard heads come in handy sometimes. How long has he lived with you?" Riley asked.

"Six years. He had a fall not long after my grandmother passed and we forced him to move in. He has pretty limited mobility, but that's only been in the last year or so since his diabetes got harder to manage."

"He won't go into a home?"

"Mom doesn't want him to and he probably wouldn't stand for it. Plus, Chelsea likes having him around."

"But you do most of the work taking care of him, don't you?"

Olivia shrugged and dropped onto the sofa, kicking off her sandals so she could pull her knees up to her chest. "He's my grandfather and I love him. Besides, he won't listen to anyone else."

Riley sat on the opposite side of the sofa, deciding it was best to keep some distance between her hands and Olivia's body. "You are very bossy sometimes."

"And you really, really like it."

"Yeah, I do." Riley ran a hand through her hair. "You've given up a lot for your family. How do you manage?"

"By dropping out of art school." As soon as the words were out of her mouth, Olivia looked embarrassed to have said them. She looked at her toes and continued quietly. "That's not Poppa's fault, though. I was already juggling a lot after my stepdad passed."

"Chelsea's dad?"

"Yeah. He was a contractor for the military. Died in Iraq when Chelsea was still a toddler. Mom needed help."

"I can imagine. Still, you couldn't have been that old."

"Nineteen." Olivia squinted and looked back out the window, though from this angle all she could see were rooftops. "I was about to start my sophomore year of college. They let me take a year off to help. Grief plus a toddler, it was a lot."

Riley tried to imagine herself at nineteen, trying to take care of a toddler and a grieving mother. She spent all her money on cheap beer and expensive weed back then. She partied and ate junk food exclusively and it was the best time of her life. The idea that Olivia had missed out on all that made her heart ache.

"They weren't as understanding when I had to leave school again to help with Poppa," Olivia said. "But I reached out to my advisor a few months back and he was willing to work with me."

"That's great." Riley sat a little straighter. Maybe all the fan art stuff was a way for her to keep her skills up until she got back into school. "You're going to finish your degree?"

"Definitely." There was a determination in Olivia's tone Riley liked to hear. When this woman set her mind to doing something, she did it, and she had set her mind to going back to school. "I just have to pay for the classes myself now. No more grants or loans. The commissions will help a lot."

"What's your dream job?"

She answered without hesitation. "Graphic animator. I'd love to draw for Pixar or a studio like that. Maybe do some comics. Anything that'll get me out of Florida and into the business."

"LA?"

"That's the dream. But isn't that everyone's dream?"

"It's certainly mine."

Olivia leaned forward, her chin on her forearm where it rested on the back of the couch. "Not New York? Don't all journalists want to be in New York?"

"Not the ones who write about the entertainment industry." Riley took a deep breath and decided to admit her real dream. "But that's not what I want. I want to write for TV."

"Scripted TV? Like a real Hollywood writers' room? Is that what the agent is for? I thought it was a celebrity thing."

"No, for writing. I know I don't have any experience with it, but I know a lot about TV and there should be more lesbians in writers' rooms."

"You'd be perfect. You have such a dry wit and you obviously know how a story should be crafted. You tore apart enough of the weaker Middies episodes for their lazy storytelling."

Riley cringed, thinking she'd been more subtle about her disdain for that second season. "I didn't tear them apart, exactly, but, yeah, there were some weak episodes. I think they could have done so much more."

"You're right. I can't wait to watch a show you write for."

Riley was already leaning forward to kiss Olivia when a rumble tore through their momentary silence. Olivia laughed, clutching her growling stomach.

"Okay," she said. "I might be hungry."

"I can tell," Riley said.

"I didn't exactly eat much breakfast. Or any breakfast at all." It was Olivia's turn to blush and the pink in her cheeks was a beautiful sight. "I was excited to get here. And maybe a little nervous. I've never been to Miami."

Riley thought there was likely more to her nervousness than being in a new city, but it was nice to finally feel on equal footing. She hopped off the sofa and held her hand out. "Good. I have plans to show you all around and I'd hate for you to be bored with my tour."

Olivia slipped her palm into Riley's. It was soft as sun-warmed silk.

"I doubt I'll ever be bored with you. What's the first stop?" Olivia asked.

"Lunch."

"My growling stomach approves."

"Excellent. We should leave now or we'll be late for our reservation."

Chapter Fifteen

Olivia had been on a few good dates in her life and one or two great ones. But this day exploring Miami with Riley counted as perfect. Lunch was followed by a long walk on the beach where they talked and strolled with their shoes in their hands. Riley had rolled up her pants legs, revealing a cartoonish ankle tattoo of a slice of cake. She had treated Olivia to its origin story—a bottle of cheap vodka and a lost bet with her best friend—that had Olivia so lost in laughter they covered a large swath of South Beach without realizing where they were. They had veered off the beach and walked, arms entwined and the sun setting at their backs, to Joe's Stone Crab where they had indulged in a decadent dinner of conch fritters and stone crab claws before heading to Riley's favorite club.

Now they stood close at a high-top table in the corner of a neon-drenched nightclub. The song blasting from nearby speakers had a quick, almost frantic beat. Riley was driving, so she'd been nursing her beer. Still, Olivia had noticed the way Riley's eyes returned to her lips and hips more often the deeper into the bottle she dove. Olivia's nerves tingled and her heart thumped along to the bass. Her thoughts drifted back to the farewell party at QueerCon, when they had danced in perfect rhythm, their bodies close but rarely touching.

She wanted to touch Riley's body now. "Come with me." She grabbed Riley's hand and dragged her to the center of the crowded dance floor.

Riley came willingly and there was a sparkle in her eye when Olivia stopped and turned to her. Riley started to move her hips, a slow smile creeping onto her lips. Those lips. Olivia moved closer, slipping her hand onto Riley's shoulder. She moved closer, matching her hips to Riley's rhythm. She didn't stop until she could feel Riley's breath hitch. Then she moved a fraction closer.

"You're an amazing dancer," Olivia said. She was so close to Riley's ear she could feel the heat of her skin.

Riley's steps faltered, but she recovered quickly. They danced through three songs and, with each new verse, she did her best to make Riley squirm. They were hardly the most provocative couple on the dance floor, even when she slipped one hand into Riley's sweat-soaked hair and the other into the back pocket of her pants. The song ended and Olivia drew Riley close, lightly biting her earlobe.

When Riley groaned, Olivia said, "I'm ready to go home when you are."

The moon threw cold light over Riley's building when they arrived back home. Sweat had dried on Olivia's back and neck under her frizzing hair, but she'd had so much fun she didn't mind the state of her hair or the stickiness of her skin.

Riley's hand shook ever so slightly as she fit her key into the lock. A single lamp glowed beside the sofa, mingling with the full moon through the sheer curtain. When Riley reached for the light switch, Olivia caught her fingers, bringing them to her lips and kissing them one by one before turning her hand over and pressing her lips to the inside of Riley's wrist.

Desire clouded Riley's eyes, dark in the dimly lit room. She stepped forward, moving into the circle of Olivia's arms, her strong hands wrapping around Olivia's waist. Riley turned her face up, capturing Olivia's lips in a hungry kiss. Since they'd met, Olivia had made all the moves, taking the lead and unsettling this intoxicating woman. Now Riley took the lead, pressing deep into the kiss and exploring Olivia's willing mouth with her tongue. Far from being unsettled by the role reversal, Olivia thrilled at the taste of confidence, encouraging more with an involuntary groan of pleasure.

The groan had a welcome effect on Riley. She pressed Olivia back against the door, her hands moving lower on her hips to pull the length of their bodies closer. Olivia reveled in the warmth of Riley's body and the scent of her new cologne mixed with the enticing tang of sweat. Olivia looped her hands under Riley's arms so she could scrape her nails down her shoulder blades through layers of fabric.

Just when things were starting to get interesting, however, Riley pulled back, breaking the kiss with obvious reluctance. She stood panting for a moment, staring into Olivia's eyes, her body still pinning Olivia to door. Then, with a wink Olivia could only describe as cheeky, she pushed away and strolled into the kitchen.

"I have some wine," Riley said, her head buried in the fridge. "It's nicely chilled if you're interested."

Recognizing her own teasing moves, Olivia strolled to the sofa. She dropped onto the cushions and kicked of her sandals. "Just water for me."

Riley brought two sweating bottles of water with her. She sat, leaning against the far arm of the sofa as she tipped hers back, half-draining it. Olivia allowed herself a long moment to watch Riley as she swallowed, the muscles contracting at the open throat of her shirt.

"Not thirsty?" Riley asked with a teasing twinkle in her eye.

"Oh, I'm very thirsty."

Her comment was rewarded with a sputtering choke and Olivia laughed, taking a sip of her water and leaning forward to pat Riley's knee. "Sorry. I couldn't resist. You okay?"

Swiping her cuff along her chin, Riley shook her head. "You like doing that, don't you?"

"Very much. You don't mind, do you?"

"Far from it." Riley ran a hand through her hair. "I like a woman who can keep me on my toes."

"Good to hear. I've messed up more than one relationship with my big mouth," Olivia said.

"I find that hard to believe."

"It takes a lot of self-confidence to let a feminine woman take charge. A lot of the people I've dated couldn't handle it."

"Sounds like you've been dating the wrong kind of person," Riley said. Olivia was surprised to see an absolute lack of jealousy in her calm features. Yet another major point in her favor. "What is your type anyway? I mean apart from short, awkward bloggers, of course."

"That's my favorite type." Olivia lifted an eyebrow and ran her fingertip across her teeth. She was having a very hard time keeping her eyes off the barest hint of Riley's cleavage visible at this angle. "I prefer folks on the androgynous side."

"Men and women?"

"I don't get hung up on gender. I'm more interested in people. Especially short, awkward bloggers."

A small smile pulled at the corner of Riley's mouth. "Lucky me."

"How about you?" Olivia asked. "What's your type?"

"Supermodels."

"Seems like a reasonable standard. There are quite a few in Miami."

"Could be, but I've only ever found one in Tampa."

Olivia grinned. "Good answer."

Riley winked and Olivia's heart actually skipped a beat. Now it was Riley's mouth that held Olivia's attention. She had a small mouth with an exaggerated bow and plump lips that were more expressive than any other part of her. They were also deliciously inviting as she spoke.

"Seriously, though, I do like tall, very feminine women. Especially brunettes," Riley said.

"Only women?" Olivia asked. Riley nodded. Olivia flipped a dark curl from her shoulder, "Why brunettes?"

"Too many blondes in Florida."

"But aren't you from Upstate New York?"

"Too many blondes there, too."

Olivia scooted forward on her cushion, her knee within inches of Riley's. "Well, I'm all for your brunette preference. I won't even point out that you're blond."

Riley leaned forward, closing the distance between them until Olivia could feel the warmth of her skin. "Very kind of you not to say anything."

Olivia laughed, watching Riley's eyes sparkle and darken at the sound. She touched her lips to Riley's earlobe and whispered, "I can be extremely kind."

Taking Riley's earlobe into her mouth, she scraped her teeth until she felt Riley's breath hitch, then she released it and moved down her throat. She let each kiss linger for a heartbeat before dropping the next, leaving a line of lip gloss across the column of Riley's throat. When her lips pressed against Riley's pulse point, Olivia felt the blood thundering beneath her skin. Riley groaned and let her head fall back, revealing more skin for Olivia to pepper with kisses.

She took her time working her way back up Riley's throat, lingering on the hinge of her strong jaw before trailing across her chin. Riley was quivering under her attention, the tension in her body palpable. She slowed her progression for no other reason than to prolong the slight torture she was inflicting. Riley gripped the back of the sofa, her knuckles white against the navy fabric. Olivia was just wondering how long it would take for Riley to push her back on the sofa and rip her clothes off, when her phone rang.

"Shit." Olivia tried to silence her phone without breaking her focus.

"Jesus." Riley pulled back. "You should, um, you should get that." Riley's hand trembled as she released the cushion she'd been gripping.

Despite the interruption, Olivia couldn't help grinning at how unsettled Riley looked. She'd made such a big deal about the lack of expectations for this visit and it looked as though she was intent on sticking to that conviction despite what they both clearly wanted.

Grabbing her phone, Olivia intended to silence it and ignore the call, but she saw Allison's photograph on the display and knew she couldn't. She pushed off the sofa with reluctance and answered the phone, mouthing an apology to Riley as she turned her attention to her mother.

"I am so, so sorry to interrupt, Liv." Allison didn't sound frantic yet, but there was certainly the potential present in her rapid speech. "I'll be quick. I'm sure you can make it up to Riley."

Not only did she have no intention of discussing the details of her sex life with her mother as they were happening, but Olivia was also distracted by the sounds of Riley leaving the sofa. Turning, she saw Riley disappear down the apartment hallway carrying Olivia's overnight bag with her.

"What's up?"

"Poppa's medications. I can't remember which one he gets at bedtime."

"He can't tell you? Is he okay?"

"He's fine, he just said he didn't bother to learn because you knew what to give him."

Olivia rolled her eyes, pinching the bridge of her nose and going through the list of meds slowly. She had written all of it down on a notecard in the kitchen, but she knew Allison had probably lost it within an hour of Olivia leaving. Pacing closer to the hallway, she thought she heard Riley opening and closing drawers in her bedroom and the thought of what she might be putting away or retrieving was enough to make her mouth go dry.

"What was that last one again? You trailed off."

"Coumadin. Twice a day. Breakfast." The sound of water running caught her attention and she tried to decide if it was the shower or the sink. "Bedtime."

"Uh-huh. Not for you I think."

"Good night," Olivia said in a singsong voice.

Allison laughed and wished her good night before quickly hanging up. Olivia tossed the phone on the couch, hoping to catch Riley while she was still in her bedroom, but she turned to find her exiting the hallway dressed in matching button-up cotton pajamas.

"Cute pj's," Olivia said, imagining interesting ways to wrinkle the neatly ironed cotton.

"Thanks," Riley said, fidgeting with the cuff of her pajama shirt. "Everything with your family okay?"

"Everything's fine. Except Allison's reading comprehension." She took a moment to gauge Riley's reaction, worried the interruption had upset her. Riley only laughed self-consciously and scratched the back of her neck in that adorably awkward way of hers. "Sorry."

"Totally fine. It's, um, late. Let me show you to your room."

Olivia followed her down the hall, noticing an office along the way with a day bed that had the covers turned down. Riley stopped in front of the only door on the left side of the hall.

"I've set up the primary for you," she said. Olivia looked in to see her duffel bag perched on a king-sized bed draped with a brightly colored quilt. The bed was so neatly made it could be a photograph from a catalog. "Bathroom's at the end of the hall. I'll be in the guest room down there if you need anything."

Olivia leaned against the wall, crossing her arms and using them to push up her breasts. "I can't take your bed. Not without you in it, at least."

"The guest room has a day bed. You're way too tall for it."

"Then why don't you join me in here?" Olivia asked.

Riley shook her head. "I told you there were no expectations and I meant it. Separate bedrooms, remember?"

"You're not gonna budge on this, are you?"

"Nope. I keep my promises."

As Olivia strolled past, Riley leaned up and kissed her cheek. With her lips still close to Olivia's flushed face, Riley whispered, "Sleep well, Olivia."

Chapter Sixteen

Just above the headboard of the day bed there was a smear of gray on the white ceiling paint. Riley was aware of the imperfection because she had been staring at that spot for a half hour. The cold moonlight bleeding in above the curtains was angled perfectly to illuminate the spot and, now that she had seen it, Riley couldn't notice anything else. She lay in bed, the sheet twisted around her legs, and wondered if it was worth calling the rental office on Monday to come fix the terrible paint job.

"Stop being an idiot," she whispered. "You don't give a shit about the ceiling paint. You shouldn't even be seeing it right now."

She was a coward. That was the conclusion she'd come to since flipping off the lights in her guest room and climbing, alone, into bed. It wasn't that the day bed was uncomfortable. Far from it, the firmness of the mattress was a welcome relief from the enveloping foam and goose down of her own bed. On a night like tonight, when her skin was on fire and her mind was reeling, she couldn't deal with that softness.

Realizing her mistake a moment too late, Riley's thoughts wandered to her own bed down the hall. It was, after all, what had kept her awake, staring at the ceiling and barely seeing it. Riley was not in her bed. Olivia was. Riley's navy sheets, freshly washed this morning, were soaking up the warmth from her tanned skin. The yards of rich brown curls were spread out over Riley's pillow.

And Riley was in here, alone and staring at a bad paint job. Olivia had clearly wanted her. With her words and her touch and her delicious lips she had begged Riley to take her to bed. But Riley had promised they would sleep in separate rooms when she'd invited Olivia down here and she meant to keep her word. It had felt at the time like a matter of honor and respect—a way to show Olivia she wanted more than her body—but now she wondered if she had come across as disinterested. Had Olivia felt rejected when Riley had settled into her guest room rather than continuing what they'd begun on the sofa?

"Of course she did, and now she'll go back to Tampa and never talk to you again."

Riley forced her eyes closed. There was nothing she could do about it now. She'd just have to prove to Olivia tomorrow how important she was. The only problem was that the moment she closed her eyes, she pictured Olivia in her bed again. This time she didn't try to stop the image. She let it play out in her mind, hoping the view would lull her to sleep, but it had the exact opposite effect.

In her mind's eye, Riley watched Olivia tossing and turning just like she was doing now. She watched her flip back the sheet and expose long, bare legs, the slightest flash of bright red panties visible between. She imagined walking into the room, Olivia's gaze shifting to her, her pupils wide and begging in the semi-darkness. Fantasy Olivia slid back, making room for Riley on the mattress. She imagined crawling onto the mattress, pressing her body flush against Olivia's. She leaned in, the taste of Olivia's mouth and the smell of her skin overwhelming her senses.

The fantasy kiss made Riley's body ache. She could almost catch the flavor of Olivia's tongue in her mouth. Her body hummed at the thought. Her core flashed white-hot with need. She felt that reckless pull their first kiss had started. She had no chance to settle her overstimulated body with Olivia, her own hand would have to do. Wetness pooled around her fingers as soon as they slipped below her boxer briefs.

A noise by the door snapped Riley from her fantasy. Her eyes flew open and she yanked her hand out of her underwear, taking the thin blanket in a white-knuckled grip. Just as her eyes adjusted, Olivia stepped into the room looking even more tempting than the fantasy she'd conjured.

Olivia wore an oversized T-shirt that barely grazed her thighs. The wide, stretched collar hung off one shoulder, displaying smooth skin that glowed in the moonlight. Her legs looked even longer with nothing to cover them. Her hair hung loose over one shoulder, reaching low enough to hover just over the swell of her chest through the thin fabric. She lifted one arm and leaned against the wall. Her unsmiling eyes were focused on Riley.

Riley lifted up to lean on one elbow. "Is everything okay?"

Olivia took a long time answering. Her eyes glowed as they trailed over Riley's body. Her voice was a low, husky whisper when she said, "Everything's great."

Her hunger was unmistakable and a perfect reflection of Riley's. Olivia's body was rigid as she stood waiting in the doorway. Riley searched for something to say that would make her stay. Make her come closer. Make her Riley's. Her mind was blank as warmth spread through her like a fever. Without words to do the begging for her, all she had was action.

With a flick of her wrist, Riley pulled back the blanket. She slid back on the mattress and Olivia immediately slipped between the sheets. Riley watched her move with liquid grace, leaning on her elbow and letting her hair cascade down until it brushed the pillowcase. Their thighs grazed against each other and then shifted apart. Then their arms did the same. When their breasts came within a whisper of touching, Riley finally realized Olivia was doing it on purpose—making those little connections and then breaking them. Her pulse pounded so hard in her ears she missed Olivia's whispered question.

"What?"

Olivia smiled wickedly. "I said, is this okay?"

Riley's voice was a harsh croak as she said, "Almost perfect."

Olivia leaned in close, this time letting her breast brush against Riley's. Even through the T-shirt and Riley's pajama top, she could feel that Olivia's nipple was rock hard. Her breath caught as she wondered again if Olivia was wearing anything beneath the thin cotton.

"How do I make it all the way perfect?" Olivia asked, her lips against Riley's ear and the long, glistening column of her throat inches from Riley's mouth.

Her mouth was so dry, Riley could barely force the words out. "That's a good start."

Olivia actually purred, her throat vibrating against Riley's skin. "Which part?" she asked. "This?" Olivia took Riley's ear between her lips, sucking the lobe into her mouth and flicking the end with the tip of her tongue. "Or maybe you prefer this?" Olivia ran her teeth down across the throbbing vein in Riley's neck to nip at her collarbone.

When Olivia started painting wet circles around the hollow of her throat, Riley couldn't hold back any longer. She grabbed Olivia's hips hard and pulled their bodies flush.

"Christ, Olivia." She groaned and slipped her hands beneath the T-shirt where she found nothing but acres of bare skin. "Are you trying to kill me?"

Holding Riley's hands in place on her bare thighs, Olivia sat up, straddling her hips. Using Riley's hands, she lifted her own shirt slowly, revealing one glorious inch of flesh at a time.

"There are a lot of things I'm trying to do with you, Riley, but killing you is not one of them." She held still, her shirt hovering just high enough to show the lusciously rounded bottoms of her breasts. "If that's what you want?"

Life held very few absolute certainties for Riley. Wanting Olivia here and now and exactly like this was one of them. Watching this incredible woman—this beautiful, kind, funny, talented woman— hesitate was enough to shatter any of her own doubts. She moved like lightning, wrapping her arms around Olivia and reversing their positions. Olivia moved with her, allowing herself to be led, though her eyes went wide when she found herself on her back with Riley's hand cradling her head.

"Lots of things, huh?" Riley said with a fair imitation of Olivia's confident smirk. She settled between her thighs, reveling in the long legs twisting around her. "I can't wait to see what you have in store for me."

Olivia dragged her shirt over her head, revealing a pair of large breasts topped with pink-brown nipples that begged for Riley's mouth to envelop them. The curl of her lips made it clear she had a witty retort, but Riley decided she was going to take over the teasing for the evening. She ran her tongue along Olivia's shoulder, stopping just where it met her neck, and followed the path with several wet kisses. Olivia gasped beneath her and bucked her hips, grinding against Riley.

For a moment the pressure between her legs was enough to make Riley's vision go blank, but the smell of Olivia's skin and the sound of her ragged breathing helped her focus again. She continued the trail of kisses, zigzagging down Olivia's chest and intentionally avoiding her breasts. With each new press of her lips, Olivia groaned a little bit louder. With each swipe of her tongue over hot flesh, Olivia squirmed a little bit more insistently. When she finally took one plump nipple into her mouth, Riley discovered that Olivia was as expressive a lover as she had hoped. Her throaty moan left Riley chuckling. Riley released her and went back to gentle, chaste kisses across her ribs.

"Are you trying to kill me?" Olivia emphasized the last word.

"It's an appealing thought." Riley laughed when Olivia lightly smacked her shoulder.

"If you don't get naked soon, I'm going to scream," Olivia said.

"I fully intend to make you scream."

Olivia's jaw dropped. Apparently, she hadn't expected Riley to give as well as she got, but she had a feeling Olivia appreciated the sparring as much as the kissing. Riley rocked back on her heels, making sure to stay close to the circle of Olivia's legs while she popped one button open on her pajama shirt.

"I'm sure you can do better than that," Olivia said. When Riley shook her head, she broke out the pout, but there was genuine strain in her voice when she said, "Please, Riley. I want to see you."

Riley's fingers fumbled on the buttons in her haste to open them. Olivia watched her with naked hunger, staring at each new patch of flesh. Struggling out of her shirt at last, Riley kicked out of her pants and settled back between Olivia's legs. Olivia's eyes sparkled in the moonlight, inspecting every inch of Riley. Far from shriveling under the inspection, it was Riley's turn to preen. She knew her body was firm in all the right places and soft in all the rest.

Olivia began to move beneath her again, her eagerness evident, and Riley hastened to fill her needs. She bent again, careful to let her breasts rub against Olivia's skin as she focused her attention on first one breast, then the other. Her skin was like gold in the pale glow from the window and she tasted like sweat and tropical fruit. The lower she tasted, the sweeter Olivia's skin until she hovered over the apex of her thighs. Olivia dragged a pillow over her mouth to muffle her moans.

Her back arched off the mattress the moment Riley's tongue found the source of her heat. Wrapping her arms around Olivia's hips to hold her in place, Riley drank deep from her folds, teasing and tasting as her mind spun with sensation. Pressing the flat of her tongue against Olivia's clit, she released a moan of her own, the relief of finally making love to this woman flooding her senses.

Olivia responded with her whole body. Her enthusiasm was a guide that allowed Riley to make the most of every movement, every touch. Kissing Olivia's core made her feel alive. Energy radiated between them, replacing all the previous hesitancy with delicious anticipation. Within moments she felt Olivia tense beneath her and she picked up her pace, desperate to please. The screams she released were euphoric, nearly enough to take Riley with her over the edge.

Riley forced herself to focus on the little details to distract from her own desire. The curl of Olivia's fingers around the pillow. The arch of her foot pressing hard into Riley's back. The erratic rise and fall of her chest. Riley released one hip to spread her fingers across Olivia's abdomen so she could feel the clench and release of her muscles. She didn't allow Olivia a moment to rest, continuing to tease and touch and earning another orgasm just as the first ebbed away.

Olivia dragged the pillow away from her face, panting, "Don't stop. Please, Riley. More."

Riley obliged, sliding first one, and then a second finger into Olivia as she continued her attentions with her tongue. Sweat pooled at the back of Riley's neck and her jaw ached, but she was a woman possessed, ignoring her own body in favor of Olivia's. When she crested for the third time, Riley felt the release from inside and out, reveling in the pleasure she was providing.

When Olivia finally relaxed beneath her, Riley reversed the trail of kisses she had taken down that glorious body and stretched out beside her, content to watch the aftershocks play across her body and face. The vision wasn't all that different from her fantasy. Olivia's hair was strewn across Riley's pillow, though there was an inch of darker brown at the roots where sweat had soaked into the curls. Her skin was just as luscious against these pale green sheets as they would have been against the navy, and the way they were twisted told an eloquent tale. Her brown eyes fluttered open and fixed on Riley, a smile stretching her lips.

"Is that what you had in mind?" Riley asked.

It was Olivia's turn to put Riley on her back. "Oh, we're just getting started."

Riley's mind and body were trapped in the insurmountable gravity of impending sleep, but she was conscious enough to feel Olivia slip out of bed. One moment her arm was wrapped around Olivia's waist, holding her tight against Riley's still-tingling flesh, the next, only damp sheet and blanket. She tried to speak but couldn't. She drifted off to sleep with a vague, clawing loneliness.

She knew she was alone in her guest bed before she woke to the flare of morning sunlight against her eyelids. The cruel mixture of her tired, cramped limbs and the chill of the sheets beside her made Riley keep her eyes closed and beg for more sleep. But knowing Olivia had left in the night worried her. The pleasant ache of her body told her she hadn't dreamed the sex they'd shared, but why had Olivia left?

Finally bowing to the inevitable, Riley opened her eyes. The first thing she saw was the ruin of the sheets beneath her. Olivia had been just as lively in giving pleasure as she had been in receiving it and the fitted sheet had come off the mattress in one corner. For a long while Riley waited, staring again at the paint imperfection on the ceiling in case Olivia had just gone to the bathroom. She knew it was wasted effort, however, and eventually she couldn't lie there any longer.

Though her pajamas hadn't fared much better than the sheets, they were the only clothes she had in the room. She pulled them on and tried to smooth out the worst of the wrinkles. The apartment was silent as she emerged from the guest room. She spared a quick glance toward the empty living room before dragging her steps down the hall to the primary bedroom.

Olivia had made herself a cocoon in the very center of the bed, every pillow and blanket piled around her. The morning sun cut a bright path across her nest and the edges of her messy curls glowed like a halo around her. The largest of the pillows piled on top of Olivia purred and rolled over, exposing four paws and a comically large white belly. Olivia scratched Nicodemus's cheeks, making his mouth loll open and his purrs intensify.

"You're a big flirt, just like your mom, aren't you?"

"Nicodemus is way more of a flirt than I am." Riley leaned against the doorframe. "Sorry if he bothered you."

"Not at all," Olivia said, transferring her scratches to his chin. "He was a perfect gentleman all night. Stayed on his side of the bed until I woke him up by stretching. Didn't you, Nicodemus?"

He sneezed in answer and shook his head, making his ears flap noisily. Riley laughed along with Olivia at his antics, but the confirmation she'd spent the night in here made her worried all over again.

"Is, um, something wrong?" Riley asked

"What do you mean?"

"You left." Riley swallowed hard, fighting back her confusion. "I'm just wondering why."

Nicodemus hopped down onto the mattress, flopping on his side and commencing a thorough washing of his ear.

Olivia turned to face Riley, her T-shirt sliding off her shoulder to reveal the shadow of a bite mark. "I agreed we'd sleep separately on this trip," she said in a mock innocent voice. "I wouldn't want to break my word."

"Oh." All the disappointment that had plagued her since she woke washing away with Olivia's teasing. "I suppose we did agree to that."

"So I slept in here." Olivia stretched luxuriously. "In your bed." Riley's gaze locked onto the hard points of her nipples visible through the T-shirt.

"Hey, Riley?"

"Huh?"

Olivia pulled back the sheet. "I'm not sleeping anymore."

Nicodemus meowed indignantly as Riley dropped him onto the carpet in the hallway. He ran off with a hiss as the door slammed behind him.

CHAPTER SEVENTEEN

It was late afternoon when Olivia pulled into her assigned parking spot in her family's townhouse community. Because the neighborhood was so tightly packed, her spot was far enough away from her house that she could sit in her car in relative seclusion. She switched off the car and let her head fall back against the headrest.

It had been a long drive back from Miami with traffic and construction and all the usual frustrations of a road trip, but Olivia wanted it to last a little bit longer. She wanted to sit here in the cocoon of her car and relive her incredible weekend. With her eyes closed she imagined herself back in Riley's arms. Beneath her and above her and wrapped inside her strong, electric presence.

For all Olivia liked being the one to take the lead, she wanted a lover who would assert themselves at the right moment. It was a difficult line to walk, Olivia knew that, and the nuance had ruined relationships for her in the past. Olivia smiled as she looked back over the previous night and morning with Riley. That would not be a problem this time. More than anyone she'd ever met, Riley matched her in passion and left Olivia utterly satisfied.

With one last wistful sigh, Olivia wrenched the car door open and shouldered her bag. She had to weave through three rows of parked cars before arriving at their building block. The end unit around the corner from hers glowed with light from all the windows. A too-loud television screamed an advertisement for a local car dealer through the walls. Lewis sat on the stoop, a tattered paperback in his hands and his shoulders thrown back. He looked up when she was a few steps away and there were familiar shadows behind his eyes. This close she could hear that the screaming television didn't quite cover the sound of his parents shouting.

"Hey there, cool kid." She injected as much flippancy in her voice as she could. She'd learned long ago that talking about his parents only made Lewis clam up. He'd ignore her unless she pretended like everything was okay. "What're you reading?"

"Tolkien. Obviously." He waved the cover at her, the black towers faded so much they blended into the orange background.

"Obviously. What about your book list?"

He returned his attention to the pages. "I promised Chelsea not to read too far ahead."

"That's nice of you. Not sure she'd return the favor."

"She won't, but it'll make her feel good to finish first."

"Coming over for dinner?"

Olivia could see the harried dart of his eyes toward his living room window before he said, "Probably."

"Cool. See you then."

"Can't wait to hear about your sleepover."

She caught the words just as she turned the corner, so she was saved a response. His emphasis on "sleepover" made it obvious he had a good idea how she'd spent her weekend and she had no intention of discussing that with either Lewis or Chelsea. They might act like teenagers, but they were only twelve.

Olivia's bag banged loudly against the door, no doubt interrupting Poppa's peaceful afternoon nap. Normally she would have berated herself for her thoughtlessness, but she was still too euphoric from her weekend with Riley to care.

"You look like you could use a beer," Allison called from the kitchen. "Come over here and spill."

Gratefully dropping her bag by the door, Olivia kicked off her shoes and joined her mother in the kitchen.

Allison took one look at her and said, "Oh, daughter of mine, you have it bad."

"I don't know what you're talking about," Olivia said, snatching the bottle from her mother's hand and twisting off the cap.

"Sure you don't. Why don't you go over there and sit? I don't trust you with a knife right now."

Olivia didn't argue, just took her beer and flopped on a barstool, absently watching her mother chop lettuce and carrots. "What's for dinner?"

"Salad and grilled chicken. What else?"

While Allison had a few wonderful attributes, culinary skills were not among them. She was moderately successful at marinating and grilling chicken breasts and had decided one meal was enough. It would be all they'd ever eat if Olivia hadn't bought herself a basic cookbook and discovered a genuine love of feeding her family.

"Sounds great."

"Bullshit." She chopped a chunk of carrot approximately the size of a golf ball and dropping it into the salad bowl. "It sounds as boring as it'll taste, but who cares? Tell me about your weekend."

The sparkle in Allison's eye, mixed with memories of walking on the beach hand-in-hand with Riley, forced a smile so wide Olivia's cheeks hurt.

"That good, huh?" Allison started rinsing a tomato.

"Better. Would you call me silly if I said I think it was the best weekend of my life?" Olivia asked.

"I wouldn't call you silly, but I would tell you to be careful. Be happy, of course, but be careful."

"I know." Olivia groaned. "It's going too fast and I'm falling too hard, but I can't help it. She's so incredible."

Before she turned away to drop the tomato on her cutting board, Olivia caught the look in her mother's eye. It was awfully close to the look Olivia gave her every time she fell for a new guy, only to be left crying a week later when they ghosted her. Being on this side of that worried glance for the first time was a strange sensation.

Despite the concern, Allison didn't warn her off. She smooshed her dull knife through the thick tomato skin. "When are you going to see her again?"

Olivia pushed aside the knot her mother's concern had formed in her stomach and sat up straight, remembering the conversation she and Riley had shared in whispers between kisses and intimate touches. "I work this weekend, but I'm going back middle of next week."

"She can come up here, you know." Allison grabbed a plastic bag full of marinating chicken from the fridge. "No one can hear what's going on all the way up in your room."

Olivia's cheeks blazed, but she had no intention of sleeping with Riley in her family's house. "I am not inflicting all of you on her."

Chelsea came bounding into the room. She threw her arms around Olivia. "I want to see Riley. Bring her here."

Olivia dropped a kiss on Chelsea's frizzy hair and gave her a quick squeeze. "Even if I did bring her here—which I won't—we wouldn't hang out with you and Lewis."

"Rude." Chelsea detached herself from Olivia to grab the cast iron grill pan from the cabinet.

"If she hung out with you instead of Olivia I'd question her sanity," Allison said.

Chelsea scowled at their mother. "Double rude. Why do I put up with either of you?"

Chelsea marched off in the direction of Poppa's room. Once she was out of earshot, Olivia turned back to her mother. "Speaking of Lewis."

"I heard them," Allison said. A frown creased her thin face. "I'll send Chelsea out to get him in a minute. Don't want it to be too obvious."

"He'll tease you about the chicken."

"Well, you can tell him you beat him to the punch."

The pan sizzled and popped as the first of the chicken landed on the surface. Allison hadn't oiled the pan, so they'd stick again, but Olivia bit her tongue. Sometimes her mom took her helpful hints as criticism and Olivia didn't want a fight tonight. Better they eat scorched, ripped chicken than hurt Allison's feelings.

Olivia's phone chimed and she snatched it up fast enough to make her mother laugh. Her smile at seeing Riley's name on the screen must've been just as ridiculous, because Allison waved her away with a set of tongs.

"You do have it bad. Go ahead to your room. Dinner'll be ready in ten minutes."

She didn't bother reminding Allison that the amount of chicken she was cooking would take longer than that to grill. She was too happy about the chance to chat with Riley. She scampered up to her room, bag in tow.

As she went up the stairs, she heard Allison shout, "You can keep her to yourself for now. I'll meet her on your wedding day."

❖

The cursor blinked at Riley as she stared at the computer screen. Nicodemus was lying on the bed behind her, his nose tucked under his paw and the occasional light snore whistling through the room. The sun shone warm through the curtains without heating the room too intolerably. Riley had taken her morning run, eaten a healthy breakfast, and luxuriated in a long, hot shower.

The day was perfect for writing, but the cursor blinked at her rather than flying across the screen. She scanned the list of tasks she'd assigned herself today. It was a long list and she really should have made a dent in it by now, but she was still staring at a blank document.

"Outline the Matthew Barnes article," she said out loud. Nicodemus's snoring cut short. "Easy. I already have it in my head. I just need to..."

She wiggled her fingers first at her head, then at the computer. She was disappointed, if unsurprised, to find the words hadn't magically transferred from her brain to the screen.

"Stop being a dork and type, St. James."

She cracked her knuckles and neck, then set her fingers on the keys again, ready to follow her own command. Her fingers, however, remained as still as her mind remained blank. She growled and flopped back against her chair. It leaned back with her weight, squealing and twirling in place. The twirl was fun, so she tapped her toes along the carpet, spinning the chair beneath her while she fixed her eyes on the ceiling.

Her eyes landed again on the smear of wall paint on the ceiling, eliciting a smile. Olivia had been hovering at the edge of her consciousness all morning, the delicious cause of her lack of focus, and she opened her mind to the memories of their two visits together. Olivia laughing at her silly joke as they strolled along the beach. Teasing her over her choice of unbuttered popcorn to go with their movie night. Screaming into a pillow as Riley's fingers and tongue took her over the edge.

She let the last image stay for longer than the others. Riley had never been with a woman quite like Olivia. A woman who knew what she wanted and was willing to let Riley provide it. She'd never had a lover so demonstrative. It had made Riley feel sexy in a way she never had before. That pride was a hell of an aphrodisiac and the need to taste it again had settled into her like an addiction. Olivia had last left Miami three days and twenty hours ago and she wouldn't be back for another eight days and thirteen hours. Not that Riley was counting.

Riley pressed her feet down on the carpet to stop her spin and turned back to the computer. She shook her body, trying to free it from the tingling thoughts of Olivia had created. She couldn't just sit here yearning for a week until she'd see Olivia again. She had a job to do and pining for her new girlfriend all day wouldn't get that done.

Ten minutes later she had forced herself into a groove and was articulating a well-formulated outline for her article. She knew enough about Barnes to have a good idea of the direction she wanted to take the interview. It couldn't be like her last article about him, which focused entirely on his role on *The Midtown Avengers*. This one would be about the man, not the character, and could propel her into the realm of celebrity above the con circuit.

She was writing the first of her preliminary interview questions when her phone rang. She didn't have any intention of answering, not wanting to disrupt the flow of words, but she snuck a peek at the screen in case it was Olivia. The name on the display made her scramble to answer the call.

"Riley St. James," she said, straightening her back to help project confidence.

"Hi, Riley. It's Lisa Winchester from *Vanity Fair*."

When Riley had programed the number into her cell phone, she hadn't honestly thought she'd ever get this call. Lisa Winchester was

Vanity Fair's executive editor and possibly one of the busiest, most influential women in the magazine world. When Riley's story idea had been green-lit, she'd received an email from Lisa with her contact information and had programmed all of it into her phone as a personal pat on the back.

"Of course. To what do I owe the pleasure, Ms. Winchester?"

"Call me Lisa," she said in clipped tones lacking either warmth or chill. "I want to talk about your Matthew Barnes story. We have a spot in the next issue and it will coincide nicely with the series premiere."

Riley pumped her fist and opened her mouth in a silent cheer before saying as calmly as possible, "That's wonderful. I'm excited about the project."

"Tell me your vision."

Forcing herself to work had been a good decision. Since she had just completed her outline, the story was fresh in her mind. She hit on the major points she would highlight about Barnes's background and life, noting that she had interviewed him before and they had a good rapport.

"I dislike the Q&A format used so often these days. It's one reason I'm so interested in working with *Vanity Fair*. I love the *VF* style of writing about an interviewee by writing about the meeting itself. Weaving tidbits into the article almost in a narrative nonfiction style."

"Is that how you generally work?"

"Not as much in my online publications," Riley said. She was distracted by the chime of an arriving text message and stumbled through the rest of her answer. "But then it's very different. Online versus in print. Of course, *Vanity Fair* has an electronic, um, version, but the reader still expects more."

"That's very true. We try to adapt our articles to be palatable to both the online reader and the print reader, but we aren't willing to compromise the journalistic integrity of the magazine."

Riley half-listened while digging through her papers for her iPad. Her phone would chime again in a couple minutes if she didn't check the message, and she couldn't afford a distraction with Lisa

Winchester on the line. She propped the iPad open on the desk while checking her outline to answer another question. While Lisa responded, Riley looked at the message and grinned to see Olivia's name. It couldn't hurt to actually read the message. Lisa sounded like she was in for a long explanation.

Olivia texted, *Miss u*

Riley awkwardly typed her response with one hand. *Miss u too*

Next Wednesday feels like a lifetime away, Olivia texted.

Riley was going to agree, but Lisa asked, "Will you be discussing his disability?"

"I'd be remiss not to. Matt is very open about having cerebral palsy and he's proud to be an actor who uses forearm crutches playing a character who utilizes them as well. He's clear that it's part of his identity."

"It would also show *Vanity Fair* in a favorable light to highlight one of the few disabled actors in a leading role. I suppose you were angling for the cover by pushing this story."

Riley opened her mouth to protest when a new text message appeared on her iPad screen.

I miss your tongue

Riley dropped the phone and it landed on her bare toe, sending a stab of pain through her foot. She swore, scrambled for the phone, and slapped the iPad closed onto the desk all at the same time. Not only did she miss in her swipe for the phone, but she smacked her forehead on the lip of her desk, eliciting another, very audible swear.

She pressed one hand over her throbbing forehead and put the phone to her ear with the other. "I'm so sorry," Riley said. "Ms. Winchester, Lisa, please forgive me." Desperately searching for an excuse that didn't involve an elicit text message from her girlfriend, her eyes landed on Nicodemus. "My cat knocked the phone out of my hand."

Nic, who was flat on his back on the guest bed, looking like his paws didn't work, let out an indignant howl at being blamed. Fortunately, his protest carried through the phone.

The sound of a low, throaty chuckle came through the line. "Not a problem. Sounds like he's quite the bossy officemate."

"Can you repeat the question?" Riley asked.

"No need. I've heard enough. I love the idea."

Riley pumped her fist in the air again, but the ache in her temple didn't allow her long to celebrate. "That's fantastic. I appreciate the confidence."

"I'm sure it's well-placed. And if the story is everything you say it'll be, I certainly will consider it for the cover."

Riley barely managed to mumble through her good-bye without geeking out, but the moment she hung up, she leaped out of her chair and shouted. It was a poor decision, given the way her big toe throbbed, but a chance at the cover article for *Vanity Fair* was worth the pain.

"Thanks for covering for me, buddy," she said, massaging Nicodemus's cheeks.

He meowed quietly and batted at her hand, clearly chastising her further.

"You're right, you do deserve a treat." She waved him on. "Come on, good boy. Let's both have a treat."

With surprising agility for his size, he flipped onto his paws and streaked off toward the kitchen. Riley followed, making it all the way out of the room before rushing back in and snatching her iPad off the desk.

"I did promise myself a treat, after all."

Chapter Eighteen

Olivia peeled her eyelids open with difficulty. It felt like she'd just closed them, but daylight was flooding her face, dragging her from the sleep she desperately wanted. She stretched out to the bedside table, slapping around on the wood a couple of times before her fingers landed on her phone.

Riley groaned into the pillow beside her. The adorable mumbling made Olivia smile, but the numbers on her phone screen, superimposed over a picture of Chelsea grinning at the camera, took the smile away.

"Too early," Riley said. She wrapped her arm around Olivia's waist, dragging their bodies together. "Sleep."

Olivia settled in, her back pressed against Riley's naked breasts, and sighed. "It's not too early, babe. It's too late. I have to leave in a few hours."

"No." Riley pouted, pulling Olivia closer still. "Sex."

Olivia laughed and spun in Riley's arms. Despite Riley's overtures, she was in no state to follow through. Riley's face was half-buried in her pillow, her eyes still firmly shut, and her limbs heavy as stone. She looked like a woman who had been up until two a.m. having extremely enthusiastic sex. Mostly because they had, in fact, been up until two having incredible sex. It accounted for the tousled hair curtaining Riley's exposed eye and the exhaustion etched into her features.

"Baby, you couldn't have sex right now if you wanted to."

"Want to," Riley said. She finally opened one eye. "Maybe coffee first."

Olivia groaned and flopped back onto her pillow. "Coffee sounds divine."

With more energy than she looked capable of, Riley popped up and threw off the covers. "On it."

"You don't have to go make coffee, babe."

"Course I do." Riley stepped into her boxers. "Be right back."

"Why'd you put on boxers?" Olivia called after her as she hurried from the room. "I'll just have to take them off you later."

Riley popped her head back into the room and smiled. "That's why I put them on."

Olivia had time to check a few emails and the latest on Twitter while listening to the gurgling and sputtering from the coffee maker down the hall. There was also an adorable exchange between Riley and Nicodemus that ended with the clatter of kibble being poured into a ceramic bowl.

Olivia propped her pillow up against the headboard and leaned back into it, taking in the peace of the morning in Riley's place. Back home, morning was never quiet. Chelsea was always up with the sun, never having embraced Allison's lazy morning routine. Olivia never got lazy mornings either, even though she wanted them.

Poppa's blood sugar levels spiked in the early morning. It hadn't always been a problem, but he'd been battling dawn phenomenon for about a year now. At first, she thought he'd been sneaking snacks before bed, but his doctor said it was a common occurrence for folks with diabetes to experience spikes in the morning. All they had to do was ensure they stayed on top of it, but that meant early mornings for Olivia.

Chelsea's early bird tendencies and Poppa's dawn phenomenon were bad enough, but the worst was Allison. Punctuality had never been her thing, and she always misjudged the appropriate number of snoozes. Between the snoozing and the distracted, haphazard way she showered, dressed, and applied her makeup, Allison was always sprinting for the door long past the right time to leave. Fortunately, her boss wasn't strict on arrival times or else Allison would be unemployed because of tardiness many times over.

"Whoa." Riley froze in the doorway, her jaw on the floor. Olivia looked around, then down at herself. Sitting up against the headboard, the sheets had pooled around her waist, leaving her breasts exposed to the air and Riley's appreciative stare.

"You know you've seen these a few times, babe."

"Yeah," Riley said, one side of her mouth twitching up and her eyes glued to Olivia's nipples. "Awesome every time."

Olivia couldn't help but laugh. Riley was so adorable, standing there in wrinkled boxers, holding mismatched coffee mugs, and grinning like a fool. It also didn't hurt that Riley's breasts were exposed, too, and her nipples were reacting either to the air conditioning or Olivia's nudity.

"Get over here and give me some coffee, you adorable nerd," Olivia said as she pulled the sheets up to cover herself.

Riley stuck out her bottom lip, but she finally let her eyes travel up to meet Olivia's. She set one steaming mug on her bedside table and carefully passed the other to Olivia.

Before she settled onto the mattress, Riley said, "As much as I hate for you to cover up, you know Nic will be in here any minute. He has an unfortunate habit of sniffing anything and everything, so a shirt might be a good idea."

Olivia was deep into her first, perfect sip of coffee. She let her eyes flutter closed and held up a finger to Riley, letting the caffeine surge through her veins before she took in the warning. There was nothing like that first sip of the day. She wanted to let it linger. When she let her eyes fall open, all she saw was Riley, staring at her with a curious mix of awe and humor shining in her eyes.

"What?" Olivia turned away to hide her blush.

"You are stunning."

Olivia's cheeks tingled at the compliment. This was her third trip down to Miami to stay with Riley and they were obviously enjoying each other's company. It amazed her how well-suited they were. Riley stared at her like she was the most beautiful woman in the room.

Sometimes it was too much. It felt too good. Too safe. Too much to hope for.

"You're not so bad yourself, St. James," she said to lighten the mood.

Riley pulled a T-shirt on, further disrupting the tangle of her hair. Olivia tore her eyes away long enough to pull on a tank top and panties. She climbed back into bed just in time. With a squeak and a slight scrabbling of paws on the bed frame, Nicodemus burst onto the scene.

"Hey there, big guy." Olivia reached out and Nicodemus whacked his head against her knuckles. "Nice of you to join us."

Riley grabbed her phone and shuffled through a few social media apps while Nic made himself comfortable. It was a delicate process. Testing a paw here and there, sniffing the duvet in a couple of spots, then pacing in a circle until he had the perfect angle to flop down.

Riley's process was just as systematic and finicky. Olivia had caught her checking out the apps a few times in their stays together. She never seemed to be looking for anything in particular from her feed, and the process always made a little crease form between her eyebrows. Olivia supposed it wasn't as fun to scroll through social media when your livelihood depended on your followers. She ached to know what cool people Riley followed because she didn't retweet or share posts too often. Nearly everything was original content, which was rare.

Nicodemus had settled on his side, paws on Riley's thigh, but apparently she wasn't interesting enough for him. He rolled onto his back, fixing his intense stare on Olivia. Holding his front paws below his chin, he looked like an innocent angel. Olivia bent forward and pinched his fluffy cheeks. He purred and tried to rub his chin against her. She transferred the pets to his chest and armpits, and that's when he really started purring.

"Traitor." Riley scolded him when he closed his eyes and lazily licked his lips. "You never let me pet your belly without leaving a few scratches."

"Oh, I've learned to avoid the belly and stick to the chest." Olivia bent down until their noses were almost touching and continued in baby talk, "Isn't that right, lil Nic? Yes, that's right. Auntie Livia doesn't rub the belly."

"Auntie Livia?" Riley scowled. "Wouldn't that make you my…"

"Stop right there." Olivia put a finger on Riley's lips. "Don't make it weird."

"Who's making it weird?" Riley mumbled around her finger.

Olivia pulled her finger away and leaned in to replace it with her lips. Unfortunately, that transferred the cat hair she'd pressed to Riley's lips to her own. She sputtered and pulled back, swatting the fur off her lips.

"Oh, that's nice." Riley pretended to pout. "Swatting away my kisses?"

"Swatting away Nic's contribution to our kiss." Lips cleaned, Olivia leaned back in, close enough to kiss but not making contact. "Shall we try again?"

Nicodemus yowled and swatted at Olivia's arm. She jumped back, having learned that his warnings got more pointed with each repetition.

"We can't disturb the master of the house." Riley laughed, tossing her phone onto the bedside table and retrieving her coffee. "Can you stay for lunch or do you need to rush home?"

Olivia sighed and leaned back against the pillow. She had a million things to do around the house. All of these trips really cut into her housework time and she didn't want Chelsea to have to start doing laundry yet. Still, she thought as she watched Nicodemus settle down and Riley booped his nose, this was where she wanted to be.

"I can stay for lunch, but I really should leave right after."

"I can work with that." Riley took a sip of coffee.

"So why Nicodemus?" Olivia rubbed his ears.

"*The Secret of NIMH*," Riley answered, nestling into her pillows. "I loved NIMH as a kid, so I borrowed the name of the wise rat. Turns out this guy doesn't live up to the wisdom." Nicodemus ignored her, choosing instead to run a low-grade purr and lean into the ear rubs. "But I couldn't change his name again. I got him as a kitten and they told me he was a girl, so I named him Miss Kitty Fantastico."

Nicodemus sneezed and swatted at Olivia's hand. "Yeah, that doesn't really suit him. *Buffy*, right? Willow and Tara's cat?"

"That's right. I couldn't think of any other cats to name him after, so I decided to torture him with a rat name."

"What about the cat from *The L Word*?"

"Was there a cat in *The L Word*?" Riley asked.

"Just season one." Olivia decided to rub it in with her detailed knowledge. "He was Dana's cat. Mr. Piddles."

"Oh, right. Tonya killed him. I completely forgot about that."

"I have a pretty good memory for entertainment trivia," Olivia said. Riley smiled up at her and it made her stomach flip pleasantly. "Want to test me?"

Riley's eyes smoldered as she caught Olivia's gaze. Her voice rumbled as she said, "Sounds like fun. What do I get if I stump you?"

Olivia leaned over Nicodemus, brushing her lips against Riley's jaw, then capturing her lips. She kept the kiss slow and sensuous until Riley trembled against her. Then she pulled back and whispered, "You won't."

Riley's laugh was more of a strangled gasp. She recovered quickly, though. Leaning back into her pillows, she tapped a finger against her chin. Olivia let her think, knowing there was no chance Riley could out trivia her on queer media. She spent the time playing with Nicodemus's big fluffy paws.

"Okay," Riley said. "I'll give you an easy one to start. What were Elena and Syd's couple's Halloween costume in the final season of *One Day at a Time*?"

"Greta Thunberg and an iceberg," Olivia said. "And they didn't go trick-or-treating, they went door-to-door informing people about the dangers of climate change."

"Okay, yeah, too easy." Riley took Nic's other paw and he closed his eyes and indulged in a double paw massage. "What was Alice buying in the gift shop while Dana was dying in *The L Word*, season three."

"Hey, spoiler alert."

"It was 2005."

"Yeah, well, the wound is still fresh. Also, that's still too easy. It was a dancing sunflower singing 'You Are My Sunshine.'"

"Okay, those were just warm-up." Riley released Nic's paw and turned to face Olivia. Clearing her throat, she said, "I didn't want you as a cellmate then and I still don't. Not because I hate you, but because I love you."

"Um, what?"

"It's a quote from a show. Name the show."

"Oh, um," Olivia racked her brain but the words didn't ring any bells. "Say it again?"

Riley laughed and leaned in close. "You heard me. Are you ready to admit defeat?"

Olivia lost herself in the shimmering depths of Riley's eyes. Her gaze dropped to Riley's lips, plump and inviting and so close. "Never."

"Then name the show."

"Okay, fine. I give up," Olivia said. Riley tucked her hands behind her head and preened. The movement stretched her shirt across her breasts, but Olivia refused to be distracted. "But you have to tell me to get your reward."

She ran her tongue along her bottom lip to emphasize the demand and Riley's eyes clouded with lust. "*Cell Block Six.*"

"Huh?"

"*Cell Block Six.*" Riley went from gloating winner to straight-up nerd in two seconds flat. "It was an Argentinian TV show back in the early 2010s set in a women's prison. Kind of a thawing the ice queen with two cellmates falling in love. So hot. Completely ridiculous, but so hot."

"How have I never heard of this show?"

"Well, it was hard to watch in the States. I had to hack the region code on my DVD player to watch it."

Olivia dropped Nicodemus's paw and crossed her arms. "That's totally cheating."

"No way. You never said it had to be US trivia."

"It was implied." Olivia tried and failed to hold back her grin. "I think we have to call this one a draw."

"Oh, no you don't." Riley pushed up onto her knees and Nic bolted out of her way when she lunged for Olivia.

Rolling around on the mattress, Olivia gasped for air as she giggled and dodged. Riley was smaller, but she was wicked fast and she'd learned all of Olivia's most ticklish spots.

"Ah! Okay! Okay! I give up! You win!"

"What was that?" Riley continued tickling Olivia's side.

"You win. You win." Olivia fought to catch her breath as Riley finally stopped, settling in to straddle Olivia's hips. "You know more useless entertainment trivia than me."

Riley flexed her biceps. "Damn right I do."

"Now about your prize." Olivia slipped her hands under the hem of Riley's shirt.

CHAPTER NINETEEN

R iley gave her query letter one last read and finally deemed it ready to send. She'd been agonizing over this since QueerCon. After all, it wasn't every day she got a personal introduction to a successful showrunner. If this worked out, she could skip the laborious, often fruitless process of getting an agent. Plus, an agent would try to get her any old show, even if she had no interest in writing for it. That was if she could get one to take her seriously, unlike the one from QueerCon who, unsurprisingly, had not been in touch. This was a chance to write for one of her favorite shows in one of the only writers' room in Hollywood that was majority queer and people of color. It was the dream job.

Honestly, Riley had probably leaned a little too hard on the flattery in her letter. It was common knowledge Ashton had pushed hard for the finale scene with Carmen and Erin. The studio wanted shock and gore in the style of *The Walking Dead*, but Ashton wanted to take *The Railyard* in a different direction entirely. She wanted to find the glimmers of hope in the darkest nights, and that appealed to Riley. Her spec script hinged on the lesbian leads getting away after the "I want better for us, not just good enough" speech.

"Okay, Nic," she said to the ball of fluff on the guest bed. "Here goes nothing."

She pasted her query letter into the email, attached her spec script, and smashed the send button before she lost her nerve. She let out a low, slow breath and stared at the screen.

"Done." Nicodemus slept soundly through Riley's hopes and dreams whooshing away in an electronic envelope. "Now it's one hundred percent Olivia time for the next three days."

Riley spun her chair around, happier than she had any right to be. She still got butterflies in her stomach when it was time for Olivia to visit. In fact, the butterflies multiplied with each reunion. Every day in between her visits felt like a lifetime. Riley tried not to dissect her feelings. If she thought about how much she craved seeing Olivia, she'd start to try to name those feelings, and Riley wasn't the type to name feelings after only a couple of months.

She'd changed up her routine to accommodate this visit, working through last weekend so she'd have all her articles submitted by midweek when Olivia had time off. With summer tourist season in Florida, they had no choice. Olivia would be working more weekends for the next few months and Riley had enough established deadlines that she could easily adjust.

Riley was shutting down her computer when her phone rang, Olivia's name on the display.

"Hey, babe, you here already?"

Rather than the usual teasing, throaty purr, Olivia's words were rushed. "Hey, Riley. I'm sorry. Something's come up and I can't make it."

Riley's smile dropped. "Can't make it? I thought you'd be on your way."

"Yeah, me too, but Poppa has a doctor's appointment and I can't get away."

"Oh, no, I'm so sorry. Is he okay?"

"He's fine. It's his usual checkup."

Riley's head snapped up in confusion. "It was already scheduled? Can't Allison take him?"

"Yeah, she'll be there, too. The nurse called this morning and said they'd be changing some of his meds, so I need to be there."

"Allison can't get them?"

Riley knew she was pushing it when she heard the snap in Olivia's reply. "This is an important visit. He takes several medications and if only one dosage is off, he can spiral before we know it. Allison is hopeless with this stuff. Don't you remember how she had to call me about his meds on my first visit?"

"Of course, you're right." Riley forced herself not to let her disappointment show in her voice. "You're amazing with Poppa and I know your family is important." I just wish I was as important, she thought. Riley tried to stuff the thought away, but it kept repeating in her head as she faced yet another week or two without seeing Olivia.

"Of course, my family is important," Olivia said. Riley could almost hear her hand on her hip and the challenge in her eyes. "What are you trying to say?"

"Nothing." Riley hesitated, then continued in the calmest, kindest voice she could muster, "I just wonder if they really need you for this. Allison will be there and I'm sure you can call the office to clarify if something is lost in translation."

"So you think they don't need me?"

"No, I know they need you. I just wonder if they need you as much as you think they do. That's all."

The silence on the line was enough to tell Riley she'd made a mistake. It lasted far too long. The urge to fill that silence nearly overwhelmed her, but then Olivia's voice came through, dangerously slow. "Oh, that's all?"

"I didn't mean it like that," Riley said.

"Are you suggesting taking a few days away should be more important than maintaining my grandfather's health? Because it really sounds like that's what you think."

The words dropped like ice into Riley's gut. "Taking a few days away" felt so flippant. So unimportant. Did their time together really mean so little to Olivia?

"Of course not. I just miss you," Riley said.

"I miss you, too." Olivia sighed and continued in a calmer voice, "Look, Riley, I have to go. My family needs me."

"Can we talk after the appointment? I don't feel good leaving it this way."

"Yes. I'll call you later, but I have to go."

Olivia hung up without another word, leaving Riley alone, disappointed, and more than a little confused. A million thoughts chased each other through her head, most of them about whether or not Olivia would ever call her again.

"What just happened?"

Nicodemus didn't answer, but watching him yawn and settle back to sleep helped quiet Riley's brain. There was no use pouting over canceled plans. That happened all the time, and it was a miracle they'd been able to see each other as often as they had. Riley kept reminding herself this was how long-distance relationships worked. And couples fought. This was nothing to worry about. Sure, she thought Olivia was being overly cautious, but Riley had never had the sort of familial obligations Olivia lived with every day. It was selfish of her to want to come first.

"You're allowed to be disappointed," Riley told herself. "But Olivia needs you to be supportive. When she calls back, you'll talk it out."

The pep talk gave her the energy to go to her bedroom and change out of her good khakis into comfortable sweats. She'd pre-ordered pizza for them tonight, assuming they wouldn't want to leave bed for dinner, and she'd saved an episode of *Killing Eve* to watch together. On their nightly phone call the previous evening, Olivia had correctly identified the object Villanelle's ex was retrieving from the trunk when Villanelle ran her over. Maybe Riley could watch it and write something extra. Selling another article could fill the next few days since Olivia couldn't.

It took her the rest of the day to absorb the episode and work up an idea for an article. She couldn't bring herself to care about Eve having yet another inappropriate sexual relationship with a coworker when she should've been diving into bed with Villanelle. She ate way too much pizza and sulked on the couch until Nicodemus finally wandered in to join her.

"Don't worry, Nic," she said. "She'll call. It's just a silly fight. Not the end of the world."

That got harder and harder to believe as the sun set and Riley switched to numbly watching old episodes of *RuPaul's Drag Race*. She wavered between annoyance that Olivia had canceled and terror she wouldn't call back through three queens failing to lip synch for their lives. Just when she was concluding Olivia wouldn't call, her phone rang. She scrambled to answer so quickly she dropped the phone.

"Hey, babe." Olivia sounded exhausted and more than a little sad. "I'm sorry about this morning. I was a jerk."

Relief flooded into Riley. "It's okay."

"No, it isn't. Our time together is important to me and I hate that I'm not there."

"I know." Riley tried to lighten the mood with teasing. "Nicodemus blames me. I think he likes you better now."

"Aw, poor guy. Well, tell Nicodemus I'll be there to pet him again real soon." Olivia laughed. "I know I get a little silly about Poppa. It's just that Allison is so flighty, it's better if I'm there, even if I'd rather be with you."

"I'm sorry, too. It's not my place to interfere with your family obligations."

"Well, it does concern you when it interrupts our time together."

Riley still thought Olivia was being overprotective of Poppa and unfair to Allison, but she was apologizing, so Riley let it go. She was more interested in trying to salvage their plans anyway.

"Maybe it's not a total loss?" Riley looked at her watch, discovering it was well past time when Olivia could drive to Miami. Instead, she asked, "Maybe you can leave in the morning? We'd only lose one day together."

"I wish I could, but I'd have to wait until after Chelsea goes to day camp, so I wouldn't make it until late afternoon. Then I'd just have to turn around the next morning."

Annoyance flared in Riley again. Surely Chelsea could handle a morning alone in the house before summer camp? The last thing she wanted, however, was another fight.

"I understand. I don't want you tired on the road," Riley said.

"I'll get my new schedule next week and we can make plans for the next trip. Okay?"

"Yeah, that works. As long as—" Riley swallowed hard. "We're okay, right?"

"We're definitely okay."

There was no hint of doubt in Olivia's words, and that helped settle Riley. They said their good nights and Riley trudged off to bed. She settled in for yet another lonely night, determined to clear her schedule the minute Olivia was available again. Maybe it would be easier if she went to Tampa. She'd suggest it as soon as she could because she was not thrilled about sleeping without Olivia curled up beside her.

CHAPTER TWENTY

S un sparkled off a sea of parked cars to either side of Olivia. The horn blasted from a departing cruise ship, and soon the sun would sparkle off the actual sea behind her. In between handing out tickets to new arrivals, she turned to watch the lumbering ship pull into open water. The line of cars waiting to park hadn't slackened with the ship's departure. There were another two in the process of boarding. Her whole day would be like this.

The steady work kept her hands busy and her mind free to wander. Unfortunately, her mind today was full of her fight with Riley. It was inevitable Olivia's family obligations would cut into their time together. That had been a major factor in her last breakup, too. Most people found it hard to accept a partner tied to an ailing grandfather and a pre-teen sister who needed constant attention. It just usually took longer than this.

The main thought clattering around in her brain was Riley's accusation that her family didn't need Olivia as much as she thought they did. That one stung. If Olivia was honest with herself, it stung because Riley might be right. Allison was flighty, but she wasn't incompetent. The dosage change for Poppa's Coumadin wasn't extreme. Even Allison could swap one strength pill for another without difficulty.

Why had Olivia been so insistent she go? Especially when it meant missing a trip to see Riley. A trip she'd been desperate for. Every time she went to Miami, it got harder and harder to leave. Last time she'd almost suggested staying an extra night, leaving at sunrise to make it to work on time just so she could have another few hours with Riley. Then she'd blown Riley off to hold Poppa's hand through a routine appointment?

Maybe you just want Poppa and Allison to need you, she thought.

It wasn't the first time the idea had occurred to her, but Olivia didn't want to dive into her psyche while handing out port maps to strangers. That was a line of thought for another day.

An unexpected lull in traffic gave Olivia a chance to check her email. The envelope icon sported a red dot with an outlandish number inside. Ever since QueerCon, she had been inundated with commissions. Her Twitter and Insta DMs were similarly full of requests, but PayPal was the app getting the most love. She was now making more from fan art than she was from her day job. She didn't have any illusions the onslaught would continue—once the con was out of memory, requests would dwindle. Still, she'd take the opportunity to make a living from art for as long as it lasted.

Another burst of customers pulled her focus, but she checked through a few messages while each car pulled away. One caught her eye and piqued her creative instinct, and she let the idea roll over in her mind until it was time for her lunch break.

"Hey, Liv." Annie wrenched open the booth door, swearing when it caught on the track. She was as tall as Olivia and broader across the shoulders, but her frame lacked even the illusion of muscle. Her frizzy ponytail flopped over her shoulder as she yanked ineffectually at the door, managing only to get it twisted.

"Here, let me help with that," Olivia said.

Together they pushed and the door finally opened, banging hard against the back wall of the booth.

"Ready for lunch?"

"Totally," Olivia said.

Annie plopped onto the stool and helped the next car in line, somehow managing a smile even though the driver was being a total jerk. She was unfailingly friendly, a trait Olivia tried to emulate but rarely managed. It wasn't in her nature to smile and take it when someone was rude. Fortunately, she was pretty enough to get away with sarcastic remarks most of the time.

Olivia decided to wait and chat with her friend before heading to the office for lunch. Their job was lonely most of the time, with coworkers manning other booths and thus out of contact. She and Annie sometimes hung out after work, but it had been a while. They'd tried dating early on, but weren't compatible, so they fell into that stereotype of exes who became friends.

"How's life?" Olivia asked once the customer had pulled away.

"Same old thing." Annie flashed her a smile before turning to an approaching minivan. "How about you? Going back to Miami this weekend?"

Annie had been the first coworker she'd told about Riley. Annie had wanted to go to QueerCon too, but her girlfriend didn't like crowds and she chickened out of going alone. Now that her relationship with Riley was heating up, Olivia had picked up the habit of gushing.

"No, I have to work. I have three days next week, though, so I'm heading down then."

"This is becoming a regular thing, huh?"

After their first weekend together, Olivia had been desperate to go back. She'd even bribed Annie to take her weekend shift once so they could see each other sooner. The drive was wearing on her, but the reward was too sweet to give up.

"As regular as we can make it. Thanks again for covering my weekend."

"Just name your firstborn after me," she said.

"Deal." Olivia laughed. She was turning to go when a thought struck her and she stopped. "Hey, Annie. You're an Earper."

"Absolutely. CeCe and I have watched the entire series seven times. We're thinking about doing a marathon again next month." She froze, her jaw dropping. "Oh, my God. You got a commission, didn't you? Is it Dom? Kat? Who is it?"

"It's not one of the actresses," Olivia scrolled to the message that had caught her eye earlier. "Unless one of them has the Instagram handle EarpyForLyfe97."

"Yeah, I doubt it, but a girl can dream. What's the piece?"

"That's just it. They didn't say."

Most of her clients had a specific theme they wanted for their fan art. A scene they loved or a look for the characters. Whether it had happened in the show or it was inspired by fan fiction, they usually knew what they were paying for. This client was different.

"What do they want then?"

"It says." Olivia cleared her throat and read from the email. "I want a WayHaught piece. Something that shows Waverly and Nicole happy and in love. Like the perfect moment of them as a couple. No demons or monsters or Wynonna. Just the two of them. Can you do that?"

"Can you do that?" Annie repeated, her eyes practically glowing. "It sounds amazing."

"Yeah, but what does it mean?"

"Okay." Annie sat straighter and squinted into the distance. "How about the sex scene with the blue button-up? I love that scene."

"It's super-hot, sure, but wasn't Waverly possessed by a demon at the time?"

"Yeah, and they were just finishing up a fight. So maybe not the perfect moment."

"Definitely not," Olivia said.

"Maybe the first kiss in the sheriff's office?"

"It doesn't feel quite right." Olivia waited while Annie helped an older couple in a Mercedes. "Is that a perfect moment? I mean, there's so much potential in a first kiss, but there's also so much that could go wrong. They're not even in love yet."

"So what does the perfect moment for a couple look like to you?" Annie asked.

"I dunno. I'm not sure I've had one."

Annie gave her a withering look, followed by an eye roll.

"What?" Olivia asked.

"You have spent a cumulative, what, thirty hours on Florida highways in this swampy summer heat and you don't know what a happy couple moment looks like?"

"I know what it looks like for me, but I don't know what it looks like for Waverly and Nicole. Or for my client."

"Happiness looks remarkably similar for all of us."

"What does it look like for you and CeCe?"

Annie was a big softie at heart, and Olivia could tell the moment she started thinking about her girlfriend. Her eyes went glassy and her whole body smiled, making her look stronger and softer at the same moment. It made Olivia miss Riley even more.

"If I have to keep it rated PG, I'd have to say Sunday nights."

"Okay, I'll bite. What does a Sunday night look like for you two?"

"Well, I'm exhausted, obviously." They nodded at each other, acknowledging the parking lot full of cars and the roar of another ship's engine warming up. "And I'm not up for much, so we curl up on the couch with a pizza or some Chinese food delivery and watch old movies that make us laugh."

"And then what?"

"That's it." Annie shrugged. "We just laugh together, snuggled up on the couch. We don't perform for each other anymore. We're comfortable being with each other and not having to go out or look great. I can wear sweats and snort when I laugh and she loves me just the way I am. That's real love."

Before she could say anything more, a line of cars backed up behind Annie's booth and Olivia left her to her work. She dodged exiting cars and waved at another two coworkers on her way to the little corrugated aluminum shelter they called an office. It was two big rooms, one with a safe for their cash drawers and the other with a few battered lockers and an even more battered refrigerator. She dropped into one of the folding chairs flanking the card table in the center of the break room and pulled a turkey sandwich from her lunch bag.

While she munched on her sandwich and chips, she thought about her commission. Annie's happy moment sounded lovely, but it didn't quite fit her vision. She did like the idea of not having to perform. So much of dating was playing a part. The best version of yourself for each other until you're too deep in to be disappointed when the real version shows up. It had always been her intention not to hide who she was when she started dating someone. Sure, she'd scared one or two folks off, but they wouldn't have lasted anyway.

Riley seemed to accept everything about her from the start. It helped that they shared the same obsessive love of lesbian television, but there was more than that. The way Riley was with Chelsea. The way she always asked about Poppa. The way she encouraged Olivia to pursue a career in art. She'd never had that sort of thoughtfulness from a partner before. Not to mention the connection they shared in the bedroom. They just fit together.

Olivia sighed, forcing herself to focus on the commission and not the far more pleasant thoughts of Riley.

She yanked her sketchpad from her bag and propped it between her lap and the tabletop. She had a good enough idea of Waverly and Nicole to start a preliminary sketch. Three of her jobs since QueerCon had been one or both of them and her hands could work on their own, drafting the contours of their faces. Without anywhere else to start, she went with the idea of snuggling on a couch together. She just couldn't figure out where they were. She outlined Nicole's high cheekbones and slightly hollowed cheeks. Maybe they were on the Homestead? Did they even have a TV at the Homestead? Maybe Nicole's place? Nicole's apartment had been the backdrop for a couple of scenes. Nicole had even sat on her couch for one of them. Olivia played the scene through her mind's eye as she sketched. A snobby, homophobic councilwoman had most of the lines, but Nicole's fluffy orange cat, Calamity Jane, had stolen the scene.

Olivia chuckled. Calamity Jane was a cutie but no match for Nicodemus.

The pencil slipped out of Olivia's hand, clattering to the linoleum floor. She blinked twice, then closed her eyes to formulate the image in her mind.

A late Sunday morning in Miami. Riley made coffee. Olivia teasing her for putting on a pair of boxer briefs before scuttling out to the kitchen. It had been fun taking them off her later. But it wasn't the memory of removing Riley's underwear that stuck in her mind. It was the two of them, sitting up in bed with steaming mugs of coffee in their hands. Nicodemus stretched out between them, purring his little heart out while they played with his paws.

A perfect morning, Olivia thought, tearing her sketch from the pad to start a new one.

She was late getting back to her booth, but Annie took it in stride, seeing the joy in Olivia's smile.

Before she got out of earshot, Olivia called out, "How do Waverly and Nicole take their coffee?"

Chapter Twenty-one

W hen do you head out to LA?" Dani shoved a handful of fries into her mouth.

"Not for a while yet." Riley wiped her fingertips on the napkin in her lap. "We're doing a preliminary interview on the phone next week. Setting the groundwork. After that I'll coordinate with the photographer and his manager to find a good day for all of us."

"Think they'll fly you first class?" Dani's eyes sparkled and slipped out of focus. Riley knew her thoughts were impure, and the next sentence sealed it. "Bet you could nail a flight attendant in first class."

Riley shook her head and reached for her beer. "You're disgusting."

"Come on. You trying to say you'd turn down membership in the Mile High Club?"

"Yes, I would turn it down," Riley said. "Not that there would be the slightest chance."

Dani took a massive bite of her burger and said through a mouthful of meat, cheese, and bread, "Bullshit. You tell her you're interviewing Matthew Barnes for *Vanity Fair* and those panties will melt right off."

"You're interviewing Matthew Barnes?" a blonde from the next table asked, her eyes wide with excitement.

"It's not a done deal yet." Riley's cheeks heated up.

"But you write for *Vanity Fair*?" She turned from her friends to give Riley her full attention.

"Freelance." Riley shuffled in her seat. "It's not that big a deal."

A muscly guy at the blonde's table caught her attention and she turned from Riley with obvious reluctance. Riley looked across the table and found Dani smiling at her and wiggling her eyebrows.

"You've got ketchup on your chin," Riley said.

"And if you wanted, your chin could be covered in that blonde's—"

"Stop," Riley said. She only hoped Dani hadn't been loud enough for the blonde to hear. "What is wrong with you?"

Dani leaned back in her chair, giggling. "It's so easy to fuck with you. Damn, you're a lot of fun, St. James."

"And you're none at all. Why do I even hang out with you?"

"'Cause I'm your best friend and I keep you from getting that stick permanently lodged in your ass. Relax, I'll leave you alone now."

"I'll believe that when I see it."

"True, but you can't resist my charms. No woman can."

Their waitress arrived, bringing Riley a fresh beer. Not that she looked at Riley when she delivered it. She only had eyes for Dani. They shared a look that told Riley she was destined to be ditched for a tryst in the restaurant bathroom.

"Anyway," Dani said, following the retreating waitress's ass with her eyes. "Make any headway getting your script seen?"

"Yeah, actually." Riley shook off her annoyance. "I sent off a spec script a week ago to that writer who works on *The Railyard*. Hopefully, it's good enough to get a foot in the door."

"Of course it is. You're the most fucking talented person I've ever met. Your scripts are golden."

Riley tried not to preen, but the compliment felt good. "That sucking up is the real reason I keep you around."

Dani drained her beer and looked around the restaurant, a telltale gleam in her eye. Barney's was a dive sports bar, but they had amazing burgers and served them early. A little over a year ago, Riley had decided it was time for her to get back in shape. She'd been an athlete in high school, but turning thirty hadn't done her metabolism any favors. Dani had always been obsessed with working out, so they'd started running together several days a week. Once Riley had hit her goal weight and mile time, they'd changed the routine. One afternoon a week they'd take a longer than usual run and end it at Barney's, where they'd consume far more calories than they burned and Dani would find someone to spend Friday night with. The dining room at Barney's was starting to feel more like home to Riley than her own apartment.

"So how are you and the Mrs. getting along?" Dani asked, settling back into conversation when scoping for chicks didn't work out.

"We're hardly married." Riley avoided Dani's eye so she could hide her smile. "We barely get to see each other."

"What're you talking about? You're always ditching me 'cause she's coming to visit."

"Four trips down here isn't exactly a lot." There'd been more than one run Riley had missed in favor of chatting with Olivia, but she didn't want to bring that up now. "But speaking of ditching plans, I'm going to have to cut out in a few minutes."

"You're kidding." Dani sighed.

"It's just that her mom is taking her grandpa to physical therapy this afternoon and her sister's doing a sleepover. We can talk without being disturbed. We never get that."

"We never get to go out together either. I miss my best friend."

"We're literally out right now. I'm not ditching you, I'm just leaving early," Riley said.

"That's ditching me."

"Come on, Dani. I need to talk to her. Hear her voice, ya know?"

"Oh, sure. Talking. That's what you'll do." Dani scoffed and waved to the waitress for another beer.

"What's that supposed to mean?" Riley asked.

"Like you don't know." Dani smiled, her eyebrows dancing. When Riley continued to stare at her, trying to work out the joke, the smile slid off Dani's face. "Oh, my God. You don't, do you?"

"What are you talking about?"

Dani pinched the bridge of her nose, speaking very slowly. "Look, she has the house to herself."

Riley nodded.

"And she's calling you." Dani waved her hand, encouraging her to come along for the ride. "Her girlfriend."

Riley was starting to think they were never going to arrive at their mental destination.

"Jesus, St. James, you're gonna have phone sex," Dani shouted.

Every face in the now busy restaurant turned to stare at Riley. It was as though they all knew just how thick she was. A blush heated her face. Barely controlling her instinct to crawl underneath the table, she turned to Dani. "Keep your voice down. What are you trying to do to me here?"

Dani's face reddened, too, but in her case it was from holding back laughter. "If you could see your face. That's some funny shit right there."

"You're a real pal, you know that?" Riley pushed her chair back. "Come on, don't leave."

"I definitely don't want to hang out with you now," Riley said. She could hear the pout in her voice.

"Oh, shit." Dani's expression and voice softening. "You've never had phone sex before, have you?"

Riley thought about denying it, but Dani knew her too well. Besides, fear was creeping in. Was Dani right? And if she was, how did that even work? She slipped back onto the chair and leaned close. "No. I mean, come on, you know me. That's a little out there for me."

Dani put a comforting hand on her shoulder and leaned in so they wouldn't be overheard. "I get it. This is new territory. It's okay to be nervous. It's even okay to tell Olivia you don't want to do it."

"But," Riley swallowed hard and asked, "what if I do want to do it?"

Dani's smile was a little too knowing. "Then you're in for a really fun afternoon. I get the feeling Olivia is someone you can trust, right?"

"Yeah."

"And someone you have good chemistry with in person?"

"Definitely."

"It'll be just like that on the phone." Dani gave her shoulder a little slap. "Don't get in your head about this. Olivia will walk you through it."

"You think she's done this before?"

"Oh, yeah."

"How do you know?" Riley asked.

Dani's only reply was another slap on the shoulder and a wink as she leaned back into her chair.

"Seriously," Riley asked. "How do you know?"

"Lesbian intuition."

"I'm a lesbian. Don't I have intuition?"

Dani was swallowing a mouthful of beer, so she didn't answer with words. Her scoff and slight head shake ruffled Riley's feathers though.

Riley said, "Whatever. I have to get home. So I can talk—just talk—to Olivia."

"Okay, sure. If you say so. You'll know for sure if she wants to FaceTime rather than voice call," Dani said.

Riley's blush didn't fade until she was safe inside her own apartment. Checking her watch, she saw there was a good hour until Olivia called. She took a quick shower and changed into jeans and a T-shirt.

"Just a call. Nothing more. She would've said something."

But the more she thought about it, the more the idea of phone sex with Olivia excited her. Turned her on even. The butterflies that always filled her stomach in the hours before Olivia arrived on her doorstep were starting to appear. The anticipation of flirting. Of touching. Sure, she wouldn't be the one touching Olivia, but she would have a front row seat to Olivia touching herself.

There had been times when Olivia was laid out across the mattress beneath her that Riley had lost herself in the vision of Olivia's pleasure. Watched her eyes flutter shut and her back arch. This would be the same thing, right? And Riley had touched herself enough times when memories of Olivia's body had been too much. Surely Olivia had done the same while they were apart? A bolt of arousal coursed through Riley at the thought.

"Maybe we should've done this sooner," Riley said to the empty room.

Cursing herself for showering so quickly, Riley set about cleaning her kitchen and washing the dishes from breakfast. That task, too, took remarkably little time and the beer she'd had with Dani wasn't helping her relax. Her nerves thrummed and she couldn't keep her hands from shaking.

"Nicodemus." She grabbed the feather toy he liked so much. "Want to play, good boy?"

In his youth, Nicodemus had been a master hunter, helping Riley burn away the hours chasing a feather until they were both exhausted. Now, with considerably more weight slung low around his middle, he was more content to flop on his back and wave his paws in the general direction of the toy hovering above him. At least he wiggled his hindquarters in a fair imitation of his kittenish fighting stance, but his sprint was sluggish and he only batted at the feather for two minutes before falling asleep on his back.

"Traitor," she said to his snoring form. "Just when I need you most."

She dragged her fingers through his soft fur without feeling it.

"I dunno, Nic. What do you think? Is this, like, a date? Are we going to, you know?" He sneezed and opened one eye to look at her. "Yeah, okay. You don't want to hear your mom talk about her sex life."

He scooted closer to her and purred as he fell back into a doze.

"But if she does want to do that, do I?"

Before she could let her mind wander into that minefield, her cell phone vibrated in her pocket. Nicodemus swatted at it, toyed with the idea of attacking the sinister moving object, and ultimately chose to nap instead. Riley fished the phone from her pocket, and her mouth went dry as she read the screen.

Hey sexy. How about we FaceTime our call? XOXO

"Oh, God. Dani was right. This is happening."

Before she could chicken out, she agreed, then tossed her phone onto the couch. Her skin tingled from the top of her freshly washed scalp down to her core. Maybe she hadn't had phone sex before, but it had been almost two weeks since she'd seen Olivia and her body was certainly approving the plan. The butterflies in her stomach were now a positive storm. The mental images of Olivia touching herself were lodged permanently in her mind. Riley allowed herself a few, tantalizing moments to imagine the pleasure to come, but didn't let herself get too lost in fantasy. If she did, she'd never make it to the main event.

She scrambled to her feet, then ran to her office. The first thing she noticed was how messy the bed looked. With all pretense out the window, Riley hadn't slept in here since their first night together. Still, Nicodemus was an active sleeper and the guest bed was his third favorite nap location. The blanket was twisted and covered in a shockingly thick layer of black cat hair. The pillows were all flattened and equally furry. Riley stripped the bed, sending the pillows flying, only to discover she hadn't washed the other set of sheets. Examining the sheets she'd removed, she determined they were in good enough shape, it was only the blanket that had to go.

She remade the bed with the old sheets and snagged a new blanket from the linen closet. Several of the hairier pillows ended up at the bottom of the closet. Riley had to hold them in with her foot to get the door shut. This left the bed looking a little bare, so she collected all the throw pillows from her bedroom and the living room. It was a hodgepodge of colors, most of them clashing with each other, but she reckoned Olivia would be too occupied to notice.

Next, she positioned her iPad on the desk, checking the camera angle to ensure the bed was in the shot.

"Unless she wants me in the chair?"

Riley was about to go get a towel for her leather office chair when she noticed what she was wearing. A faded Orlando Pride T-shirt and worn jeans didn't exactly scream sexy. Her closet, however, gave her little inspiration. Nicodemus wandered into the room.

"I can't exactly wear a suit and tie for a phone call, even if it is a date," she told Nic. "What about a polo and khakis?"

He settled into favorite sleeping spot number two—between the pillows with his tail on the upholstered headboard—and scowled at her new outfit.

"What?" She checked herself in the mirror. "Oh, I look like I sell cell phones at the mall. Okay, Nic, I'll try again."

She had stripped down to her boxer briefs and sports bra, searching through her closet for a new outfit, when she caught sight of herself in the mirror. She'd chosen a matching set of underwear, a freebie from the photo shoot she'd done with Tomboy X. Her current stance, her torso twisted and her body in three-quarter profile, reminded her of the picture they'd chosen for the ad. The ad Olivia had admitted was a huge turn-on.

"What do you think, Nic? Should I give Olivia the underwear model fantasy?"

When she turned to get Nicodemus's approval, however, he was fast asleep. More importantly, the clock on her bedside table told her she didn't have time to fuss any longer. Underwear model it was.

On her way back to her office, she grabbed every scented candle in the house, distributing them around the room as she lit them. No sooner was she done than she decided it was too much and blew them out. Then she decided it wasn't enough and lit them again. Before she could second-guess the decision again, the iPad on her desk buzzed with an incoming video call.

Running a hand through her hair, she said in a low voice, "You got this. It'll be amazing. Just relax."

She shook out her shoulders at the last word and settled into her office chair, trying to ignore the way her stomach was curling and uncurling in knots of anticipation. Tapping the button to connect the call, she scrambled to adjust the camera to show her bra and naked abdomen. She propped her feet on the desk to show off her bare legs, then leaned back against the chair. Hopefully, the posture showed her body to best advantage.

"Hey you." Olivia came into view on the iPad screen. "What took you so long?"

Riley's stomach sank. Olivia was sitting on her living room couch, an open bag of potato chips in her lap. Her hair was pulled up into a messy bun and she was wearing a terry cloth robe. The outfit was sexy as hell—Olivia could make a burlap sack look great—but she was clearly not setting a seduction scene.

"Hey, babe." Riley swallowed hard, trying to settle her squeaking voice. She could feel the overwhelming heat on her face for the second time today.

Clearly Olivia could see the blush, too, because she sat forward and squinted at the screen. Riley watched her eyes travel all around, starting on Riley's bra and flicking from candle to candle. "Um, babe." Olivia's smile grew and her eyebrows climbed. "What're you doing over there?"

"Just, uh, waiting for your call." Riley dropped her feet to the floor and angled the iPad away from her half-naked body.

"In your underwear?" Olivia asked.

"I was running late."

"Are there candles lit?"

"No." Riley's voice squeaked. She gave up, slumping in her chair and dropping her face into her hands. "Yes. Maybe. I had lunch with Dani and she thought, since you're alone and wanted to FaceTime, maybe you wanted to, you know, do some stuff."

Olivia's eyes widened. "You thought this was a literal booty call?"

"Oh, God, Olivia, I'm so sorry. Please forgive me. I'm such an idiot."

Riley finally looked up as Olivia's laughter turned to movement on the screen. The rest of Riley's explanation and repeated apologies were swallowed by the sound of Olivia washing her hands and her continued laughter.

"You're so cute, you know that?" Olivia appeared onscreen again as she walked across her house. "Have you ever even had phone sex before?"

"No. I don't know what I was thinking. Dani made it sound like it was obvious and she was so convincing. I'm sorry. I don't want you to think this is all about sex for me."

Olivia stopped, adjusting her camera angle to show her leaning against a bedroom door, her face suddenly serious. "What is it about then?"

Blood roared in Riley's ears. Her vision pulsed with each pounding heartbeat. She wanted to say it. She needed to say it. To tell

Olivia she was in love. That she'd never fallen for anyone this fast before, but she knew exactly how she felt and she was in love. She opened her mouth to say it, but she chickened out as usual.

"I care about you," she said instead, her throat dry. "A lot."

Olivia smiled and Riley could've sworn her eyes were shining, but the light wasn't quite right to be sure. Then she pushed open the door behind her and walked into what Riley had to assume was her bedroom. The walls were covered in prints. Some of them looked like Olivia's work, some of them looked like publicity stills and posters from several different shows, mostly Middies. Riley couldn't be sure because the room was dimly lit with a flickering, orange glow.

"Are those candles?" Riley sputtered, her heart pounding in her ears again.

Olivia's laughter echoed in the candlelit room. The double bed wedged into the corner of the small room had the sheets turned back and pillows stacked around the headboard. With a muffled swish of fabric, the robe dropped from Olivia's shoulders, revealing the rippling silk of a creamy white slip. The fabric puckered around her erect nipples and fell to just below the apex of her legs.

"Of course I want to have phone sex with you." Olivia stretched out on the bed. She propped her phone against the wall by her knees, giving Riley an excellent view up the length of her body. "It's been too long. I want to have my hands on you and inside you, but I can't. We can pretend though. Do you want to pretend?"

Riley tried to swallow, but all of the moisture had migrated from her throat to her core. She nodded, snatching up her iPad and scrambling onto the bed behind her. It took her several tries to find an angle that showed both her face and the highlights of her body. Olivia's hands roamed over the slip as she watched Riley.

"How, um." Riley's gaze locked on the journey Olivia's hand was taking down her abdomen. "How do we do this?"

"Nice and slow. You chose the right outfit." Olivia's eyes sparkled. "You're so sexy."

"So are you. Are you wearing a bra?" Riley asked.

"I'm not wearing anything but this." Olivia tugged at the strap of her slip. "Touch your breasts. Are your nipples hard?"

Riley slid a hand under her bra, cupping her breast. "Not, um, not yet."

"Pinch your nipple." Olivia moaned as she demonstrated on herself. "You like it when I'm a little rough with them, right?"

"Yes," Riley said. Her eyes fluttered closed as she remembered the afternoon Olivia spent testing different methods of teasing her breasts. "When you pinched and twisted just a little."

"Do that to yourself, but keep your eyes open, baby. Watch me touch myself. If I was with you, how would you be touching me?"

"With my tongue," Riley said. She was warming to the adventure now. Phone sex wasn't scary or embarrassing. It was just like being with Olivia in person. Safe and so very sexy. "I'd probably flick it with my tongue."

Olivia moaned, licking her fingers and caressing her nipple. "I like it wet."

The words, along with the way she was touching herself, sent a jolt directly between Riley's legs. Her hips bucked and she heard Olivia let out a ragged breath. Looking at herself in the iPad's screen, she noticed her bra was covering her efforts. She pulled back the fabric with her free hand, adjusting her angle so Olivia could see how hard she was.

Olivia groaned again, running the tip of her tongue over her lips. "That's it. Touch yourself like I want to touch you. Are you wet?"

"Yes."

"Take off your underwear, baby. Let me see."

She struggled to obey, desire making her hands shake as she forced the waistband of her boxer briefs down. She lost her patience when they were around her knees and slid her fingers down, spreading herself wide for Olivia to see.

"Oh, God, you look so good. I want a taste," Olivia said.

Picking up on the request, Riley slid two fingers through her wet folds and then lifted them to her mouth, licking them clean to the sounds of Olivia's grateful moans. When she looked back at the screen, she saw Olivia's slip was pulled up, revealing the neatly trimmed hair between her thighs. Riley's mouth gaped as Olivia pressed a finger in herself, her other hand still flicking her nipple.

Riley ran deliberately slow circles over her clit. "If I was there, I'd use two fingers."

Olivia gasped, her grin widening as Riley warmed to the game. She slid a second finger inside, her eyes rolling back as she caressed herself. Riley was riveted, her gaze flicking up and down Olivia's body hungrily. She nearly forgot her own work as Olivia's breathing sped up.

"Faster." Riley's hips bucked as Olivia complied. "And use your thumb on your clit. Can you do that?"

"Anything you want, baby."

Riley's vision tightened as she picked up her own pace. She wouldn't last much longer, but she had the feeling Olivia would beat her to the crest.

"That's it," she said as Olivia hips ground into her own hand. "Just like that."

A heartbeat later Olivia stilled and screamed. The sound was familiar to Riley now and each time she heard it she fell a little harder for this woman who held nothing back. Olivia's hips bucked wildly and soon Riley's followed suit. She shouted, something she rarely did, but the naked sensuality of Olivia's pleasure intensified her own reaction. Soon they were both panting in the stillness of their lonely bedrooms, sneaking a glance at each other between heaving breaths.

"That was amazing." Riley panted.

"It totally was," Olivia said with a breathy laugh. "It's not usually like that when I'm on my own."

"Me either." Riley rolled to her side so she could see Olivia better. "I mean, I do all right for myself, but not that all right."

Olivia grabbed her phone, propping it on the pillow by her head. "It's still better when it's your hand. I miss you."

"I miss you, too," Riley said.

She almost said it then, with them staring at each other across all those miles. It felt right to say it. To confess the depths of her love for Olivia. The words were forming on her tongue when an almighty wail sounded from the door, followed by the scrape of feline claws against painted wood.

"What was that?" Olivia laughed.

"Nicodemus wants to know what's going on in here," Riley said. She wanted to scold him but was unwilling to turn away from Olivia's glowing eyes and radiant smile. The moment had passed and she reminded herself again that those words should be said face-to-face.

"And here I thought it was hard for me to have the house free." Olivia's smile faded and she bit her lip, her eyes roaming. "When can I see you again?"

Olivia had just sent her next month's work schedule, and it was as packed as they'd expected. Riley's schedule was far more flexible, but she was getting into her busy season and the interview with Matt was hovering. Still, it was starting to worry Riley how much time Olivia was spending on the road.

"I can come up there next week," Riley said.

To Riley's surprise, Olivia's face went to stone and she sat up in bed, pulling her slip back into place to cover her body. Worse, she wouldn't look at the screen, obviously avoiding Riley's gaze.

"You shouldn't do that. I can come down there," Olivia said.

"But we'd lose so much time with you on the road Wednesday morning. I can come up Tuesday afternoon and be there as soon as you're off work."

"I work early on Tuesday. I'll be off by three. I can drive down then."

"What about your grandpa?"

"I'm sure Chelsea can look after him." Olivia bit her lip as she said it and she still wouldn't meet Riley's eye. "Or Allison can take the day off."

"That's silly. No one needs to be inconvenienced when I can just come to you."

"It's fine," Olivia said too quickly.

The words were like a knife in Riley's gut. It was obvious Olivia didn't want her to come to Tampa. Her stomach turned over and tears prickled the back of her eyes. She pulled the blanket over her chest, suddenly cold with so much skin exposed.

"Okay, I get it," she said, hearing the pain in her own voice.

"You get what?"

"You don't want your family to know about me," Riley said quietly. She thanked her lucky stars she hadn't said "I love you" earlier.

"No, baby." Olivia sounded as hurt as Riley felt. "That's not it, I swear."

"What is it then?" She knew she sounded frantic, but she couldn't play it cool right now. "Why don't you want me there?"

Olivia waited a long time, picking at the corner of her pillowcase. Finally, she sighed and said, "I don't live alone, Riles."

Nicodemus wailed from the hallway again, and the sound was enough to cut the tension growing between them. With a laugh, Riley said, "Neither do I."

"You know it isn't the same."

Olivia sounded so defeated, but there was an edge of something else Riley thought might be shame. "What if I get a hotel for us?"

"We can't afford that."

"I can," Riley said, warming to the plan even as she formed it. "I've got the *Vanity Fair* article. It'll be in the next issue so I'll get a check soon. Of course, I might get a TV writing job first."

Excitement lit Olivia's eyes. "You heard back from the agent?"

"Um, no." Riley said. It was her turn to avoid eye contact. "I haven't heard anything else from him."

"But you said it went so well."

Riley swallowed hard. "I might've put a rosier spin on that at the time. It didn't really go that well, actually."

Olivia's voice was sharp with annoyance when she said, "You don't have to do that with me. You can tell me the truth."

"Yeah, I know." Riley hurried on, hoping Olivia would drop it. "But it doesn't matter anyway. Matt Barnes introduced me to a writer friend. He gave me Ashton Case's contact information. I sent her a spec script and I know it's a good one."

"Matt's getting you a writing job?"

"Hopefully." Riley sat up and brought the iPad with her. There was the shadow of a smile on Olivia's face and it made Riley's chest ache happily. "And the interview with him should be any day."

Olivia's face was aglow. "That's awesome. I'm so proud of you."

"I'll tell you all about it in our hotel room next week."

CHAPTER TWENTY-TWO

Olivia frowned at her latest piece of fan art, trying to decide if she had to start over. It wasn't that she didn't like her work. Far from it, this was possibly her favorite drawing ever. The problem was every time she looked at it, she didn't see Waverly beaming up at Nicole or Calamity Jane grinning out at the viewer.

She saw herself, wrapped in Riley's butter-soft sheets with Nicodemus's tail tickling her armpit. She saw Riley's strength in Nicole's shoulders and her kindness in Nicole's eyes. She saw a perfect Sunday morning lit by Miami sunshine filtering through sheer curtains. It was a beautiful drawing, but it wasn't Wayhaught in Purgatory.

Beyond that, this was the first piece in a long time Olivia had wanted to keep for herself. This was what Olivia craved most. More than the FaceTime fun they'd had a few days ago. More than the nights they'd spent in each other's arms in Riley's bed. More than the teasing and the flirting and the constant yearning. This was what she'd never found before, even with partners she'd loved. She'd never found a person she wanted to wake up next to. A person whose mind she enjoyed as much as she enjoyed their body.

But both that mind and body were a four-hour drive away. Olivia was under no illusion a long-distance relationship was going to be a tough thing to pull off with a woman like Riley. She was the epitome of a masc of center lesbian—strong, silent, and sexy—complete with celebrity status and legions of women drooling all over her. What were the chances she'd waste too much more time with an art school dropout who lived at home and sat in a parking lot booth all day? Sooner or later, she'd realize she could do better and finding better would be as easy as showing up at the next convention. But Olivia was confident in her body and she knew she could hang on to Riley for a little while longer with that at least. Until the distance effected the frequency of their intimacy enough to shake the relationship apart.

To distract herself from the negative thoughts, Olivia typed out an email to her client, explaining her concerns that she wouldn't like the piece while avoiding explaining her own personal connections to it. She attached a picture along with a request to tell her if she wanted Olivia to start something new. Just as she hit send, Olivia was startled by the blast of a car horn right outside her booth.

"I'm sorry." She plastered on her best disarming smile. "I didn't see you there."

"Maybe that's because you're too busy playing on your phone instead of doing your job."

Olivia gaped at the man, who glared at her from inside his massive SUV. He was mid-fifties and sporting a deep tan that didn't look quite natural. The rearview mirror had an ostentatious cross and a "Don't Tread On Me" placard. The woman in the passenger seat had the same fake tan and platinum hair teased into a poof on her head.

"Overnight parking or just for the day?" Olivia asked, her voice professionally neutral.

"What do you think? I've got a trunk full of suitcases."

Olivia glanced pointedly at the SUV's heavily tinted windows. "It's against our policy to violate our clients' privacy by inspecting their vehicles."

"Damn right."

She ignored the hypocrisy of his statement and asked, "So will you be parking overnight or just for the day?"

The man's face was quickly turning from red to purple. "Overnight."

Olivia handed him the appropriate tag and gave him a photocopied map of the area, indicating where the different cruise lines docked their ships.

"I can see the damn ship, and if I miss it because you suck at your job your boss will hear about it. You'd think anyone could manage a mindless job like this, but apparently not."

The SUV sped off, the man gunning his engine for the approximately ten yards before he had to slow for a sharp right turn. Olivia seethed inside, forcing herself to take a deep breath while flashing between anger and humiliation. The anger leaked away quickly, leaving the humiliation in its place. She had been on her phone rather than looking for approaching vehicles, but that didn't justify his cruelty.

She didn't have time to dwell, however, as traffic picked up. The line of cars at her booth seemed to double for each one she sent through. Olivia's phone pinged a new email. She propped the phone up out of the view of her customers and snuck peeks at the message between handing out tickets. With each new word she read, her smile grew.

Her client for the Wayhaught piece not only approved the design, she adored it. The number of adjectives crammed into the relatively short email made her happiness evident. Olivia particularly enjoyed the line when she said she'd never seen Nicole and Waverly look so happy. She also assured Olivia she was showing it to all of her friends and she should expect a lot more commissions coming in soon.

As she grabbed a fresh stack of port maps, she flipped her sketchbook open to the drawing and smiled down at it. She still saw herself and Riley in bed on a perfect Sunday morning. Maybe she knew what a perfect couple moment looked like after all.

CHAPTER TWENTY-THREE

Sun reflected at a sharp, oblique angle from the hood of Riley's Subaru into her eyes. She'd been driving in Florida long enough to be used to the glare, but not even sunglasses were enough to temper it. The blinding reflection, however, couldn't burst her happy bubble today. She'd worked late the night before, making sure to complete her articles for the week so she could focus entirely on her time with Olivia. Now, with the morning sun glancing off her car, her mind was entirely on Tampa and finally telling Olivia she loved her.

Riley was reaching for the radio, thinking some music would help settle her nerves, when her phone rang. The car's display only showed numbers, but she thought the area code matched Lisa Winchester's so she answered the call.

"Hello, Ms. St. James, this is Ellen March, senior editor for *Vanity Fair*."

"Hi." Riley's stomach clenched. Had she missed a deadline? Or a message from Lisa? "What can I do for you?"

"We're pushing your article."

There was no regret in her voice, not a hint of the kindness Lisa had shown. She just dropped the bombshell and waited for Riley to explode.

"Did something happen? When I spoke with Lisa…"

"When you spoke with Ms. Winchester we were still finalizing the issue. Now we have a more compelling article than yours."

Riley swallowed the pain of that bland dismissal. "So it'll appear in the following issue then?"

"Not sure. I doubt it."

"I can still go out to LA and do the interview."

Ellen cut her off again. "Hold off on that. We don't need the expense at this time since there's every chance the article won't appear until next quarter."

"We timed it to coincide with the premiere." Riley's heart pounded uncomfortably. "It won't have the same impact if it comes out midseason."

There was a gleeful sneer in Ellen's voice as she said, "Then maybe we'll wait for the finale."

Riley swallowed hard but the panic kept building in her chest. This was her chance. She knew how the publishing world worked. If she didn't keep herself fresh in their minds, they'd forget about the story and she'd lose her shot.

"Come on. You're a freelancer." Ellen spit the word like she was trying to get a bad taste out of her mouth. "Don't you have anything else lined up? We'll be in touch."

The line went dead and Riley stared out the windshield, listening to the hum of her tires on blacktop. That was it. The kiss of death. Roughly translated, "we'll be in touch" was journalism-speak for "drop dead." Just like the agent from QueerCon, she'd never hear from Lisa or anyone else at *Vanity Fair* again.

"It's over," she whispered to the empty car. "They're done with me."

It didn't make sense. Why would Lisa blow her off like this when she was so excited about the idea just a couple of weeks ago? She'd authorized expenses for travel. She'd talked about a possible cover. Then she sent one of her lackies to call it off?

"Maybe it's a mistake?"

The idea buoyed Riley for the next few miles until she pulled into the parking lot for a well-reviewed florist in Tampa. This was just a lower ranking editor with her own article ideas throwing her weight around. It would blow over and Riley would be back in the lineup. As she loaded bouquets into her car, she decided the worst-case scenario was the article got bumped a few issues. Not a big deal. She had her spec script in a great showrunner's hands. Not to mention, she did, in fact, have other freelance gigs lined up.

"Nothing with the paycheck or prestige of *Vanity Fair* though. I'll be just a damn blogger forever," she said.

Shaking her head to clear the negativity out, she covered the last few miles to Olivia's townhouse. She didn't have time to get down on herself right now, she had a date with Olivia and a long night in a hotel room, just the two of them. That was almost enough to make up for losing out on the *Vanity Fair* cover.

"Almost."

Riley's hands were sweating against the paper wrapping, and the mass of flowers nearly slipped from her hands as she reached out to ring the bell. She barely had time to adjust her grip and shimmy the tension out of her shoulders before the door was flung open.

"You must be Riley."

The woman standing in the doorway could have been Olivia herself, traveled from twenty years in the future. She had the same long, lean stature and the same six inches of height on Riley. Her smile was wide and her eyes, though they were pale hazel rather than Olivia's rich brown, had the same twinkle of laughter.

"Mrs. Duran-Spencer, pleasure to meet you," Riley said.

"You keep making my daughter smile the way you do, I think it'll be my pleasure."

"I'll try, ma'am." Riley held out a bouquet full of peach roses, sunflowers, and irises. "Thank you for trusting me and my intentions."

"Oh, Riley, they're beautiful."

To Riley's surprise, Allison buried her face in the bouquet and breathed deep, her eyes fluttering closed. As Riley watched her, the small differences between her and Olivia stood out. There were lines at the corners of her eyes and the edges of her mouth, though she'd done an admirable job disguising them with her makeup. They looked less like age lines and more like worry lines and Riley remembered why Olivia was still living at home. Allison had been through a great deal in her life, but there was something in the childlike way she held her flowers that explained some of why Olivia had to be an additional caregiver in this house.

Chelsea and Lewis walked up behind Allison. "Sucking up to the mom?" Chelsea said. She crossed her arms and rolled her eyes. "That's such a cliché."

"Not just the mom." Riley held out another bouquet.

Chelsea eyed the white roses with suspicion for a moment, but soon enough she snatched them from Riley's hand and hugged them close. "Excellent tactic."

"I thought so." Riley smiled.

The smile melted and bloomed into warmth in her chest when she looked over Chelsea's shoulder to watch Olivia stroll into the room, her hips swaying in a light, clinging sundress. No matter how often Riley saw her, she always had the same reaction to that sight. Olivia moved like liquid fire and Riley's blood sang to see it. She could happily stand in the Florida sun for hours if it meant she could watch Olivia walking toward her, the full power of those eyes fixed on her.

"Hey you." Riley held out the final bouquet.

Olivia's bouquet was a massive handful of stems, each topped by a perfectly puckered red rose or a delicately curled white lily. She had rummaged through the pails of flowers, individually selecting each bloom rather than grabbing a preformed bouquet. Olivia was the kind of woman one selected individual roses for, no matter the cost in time or money.

"Hey yourself." Olivia examined the flowers in her hands. "Red roses. Classic. And Lilies. Rachel's favorite flower."

"Of course." Riley noted the rest of Olivia's family didn't seem to catch the reference to *Imagine Me and You*. She hoped Olivia remembered the meaning of lilies, as told by Luce. It would make Riley's declaration of love later all the sweeter.

"Perfect," Olivia said. She leaned in, brushing her lips against Riley's cheek just in front of her ear. Every hair on Riley's neck and arms stood on end.

When Olivia pulled back, holding her arm in one hand and her flowers in the other, Riley allowed her eyes to travel over the others again. Allison was grinning at her with one perfectly plucked eyebrow arched to her hairline. Chelsea had the glassy, appreciative stare of a tweenager who wished she too was going on a date. The only occupant who looked less than impressed with Riley's effort was Lewis. He stood beside Chelsea wearing a look of disapproval similar to one Nicodemus had given her when she came home with a store brand cat food.

"Where are my flowers?" he asked with a glare.

Realizing her mistake, Riley detached herself from Olivia's grip and studied the flowers in her arms. Finding the perfect one, she gave Olivia a wink and plucked the rose from the group and held it out to Lewis.

He studied the rose almost as thoroughly as Riley had, then shrugged and took it from her hand. "I'll take it 'cause it's the first time anyone's ever given me a flower."

"It won't be the last. I promise," Riley said.

Riley caught a warm look pass between Chelsea and Allison, but Olivia's slightly wet eyes were locked on her. She wasn't quite sure what she'd done that was so great, but she had a feeling she would be rewarded later for stealing from Olivia's bouquet.

"Ready to go?" Olivia asked, taking Riley's arm back.

"Do I get to meet your grandpa?" Riley asked, looking past Allison into the living room. The furniture and rugs looked worn but comfortable, with all the warmth her own apartment lacked.

"He's sleeping," Allison said. "You can meet him at dinner tonight. I'm making him put on real pants so he can join us at the table."

"Dinner?"

Olivia clearly heard the disappointment in Riley's voice, because she turned an apologetic look on her and said, "Sorry. I couldn't get us out of it."

"You can't blame me for wanting to get to know the woman my daughter is dating."

"Of course not, Mrs. Duran-Spencer," Riley said, biting off the words but doing her best to contain her annoyance. "I can cancel our reservation. No problem."

That last part wasn't strictly necessary, she knew, but between losing out on *Vanity Fair* and her meticulously planned dinner date, this wasn't turning out to be the perfect romantic trip Riley had hoped for. The embarrassment and guilt in Olivia's expression didn't help, but she couldn't help being a little disappointed.

"Okay," Olivia said, her smile a little forced. "We'll see you guys later."

"Thank you for the flowers, Riley," Allison said. "Chelsea? What do you say?"

"Thank you, Riley," Chelsea and Lewis said in unison.

"You're all very welcome. We'll see you for dinner."

Once they were in the car, Olivia pulled Riley into a long, wet kiss across the center console. She ran a hand over the closely trimmed hair just above Riley's neck, a touch Olivia knew drove her wild. Trailing her fingertips up Riley's thigh, she broke the kiss.

"I'm really sorry about dinner. Maybe we can change the reservation to tomorrow night?" Olivia asked.

"Sure," Riley stammered, trying to catch her breath. "We can do that."

"If they're booked, I might find some other way to make it up to you."

This time it was Riley who moved, cupping Olivia's face in both hands as their lips and tongues met. When they broke apart, panting and bleary-eyed, Riley was half in Olivia's seat, the roses and lilies crushed between them. They noticed at the same moment and leapt apart, each inspecting the flowers for damage.

"Maybe we should drive somewhere and walk," Riley said.

"How about a cup of coffee?" Olivia asked. "I can take you to my favorite place."

"Sounds great."

They stole glances at each other as Riley drove. No matter how upset she was with how this trip had started, spending time with Olivia was all she wanted. Just sitting next to her, the heat of Olivia's hand on her thigh and the heat of her eyes on her face made Riley feel unstoppable. The feeling only intensified when they arrived at a coffee shop tucked into a quiet corner of the city.

The place was packed and every head turned in their direction when they entered. The two baristas acknowledged Olivia's greeting with waves. The patrons, mostly men who looked like they split their days evenly between the gym and the beach, weren't shy in their appreciation of Olivia's sundress or the long, smooth legs showing beneath. She ignored them as though they weren't in the room. Leading Riley by the hand, she pressed through the crowd to a vacant table.

"Wait here and I'll get our drinks."

She brushed her lips against Riley's before slipping off to the counter. Riley breathed the air, scented liberally with roasting beans and vanilla. The speakers overhead blasted salsa music loud enough to wipe her mind clean.

While she watched Olivia chat with the barista making their lattes, Riley's phone vibrated in her pocket. She fished it out, keeping one eye on Olivia's hips, swinging gently to the music as she waited. The alert had been for a new VIP email and she opened the app.

The name on the header was enough to rip her attention away from Olivia's swaying hips. She hadn't expected to hear back from Ashton Case so soon, but she swallowed her doubts and opened the email. It only took reading the first two lines to shatter the tentative hold she had on her annoyance.

While the script you sent is great and will certainly get you a job in just about any writers' room, I'm afraid ours is full. Check back in with me after this season wraps and we may have something.

Check back when the season wraps. So that, if they're picked up again, and if someone has quit or been fired, maybe she can score a job at the bottom of the ladder. The season hadn't even begun shooting. It wouldn't wrap for months. Then she could start this process all over again, only this time without the nod from Barnes, who would no doubt be hurt and angry his article had been bumped away from the prime spot. Her career was tanking before her eyes and she was powerless to stop it. She sighed and shut off her phone.

"You're not bored already?" Olivia's voice cut through the ache in her chest.

"No." Riley looked up and forced a smile. "Of course not."

Olivia was radiant, backlit by the sun streaming through the window. Seeing her reminded Riley of everything she still had. Olivia had liked her as just a blogger, maybe it would be enough.

"You okay?" Concern cut a line between her eyebrows, and she reached out to run a thumb along Riley's cheek. "Is it about dinner? I'm really sorry, babe."

"I'm not," Riley lied. "I want to get to know your family."

That much at least was true. She did want to get to know Olivia's family, just not now. Not when she had planned out their whole trip and spending an hour having dinner with her family hadn't been part of the plan.

Olivia's smile returned and the line disappeared from her forehead, lifting Riley's spirits a little. "Well, as much as I want to show you around Tampa, it's two o'clock. Isn't that check-in time at the hotel?"

"Yeah, it is."

"Good, 'cause I really want my hands on you."

Chapter Twenty-four

I've got chocolate syrup and a whole gallon of milk."
Olivia trailed the rose over Riley's bare chest, and recited
the appropriate line. "You really know how to charm a girl."

"Nailed it." Riley clenched one side, twitching as the petals
trailed over the ticklish spot on her side.

"Classic quote. I loved *Edison Street*. Not sure it counts, though.
I mean, that's a straight movie."

"Watching Reese Witherspoon drink that chocolate milk on
screen was the moment I realized I was gay," Riley said.

"It was hot. And you only had to wait twenty years to see her kiss
a woman." Olivia leaned in and kissed Riley's bottom lip, sucking it
into her mouth and gently biting it until Riley moaned. "Okay. I'll
accept it."

Just when things were getting interesting, Riley put a hand
on Olivia's shoulder and gently ended the kiss. Olivia scowled in
response. The last thing she wanted in that moment was to stop, but
Riley's lips had curled into the smug grin she wore when she was
taking charge. Olivia would do anything Riley wanted when she
smiled like that.

"Your turn," Riley said.

Olivia went back to tracing the outlines of Riley's naked torso
with her red rose. The rest were neatly bunched with the white lilies
in a vase the hotel had provided hours ago at check-in, but this one

flower had been Olivia's favorite. She'd plucked it from the rest to tease Riley.

It was time to turn up the heat. Sliding her body along Riley's, she waited until her lips brushed against Riley's earlobe before she started speaking. She was pretty sure she got the Lexa quote right, but her mind wasn't on swearing fealty. It was on the task of dragging the rose petals over Riley's hardened nipple. Most of her words were drowned out by Riley's groan, but clearly, she caught enough of them to correctly guess.

"Bold move," Riley said, pulling Olivia on top of her. Their bodies stretched out together, skin pressed to overheated skin. "Quoting *The 100*. Doesn't it bother you that they buried their gays?"

"Of course," Olivia said. The heat of Riley beneath her was making her head spin, so she pulled away, sitting back on her heels so she was straddling her hips. "But if it wasn't for that moment and the fandom's collective freak-out, we wouldn't have ClexaCon. If we didn't have ClexaCon, there wouldn't have been a push for a queer convention circuit. If there wasn't a queer convention circuit, there wouldn't be QueerCon and I wouldn't have met you."

Riley wrapped her arms around her. She sat up, pressing their breasts together and sending a shot of adrenaline through Olivia's body.

"It did work out pretty well for me." Riley's lips traced a path up Olivia's neck. She pressed her palms into Olivia's back, bringing her closer as her mouth moved back down, caressing her chest.

"Me too," Olivia said.

Riley's hands were moving, but Olivia could barely feel them on her skin. Her mouth had completed its journey down Olivia's chest, settling over her right breast. Riley's tongue flicked out, teasing her nipple, and forcing all the air from Olivia's lungs.

"Whoa there, hot stuff." Olivia forced her eyes open and pulled away reluctantly. Riley's gaze flicked up to her face, then she smirked as she captured Olivia in her mouth again. Olivia forced her next words out with difficulty. "As much as I want you to do exactly what you're doing now, I've got to shower."

Riley released her with a gentle scrape of teeth, but made immediately for the other side. "Just one more time."

"We can't. We'll be late for dinner."

Riley surged forward, pushing her over on her back. "I'm not hungry for food."

Olivia let Riley settle between her legs on instinct. She even tilted her chin just enough to give Riley better access to her neck. "I'm not either, baby, but we said we'd go."

"They'll forgive us," Riley said into her neck.

In that moment, Olivia finally realized Riley was serious. That she wanted them to blow off her family and spend the night in this room. As sweet as she'd been with Chelsea and Allison earlier, she was willing to hurt their feelings now.

"Riley," she said. Her voice was stern enough to stop the progress of Riley's hand down her side. "We have plans with my family."

"Yeah, but I want you to myself."

If she hadn't known better, Olivia would've thought there was annoyance in Riley's tone. Her forehead was crinkled and there was a chill to her voice that hadn't been there before. It was the chill that made Olivia push out from underneath her and off the bed.

"This is what my life is like." She hugged herself around the middle and faced the hotel room wall. "I have obligations here that I can't just ignore for sex."

"That's not what I'm asking you to do."

"No?" Olivia turned, seeing her own hurt reflected in Riley's stormy expression. "Then why did you suggest we blow off my family?"

"I'm not suggesting we blow off your family." She dropped her head and the fight seemed to flood out of her. Olivia almost asked her what was going on, but she wasn't sure she wanted to hear the answer. "I just thought we'd get the whole day together."

"We did get the whole day together, that's why I have to shower before dinner," Olivia said. Riley didn't respond, which only fueled Olivia's anger. "We were going out to a restaurant, weren't we? This is the same only it's people who are important to me." The room was so still and silent, Olivia's angry whisper was perfectly audible.

"Of course, you're right. I'm sorry." Riley sighed, the sound echoing thickly in the silence.

The apology could have done wonders, but Olivia could still detect some bitterness in that sigh. Her own words were clipped when she said, "It's fine. I'm going to shower, okay?"

She spent longer in the shower than she strictly had to, the hot water searing away the edge of her resentment. The more she thought about it, the more she decided she'd overreacted. Riley had never been anything but polite to her family. She'd brought them all flowers today and Olivia repaid that kindness by having a temper tantrum, and about what? That Riley cared about her so much she wanted Olivia all to herself? There were worse traits to have in a partner. Her embarrassment was confirmed when she emerged from the bathroom half an hour later to find Riley nervously fussing with her blazer.

"Do these jeans work with the jacket? Is it too much? I don't want to look like I'm trying too hard."

Olivia padded across the room, wrapping her arms around Riley from behind. "It's not too much. You look incredible."

The look of relief on her face made Olivia's heart sing. She melted back into Olivia's arms, her eyes fluttering shut. "I just want your family to like me."

"They'll love you."

Riley's eyes flew open and there was a hint of panic on her face, but it melted away again as they looked into each other's eyes through the mirror. "I'm sorry about earlier. I was being selfish and stupid and today was weird. I'm really sorry."

"It's okay, babe." Olivia pressed her lips to Riley's temple, feeling the vein throb beneath her lips. "I'm sorry, too."

Dinner was exactly what Olivia had feared it would be—chaos. Her mother was a terrible cook, and it appeared, to Olivia's horror, that she had enlisted Chelsea to help with the meal. When she and Riley arrived, there was the distinct bite of scorched meat in the air, and not the good kind one expects at a backyard barbecue. Olivia pushed the front door open to the sound of raised voices, and looked into the kitchen in time to see her mother clap a hand over Chelsea's mouth. Chelsea continued her complaints for a moment, then turned a sugary gaze on Riley.

"I think you have a fan," Olivia whispered as she closed the door behind them. There was still the hint of the chill from their fight in Riley's scrunched forehead, but she cracked a weak smile when Chelsea and Lewis came scuttling into the living room to greet them.

The noise level rose considerably through the greetings. Olivia took Riley's hand and led her through the house. When they trudged upstairs, Riley's features smoothed out.

"I recognize this room," Riley said.

Olivia eased her bedroom door closed. When she turned around, Riley was wearing a genuine smile for the first time in an hour. Olivia took a deep, steadying breath and stepped into her arms. She buried her face in Riley's neck.

"I'm sorry," she said into Riley's collar. "I'm sorry about this afternoon."

Riley's body relaxed beneath her and she reached around Olivia's back, pulling her close. "I'm sorry, too."

Tears prickled behind Olivia's eyes, but she willed them not to fall. She couldn't ruin her makeup, but she hated the tension that had formed between them today. She had no idea where the fight had come from or why they couldn't seem to shake it off, but fear bubbled inside her.

"Olivia, Mom says stop making out and come help Poppa to the table," Chelsea called up the stairs.

Riley laughed, the deep rumble echoing through both of them, and loosened her grip. Olivia did not let go or step away. She wanted to ask if they were okay, but she was still afraid of the answer, so she pressed her lips to Riley's neck, hoping to leave a lipstick print just for fun.

Poppa was dressed in a real shirt and pants, his hair washed and combed back off his forehead when Olivia arrived in his room with Riley in tow. He didn't complain when she helped him into his wheelchair, but he waited until he was situated to turn his attention to Riley.

"You're the one dating my granddaughter?"

"Yes, sir." Riley took a step forward and held out her hand. "Riley St. James. It's a pleasure to meet you, sir."

He shook Riley's hand. "Nice to meet the woman who keeps putting that smile on my angel's face." He looked at Olivia.

Olivia's eyes weren't exactly dry when she looked at Riley, and the warmth she saw in those ice blue eyes melted the last of her doubts away. Poppa kept up a chattering discourse on every embarrassing moment in Olivia's life as she pushed him into the dining room and up to his place at the table. Riley seemed entranced, giving him her full attention and even insisting she sit next to him at the table. Olivia couldn't help but remember her last boyfriend. Like so many people, he was nervous around wheelchairs and had never even looked at Poppa, much less given him any sort of attention.

The casserole was a disaster. The source of the scorched meat smell was obvious from her first forkful of barbecued chicken and what she assumed had once been rice. The thick layer of mostly melted cheddar cheese on top helped make the dish palatable, but it was a far cry from the meal Riley's romantic date would have provided. When Olivia chanced a look Riley's way, she saw her jaw tighten as she swallowed, but that was her only sign of discomfort. She was laughing along with Poppa, who was telling her the story of Olivia visiting when she was a young teen.

"She had braces then," Poppa said. He was eating the mushy casserole with apparent relish. "And my wife had these ribbons for one of her art projects. My dearest Sylvia was always sewing or knitting or some such. Anyway, we woke up to find little Liv sprawled on the carpet, tying ribbons to the wires."

"How on earth did she manage that?" Riley leaned over her plate toward him, her eyes dancing with laughter. It was intoxicating to see her like this. This was the charm that had drawn so many eyes at QueerCon.

"I've no idea. How did you, angel?"

Olivia swallowed another bite of dry chicken. "It was tedious work, believe me."

"She looked like she'd ripped open a Christmas present with her teeth," Poppa said.

The whole table laughed, though Riley was more subdued than her boisterous family. "I bet that was a sight," Riley said.

"The sight," Olivia said, "was a sink full of spit-soaked ribbon. Granny wanted to murder me."

"She loved you to pieces," Poppa said. He was wearing the wistful, bittersweet expression he always wore when he spoke of her.

"How long were you married?" Riley asked.

"Fifty-seven amazing years. I asked her to marry me the night we met, but she was too sensible for that," he said.

"The only sensible woman in the family." Olivia kissed the top of his head as she went around the table to gather plates. Allison stood to help her.

"Excuse me, I'm very sensible," Chelsea said.

"She said sensible, not senseless," Lewis said.

"Well, I'm much more sensible these days." Olivia winked at Riley. "After all, I'm dating a woman who's about to be published in *Vanity Fair*."

"I read *Vanity Fair*." Allison squealed with delight, a fork sliding off the plate she carried. "That's wonderful, Riley."

Riley opened her mouth to say something, but Chelsea spoke first. "You don't read *Vanity Fair*. You just look at the dresses you can't afford."

"Um, fashion is important, Chelsea," Lewis said with his nose high in the air. "It isn't about owning it. It's about seeing it. Being inspired."

"Don't pretend you know anything about fashion. You aren't that kind of gay." Chelsea rolled her eyes and turned away from Lewis's open-mouthed stare.

"Okay, you two." Allison wedged herself between them before Lewis could respond. "You'll have to take this argument to the couch. It's almost showtime."

It wasn't until Olivia saw the delight on her mother's face that she remembered the big event. "The Middies special."

"What?" Riley frowned.

"Don't you remember?" Allison looked genuinely confused at Riley's reaction. "Tonight is the pre-release special for *The Midtown Avengers*."

"Oh, right." Riley's frown deepened. "The recap show."

"Uh, it's so much more than a recap show." Lewis wedged his little fist against his hip in a fair imitation of Flame Fingers. "There's thirteen minutes of never-before-seen footage."

"In an hour-long show," Riley said grumpily.

Most of the family had already scuttled off to the living room. Allison brought out a hopefully thawed Sara Lee cream pie and a stack of plates.

Riley wasn't going into the living room with everyone else and confusion kept Olivia from going either. There had been several attempts to discuss Middies at dinner, but Riley had changed the subject. Olivia had thought at the time she was more interested in conversation with Poppa, but the annoyance clearly etched into Riley's face made her wonder. She walked over to Riley, hooking their arms together.

"There's supposed to be a lot about the proposal." Olivia leaned close. "With commentary from both actresses."

"Yeah." Riley checked her watch. "I thought we could head back to the hotel though. It's getting late."

Allison turned to them. "You aren't going to stay for the show?"

"Don't you have to watch it?" Olivia asked. "Can't we watch it here?"

"I already got an advance copy of the episode. I was planning on watching it when I got home," Riley said.

There was a long moment of silence when everyone in the living room looked back and forth between them. Poppa looked particularly crestfallen, having pulled up close to Olivia's favorite armchair for the viewing. Olivia felt like she was under a spotlight but hadn't memorized the song she was supposed to sing. She hadn't known they'd invite her and Riley to stay for the show, but she couldn't understand Riley's disinterest. Wasn't she as big a fan, if not bigger, than they all were?

In the end Chelsea broke the tension. "That's fine. She'd distract us all by taking notes for her article anyway."

With that, she and Lewis turned around and started attacking their slices of pie, wedged onto adjoining couch cushions. Allison caught Olivia's eye and gave her a look that communicated just as much confusion as Olivia felt, but she recovered quickly, turning a smile on Riley.

"You two have fun. Thanks for coming to dinner, Riley."

"Thank you for having me, Mrs. Duran-Spencer."

A moment later they were outside, the humidity of a hot Tampa night sticking to Olivia's skin.

CHAPTER TWENTY-FIVE

The drive back to the hotel was silent and Riley knew she should do something to dispel the tension. Problem was, she wasn't in the best mood. When they stepped into the elevator, she caught the glimmer of a smile sweep across Olivia's lips.

Riding in this same elevator that afternoon had been nothing short of dangerous. Olivia had pressed Riley into the wall, dragging her into a heated kiss. They had barely been decent when they'd stepped out of the car. No chance of a repeat tonight.

Trying to break the funk that had settled between them, Riley reached for Olivia's hand. Riley worried she was too upset to take it, but Olivia didn't hesitate to link their fingers. When Riley tugged gently, she came willingly, leaning against her. This wasn't what she'd imagined for their evening, but she knew they could salvage the night. Everything had gone wrong since she'd stepped into her car that morning, but this—having Olivia pressed against her—was right. This was everything she wanted.

Olivia didn't seem to notice they'd bypassed Riley's floor until the elevator opened to reveal the sun setting behind the Tampa skyline. Olivia's brows knitted together as they walked onto the pool deck, but Olivia kept her hand firmly wrapped in Riley's. She followed Riley to the railing overlooking the city.

Despite her annoyance and her doubts, Riley knew she was in love with this woman. In love with her charm. In love with her wit. In love with her talent and her poise. She was even in love with her intensity—both in kindness and in anger—so she loved Olivia as much in this moment as she ever had. Tonight, she would find a way to tell her. Tonight, she would make Olivia understand how much this meant.

Riley had intended to order them drinks. Maybe a glass of champagne or some sickly-sweet cocktail like the one Olivia had on their first trip to this rooftop bar. That plan evaporated as the orange-gold glow of evening lit Olivia's skin. It was time. She practiced saying the words in her head.

Olivia, I love you. I've loved you since the moment we met.

Excitement thrummed in her chest. The normal excitement of nearing this intoxicating woman and the new excitement of being so sure of her heart. Turning to Olivia, Riley gathered her courage and opened her mouth to say the words. But Olivia had her back to Riley, her shoulders stiff and her jaw set.

Riley wrapped her arms around Olivia's hips, pulling their bodies flush. She kissed her exposed shoulder. Olivia didn't melt against her like she usually did, but she didn't pull away either. Riley trailed her touch along Olivia's side, light against the dress.

When Olivia didn't respond to her touch, Riley asked, "What's wrong, baby?"

"I don't know." Olivia dropped her head. "It's weird. I've never missed watching an episode of Middies live. I don't know. I guess I was surprised you weren't into watching the show."

"I'm more into watching you." Riley tried seduction, but the line between Olivia's eyes didn't go away.

Olivia shook herself and smiled. "I'm being silly. Look where we are. Can you believe we talked to Jodie Gray and Carrie Nguyen here?"

She'd punctuated the question with an excited squeal, and it was that squeal even more than the reminder of Middies that stole the words from Riley's lips. That squeal reminded Riley of all the annoying fans from QueerCon who wouldn't let her rest. The ones who were so over-the-top about their Middies obsession that she couldn't talk about anything else.

Riley heard the bitterness in her voice when she said, "That wasn't exactly the best part of the evening for me."

Surprise rippled through Olivia's eyes, then her face fell. "No, of course it wasn't for me either."

Riley dropped her hand and turned back to the view, all thought of confessing her love withered.

Olivia put her hand on Riley's shoulder and the warmth of her touch melted Riley a few degrees. She trailed her hand down Riley's arm and entwined their fingers again. "We're just not communicating well today, are we? Maybe I should head home?"

"No, please don't." No matter how things got twisted, Riley knew for sure she didn't want Olivia to go home. She let out a breath and sent all her resentment with it. "Look, I know today was rough."

"It's okay. Not every day has to be great." Olivia squeezed her hand and finally smiled. "We can move past it. Most of today was fine."

Riley's mind flipped back through how terrible her day had been. Through the contempt in the *Vanity Fair* editor's voice, through the way her stomach dropped when she read the showrunner's email, and the tears she fought back while canceling their romantic dinner reservation. She pushed it all aside to be here with Olivia in this moment.

"I just want to fix it, Olivia. You deserve better, not just good enough."

She expected Olivia to be reluctant in her agreement. Or maybe to tease her for being overly dramatic. What she didn't expect was how every little bit of sadness dropped away and a wide, flirtatious smile took over her face. She cupped Riley's face.

"Of course you'd say that right now," Olivia whispered, leaning close.

"Would you like something to drink?" A waiter appeared behind them, a menu in hand and a welcoming smile on their lips.

Before Riley could speak, Olivia gave the waiter a dazzling smile and said, "No thanks. We're heading to our room."

❖

The sheets were tangled around their entwined feet and Olivia was nestled under Riley's arm. The moon was just visible through the open curtains and the room was deliciously cool. Olivia stirred against her, murmuring contentedly and pressing her body closer. Riley squeezed her tight, a wave of warmth washing through her. This was everything she wanted. The quiet moments with Olivia in her arms. The serenity of this wild woman at rest. Everything about it felt right.

Riley turned, pressing a kiss to Olivia's forehead before catching her eye. The brown of her irises was like fertile earth and she knew that, if she could bury herself in them, she would grow better for the rest of her life.

"I love you," she said, her voice wobbling with emotion.

Olivia's eyes sharpened, the sleep running out of them, then they sparkled as she said, "I love you, you big, wild superhero."

Riley's heart twisted and froze. "What?"

Olivia giggled and poked at Riley's side. "Come on, it's an easy one. I love you, you big, wild superhero."

Riley's mind felt waterlogged. She didn't remember getting out of bed, but she found herself naked in the middle of the room, looking at Olivia's confused stare. Her chest heaved with the force of her breathing.

"Are you serious?" Riley heard herself speaking from a long way off. "I tell you I love you and you quote that goddamn show at me?"

Maybe Olivia's mind was underwater, too, because it seemed to take her a long time to recognize the situation. Finally, she bolted upright, pulling up the sheet to cover her naked chest. "Wait, you were serious?"

Riley's ears buzzed and her vision blurred. Rage warred with humiliation. "Are you fucking kidding me? Yes, I was serious. Who says 'I love you' as a quote from a TV show?"

"I don't know." Olivia's eyes blazed, her voice had an edge of anger now, too. "Maybe someone who seduced her girlfriend using a quote from a TV show?"

Her mind was finally sharp again, sharp enough to run through the words they'd exchanged beside the rooftop pool. Olivia had been distant, cold even. They'd discussed their fight and how they'd get through it. Something clicked and she remembered the exact words she'd said. *You deserve better, not just good enough.* It wasn't Carmen's exact quote before she ran off with Erin on *The Railyard*, but it was close enough. Given their afternoon of flirting with movie and TV quotes, maybe it made sense, but this was totally different. Riley had put herself out there and Olivia had made fun of her for it.

"Can't we separate ourselves from television shows for one fucking minute? Especially that stupid fucking show."

"I understand you're upset and I'm sorry I misunderstood," Olivia said. Her words were grating. She padded toward Riley, who stepped back. "I do mean it, Riles. I'm really sorry."

"Funny how that doesn't make me feel better right now." She was a joke to Olivia. Just like she was a joke to that editor from *Vanity Fair* and the showrunner who thought she was perfect, just not worth hiring.

"I made a mistake and I'm so sorry."

"I don't understand how we—" Riley swallowed hard, trying to settle the throbbing in her brain and the churning in her gut. "I've been so sure we were on the same page all this time."

"We are, honey." Olivia reached for her hand. "I don't know, it's been a confusing day."

Riley turned away and riffled through the clothing on the floor until she found her boxer briefs.

"Please let me make it up to you," Olivia said. Riley couldn't look at her, but she could hear the tears in her voice as though she had any right to be the one crying right now. "I mean we both love Middies and I thought—"

Riley whipped around. "Let's get this one thing straight." She couldn't see Olivia for the red in her vision. "I hate that show. The whole premise is a cheap rip-off of much better shows that aren't trying to make a statement. The show is pathetic and the fandom is just sad."

Olivia's eyes flashed with anger, but her voice was almost meek. "But the way you write about it."

Riley yanked her shirt over her head, catching the bewilderment in Olivia's eyes. "I write about it because it's my job. I get paid to write about it. I do what I have to do to build my brand. Sometimes that means writing about bad television."

"So you've just, what? Been pretending?"

The bewilderment in her voice sparked a new surge of rage in Riley. "I'm not pretending, I'm writing. I'm a journalist."

"I mean with me. You let me believe you loved the show," Olivia said.

"You made that leap. I think I've made it clear that Middies is my job."

"But you've got other work. *Vanity Fair* and screenwriting. Why do something you actively hate?"

"*Vanity Fair* fucking dropped me, okay?" Admitting it out loud stung worse than Riley thought it would, but she was already so far gone, what was a little more humiliation? "And Ashton Case blew me off. In fact, both those jobs blew up in my face today." The air went out of Riley. What had the point even been of coming here if this was all she took away? She slumped against the wall. "Maybe that's why I'm in such a shitty mood today."

"But you talked about the article at dinner. You lied to my family? You lied to me?"

There'd been an edge of anger in Olivia's voice. What right did she have to be angry when it was Riley who'd been hurt here? Riley found herself angry again. "I was embarrassed, okay?"

"Then tell me about it. Confide in me. I've told you before you can tell me the truth. Don't you trust me?"

"Should I trust you after tonight?"

Olivia jerked back like Riley had slapped her. "I made a mistake. We've been trading TV quotes all day. I thought we both loved queer TV. I'm not the one who's been lying."

Some of the hurt leaked out of Riley. Had she been lying? She certainly hadn't been fully honest. Maybe Olivia deserved more honesty from her. "I do love queer TV. I don't want to be a fucking blogger forever, okay?"

"Sweetheart, being a successful blogger is nothing to be ashamed of."

Riley scoffed. "Like you'd be happy doing fan art forever? It's the same as blogging, just copying someone else's work."

Olivia flinched and said in a low voice, "My art isn't just copying someone else's work. It's my passion. It's also my livelihood."

"It's cool you're earning tuition money with your art, but I have to pay rent."

"Excuse me?"

"I'm a professional. I'm not some obsessed fan clinging to a crappy show to keep from realizing I'm stuck in an empty life," Riley said.

Silence rang in Riley's ears, blocking out sound. Her words repeated over and over again in her mind and each time they sounded worse. More cruel. More thoughtless. She tried to swallow but there was something large and solid in her throat, threatening to close off the oxygen from getting to her lungs. Olivia's face was stone. For the first time since Riley had known her, there was not a hint of emotion on her features.

Riley took one step forward, and Olivia didn't react. She took another two, watching Olivia breathe shallowly. When Olivia still did not move, Riley let her breath go in a careful sigh and reached for her. "Olivia, I'm—"

Olivia stepped backward, holding up her hand. Riley slammed to a halt as though Olivia's hand were against her chest rather than outside her reach.

Olivia spoke in a slow, careful voice that shocked Riley more than a scream of rage would have. "Don't touch me. Don't you ever touch me again."

Riley stumbled back, her hip banging hard into the bedside table. Olivia moved as slowly and deliberately as she'd spoken, crossing the room and slipping silently into her clothing. The calculated calm of her movements frightened Riley into action.

"Olivia, please." Riley rushed forward. Her fingertips just brushed against Olivia's skin.

"I made it very clear I don't want you to touch me." Olivia pulled her arm away. Her dress was on but unzipped, her bra in one hand as she bent to snatch up her sandals.

She didn't look at Riley again or say another word. She marched to the door with the dignity of Miranda Priestly after another employee evisceration. When she slammed the door behind her it was so close it almost snagged her purse.

Chapter Twenty-six

The front door of Olivia's townhouse was metal painted in a faded, streaky forest green. The doorknob had obviously been replaced in the last few years, much more recently than the battered kickplate. There was a bare nail between the top panels which looked to be for a Christmas wreath.

Riley took in all these details and more while she stared at the door, unable to raise her hand to knock. Her eyes burned with exhaustion. She hadn't slept a moment last night. When Olivia had stormed out of her hotel room, Riley had shoved herself into her clothes in an effort to follow, but had wasted precious time looking for her shoes. She'd run down the stairs barefoot when the elevator was too slow, but Olivia hadn't been there. She ran out to the taxi stand to find it empty, then she'd tried the ride share zone, but it was similarly abandoned. It had simply taken her too long to follow and Olivia had slipped through her fingers. She'd thought of getting into her car and driving to her house immediately, but it seemed wiser to give her the night to cool off. She'd sent several dozen text messages, but when she didn't get an answer, she stopped that, too. In the pale light of morning, that decision seemed foolish.

Riley puffed out three quick breaths, sucked in another through her nose, and lifted her fist to knock. It hovered, knuckles inches from the door, long enough to drain of blood and begin to tremble. She didn't see the door, she saw Olivia's face, twisted in pain. Just thinking the words she'd said made her cringe. Why had she said that? It was possibly the cruelest thing she'd ever said in her life and she said it to the woman she loved. The woman who trusted her and confided in her. She let her arm fall back to her side.

"Are you ever going to knock?"

Riley spun at the sound of Chelsea's voice. It was so much like Olivia's that it made her heart ache. Chelsea was standing behind her, arms crossed and fire in her eyes. She uncrossed her arms, planting her fists on her hips and puffing out her chest to reveal a bright blue T-shirt bearing the *Midtown Avengers* logo. The way she proudly displayed the shirt and stood with such defiance made Riley's shoulders sag. She wasn't that much taller than Chelsea, but she was dwarfed by this kid's nerve.

"So you know how much of a jerk I was," Riley said.

"Yeah, we know." Lewis emerged from around the corner with the rose Riley had given him the night before in his fist. He flung it at her feet and it landed petals down on the welcome mat. "You get out of here or we'll call the cops." He leaned his arm on Chelsea's shoulder and they looked for all the world like a very scrawny, very young gang.

As much as it humiliated Riley to be shunned by them, she couldn't help but admire the way they defended Olivia. She was the kind of woman anyone would fight for. Anyone except the woman who claimed to love her.

"We won't call the cops," Chelsea said.

"We won't?" Lewis squeaked, cutting a glance at her that clearly showed she'd changed the plan.

Chelsea shook her head and she suddenly looked very grown up. World-wise in a way Riley was never likely to be. She remembered Chelsea's father had died when she was only a toddler.

"No. We don't need to punish her any more than losing my sister will do."

Riley's stomach turned over and she was grateful she hadn't been able to eat breakfast. She couldn't have truly lost Olivia, could she? Not forever. Olivia would forgive her, wouldn't she?

Obsessed fan. Stuck in an empty life.

The words echoed again in her mind along with the realization she had no right to expect forgiveness. The hopelessness made her stomach twist again.

"Whoa. She's about to pass out," Lewis said.

"Am not." Riley gritted her teeth to keep her nausea at bay.

"Are too," Chelsea said.

Her head spun as her stomach lurched again and she had to reach out and grip the doorframe. "Okay. Maybe."

Lewis's smirk would have made Riley angry on any other day. "Serves you right."

Riley couldn't disagree, so she just held tight to the painted wood, hoping the world would stop heaving. Chelsea's smile faltered and she turned to Lewis. "Go home, Lewis. I'll be right there."

Lewis clearly didn't want to miss out on all the taunting. He stomped his foot and whined. "What? Why?"

"I need to have a conversation with her." She didn't sound angry anymore and that helped Riley center herself.

Lewis rolled his eyes. "Fine, but be quick. I'm so obsessed I might figure out how empty my life is if I don't latch on to you."

Lewis whirled around and stomped off with such grace Riley couldn't quite blame him for the verbal kick in the gut. Chelsea watched her swallow the last of her self-respect and stand straighter.

"I really screwed up," Riley said.

"Obviously." Chelsea didn't look angry anymore. She looked hurt in the way only a child who has discovered one of her heroes was a piece of shit could look. "But my sister is a good person and she just might love you enough to forgive you one day."

Hope blossomed in Riley's chest, but it hurt almost as much as the guilt did. Olivia didn't love Riley at all. She couldn't after last night. Not after what she said. If only Olivia had said it last night, true or not. Hearing those words once would have been enough to sustain Riley now that she was staring into the gaping maw of a future without her.

The door squealed when it opened, and Riley spun much less gracefully than Lewis had. It would be Olivia and she would give

Riley a hard time about last night—like she deserved—but she would forgive and she would forget. Riley ached for that.

It wasn't Olivia standing in the door. It was a very angry, very unfriendly Allison. If Chelsea looked like a younger version of smug Olivia, Allison looked like an older version of angry Olivia.

"Chelsea, come inside the house."

"But I'm going to hang with Lewis."

"Not right now. Come inside."

Chelsea looked unmistakably like a kid again as she stomped past Riley into the house. Instinct told her to give Chelsea a friendly pat on the back as she walked by. Riley could still remember a dozen times at least that this small injustice had been leveled at her when she was Chelsea's age. Riley wasn't the person to console her though, not when her words had broken so many hearts. Now her presence was keeping two best friends apart. Her sins were growing by the moment.

Allison pulled the door shut behind her, facing Riley alone, and though it was her back pressed against the door, Riley was the one who felt cornered.

"Mrs. Duran-Spencer."

"Don't." She held up her hand and Riley held her lips together. "There is nothing you can say that will make up for what you've already said."

Of course, she meant there was nothing Riley could say to her, but what about Olivia? Surely there was something Riley could do to win her back. "If I could just talk to her?"

"That's not for me to decide, but she's sleeping off a bad headache and needs the rest."

"Bad headache?" Riley surged forward on instinct, but the thin line of Allison's mouth made her step back and moderate her tone. "What's wrong?"

It was shocking and more than a little frightening to watch Allison snap. It was as though she had held back all of her anger until Riley said something that gave her permission to explode. "You're what's wrong. We were fine before you, do you know that? Olivia was fine before you. She wasn't happy, but she was fine. Now you've taken even that from her."

Riley felt the tears forming in her eyes but she'd already shed too many and these weren't ready to fall. The pain in her chest was like nothing she'd ever felt. She knew in that moment she had never been in love before because she had never hurt like this before.

Allison visibly relaxed, but her voice was cold and flat when she said, "You should go."

"I can't. Don't ask me to do that." Riley couldn't stop herself. She stepped forward and took Allison's hand. It didn't feel like Olivia's hand. It was thin, the bones prominent under cool skin. "Ask me to do anything else. Ask me to pull down the moon for her and I will."

Allison laughed but it was a mirthless laugh. It spoke of lonely nights and broken hearts and the sort of life Riley knew she was doomed to from now on. She took her hand back and said, "Pull down the moon? Funny you should say that. Her father used to offer me the moon. He said he would die for his little girl, but, funny thing is, he couldn't seem to live for her. At least he couldn't live with her."

Riley let the words wash over her. Olivia never talked about her dad. All she ever said was he was gone. She left the rest to Riley's imagination.

"He walked out when Olivia was nine years old and I was a wreck. I was distant and she didn't understand. I couldn't engage. I couldn't feel and she wanted so badly to help. Can you imagine that? A lonely nine-year old trying so hard to connect with her heartbroken mother?"

Riley kept her voice quiet when she said, "I can imagine it from her."

"Then Chelsea's father was killed in Iraq and guess who fell apart again? She had to take care of her mother and her toddler sister. Then my mom died and my daddy got sick and she took care of him, too. She takes care of all of us and you know what, Riley? When she met you, I thought there was finally someone who was ready to take care of her."

Riley was sick again and she couldn't stand straight. She wanted to put her head between her knees until the dizziness passed, but she couldn't look away.

"Someone who was kind and generous," Allison said mercilessly. "Someone who would sweep her off her feet."

The tears that had been filling her eyes spilled down Riley's cheeks. There was a river of them inside her and they poured out.

Allison took a step forward and her voice was sharp as a razor and solid as a whetstone. "Don't you dare cry. You don't get to cry."

Riley forced herself to calm down by straightening her spine. "No, ma'am."

Allison watched her struggle with her emotions as though this were a test. Riley was determined to pass, though she was certain there was no reward for victory.

After a long, quiet moment, Allison looked up at the pale blue sky. "I'll admit we're all a little obsessed with *Midtown Avengers.* You may think the show is silly or the fandom is sad, but it has healed this family in ways you will never understand. Chelsea has something to share with her best friend who is bullied to the point of madness both at school and in his own home. I have something to share with my daughters who slip further away with each day they age. Poppa gets to feel like the superhero he's always wanted to be for us. Olivia can see herself on screen in a show we can all share. She never thought she'd find love like Flame Fingers and Mind Bender have, so she latched onto it, you were right."

"Ma'am, if I could take back what I said I would."

"You can't." There was no cruelty in her look, nor was there kindness. "This isn't a story you can write how you want it to end."

"I love her so much." Riley let the tears fall again. She had nothing left to hold onto and no way to hold them back.

"You can say it all you want, but you have to act it, too."

All the fight drained out of her and she slumped against the doorframe. She was tired to her bones. Not just from her sleepless night, but from a lifetime of this. A lifetime of coming close to having what everyone else had, but never quite being able to touch it. Her exhaustion filled her and the weight of it was like an ill-fitting coat, itching her and annoying her. Why couldn't anything ever be easy?

"I'm surprised you don't understand how Olivia feels about this show," Allison said. "You grew up gay in a world where all you got to see was straight people. But you started writing about these shows so you must understand what they mean to people." Her words were a relentless reminder of how much Riley had fucked up. "Hasn't a show ever touched you the way Middies touches her?"

Riley's annoyance grew and spread. How could she ask a question like that? How could this woman, presumably straight based on everything Riley knew of her, lecture her on the importance of representation? Did she really want Riley to stand here and give her a full mission statement for her career? What would that prove?

"Please let me see her," Riley said.

"If I let you in there, what would you say?"

Riley opened her mouth to answer before she realized she hadn't thought that far ahead. All those tortured hours last night and all she had focused on was getting Olivia to see her, not what she would say to fix what she had broken. They were both empty and alone. What well could Riley draw from when she was so hurt? Were there words she could say that would patch over the hole she'd put in their relationship? She closed her mouth, shaking her head and staring at the toes of her shoes.

"You better figure it out before you come back."

There was a glimmer of hope in hearing there may be some reason for her to come back, but it wasn't enough to lift her. The soft click of the door closing sounded like a gunshot to her busted nerves. She shivered, despite the growing warmth of the morning. Turning to go, her boot crunched on something. She lifted her foot to display the battered rose Lewis had thrown at her feet. When she squatted down to pick it up, a few loose petals fell off. There was a smear of dirt from her Doc Martens on the stem.

Lewis was sitting on the stoop of a house a few doors down, picking at the laces on his sneakers. He looked like he would wait on that stoop for Chelsea all day. It was pretty clear he didn't want to go inside without her. Allison had mentioned him being bullied at home. Looking at his sad, disappointed face, Riley felt a new wave of shame-induced nausea. It was bad enough she'd ruined her own life and hurt the woman she loved, but this kid had enough pain in his life.

Riley knelt at Lewis's feet. He didn't look up.

"I'm so sorry for what I said." She had to take a moment to let the thickness in her throat clear before she continued. "I know I said it to Olivia, but it hurt you, too, and I never wanted to hurt any of you. You are not sad. Your lives are not empty. Mine is."

He sniffled and it was worse than the snarky remarks he usually threw her way.

It was battered and dirty, but Riley held out the rose to him anyway. "One day someone will give you one of these and they'll be worthy of you taking it from them. I promise you, you'll find your Mind Bender."

She moved to lay the rose on the step, but he reached out and took it from her. He didn't look at her, but he nodded, twirling the rose between his fingers.

CHAPTER TWENTY-SEVEN

Olivia hadn't had a day off in over a week and she was exhausted. It wasn't the work itself that exhausted her. Sitting in a glass and metal box all day, making change and giving directions wasn't exactly mentally or physically grueling.

The emptiness, though. The emptiness made her so tired she could barely lift her limbs. She had always been a crier. She cried at movies and romance novels and even those commercials about abused puppies. But she hadn't shed a tear since the night she last saw Riley.

It wasn't just crying, though. It was laughing, too. And smiling. She had lost every single emotion and was left with nothing. She was dead inside. She slept and she woke up and she went to work and she felt nothing. Allison and Chelsea had stopped asking if she was okay. She couldn't blame them. A week of monosyllabic answers and silent dinners was enough to make anyone give up on her.

Like Riley had. Given up on this empty, sad loser.

Thinking Riley's name was enough to get her up and out of bed. If she stayed lying in bed when she thought of Riley, she'd lose the will to do anything and she didn't want to do that today. She didn't want to lie there feeling sorry for herself because that wasn't her style. She wasn't some teenager with her first broken heart. She was an adult and she had responsibilities.

While she brushed her teeth and showered, Olivia made a mental list of her tasks for the day. She needed to go to the grocery store.

Chelsea being home for the summer meant Chelsea and Lewis were home for the summer and they were steadily eating their way through every unhealthy snack in the house. Normally that would be fine, but snacks were breakup fuel and she needed them for herself.

Don't think about it, she told herself. Think about the grocery store.

Drying her hair was too monumental a task for her energy level, so she threw it up into a messy bun, fully aware it wouldn't dry anytime soon. At least she'd have some serious curl in it. She forced herself not to remember how much Riley liked it when she was too lazy to straighten her hair. She did take the time to put on makeup because it made her feel good to look her best. Apparently, the feel-good effects took a while to set in, so she went back to her room to get dressed while she waited.

Even throwing on old jeans and a thin cotton tunic exhausted her, so she collapsed into her desk chair. The grocery store could wait. She'd check her messages and take it easy for a while.

Instead, she stared at the blank wall for fifteen minutes. She wanted to be sad or angry, but she wasn't either. She wasn't anything. Time slipped past and she watched it with detached acceptance. Her mind didn't go to Riley, which was a start, but it also went nowhere else.

The sound of a door downstairs slamming shut dragged her out of her stupor. She could tell Chelsea's run anywhere, and that was definitely Chelsea. It didn't sound like Lewis was with her, so that meant there was only one place she was heading.

"Liv, I'm going over to Lewis's."

She didn't wait for permission or even a response, she just repeated her plans in a shout to Poppa. He grunted loud enough for Olivia to hear and then the front door slammed shut. The glass penguin on her desk rattled on its little glass feet.

Olivia flipped open her tablet and stared at the glowing screen without much interest. The email icon seemed as good a place to start as any, so she clicked on the app. Her inbox was still overflowing. Most messages were other fans praising her work. She spent a long time reading those, pumping up her self-esteem as much as possible.

Despite the months since QueerCon, there were still a lot of people willing to pay her for commissioned work.

She tried hard to turn that into hope. These were people who liked her art. Who respected her and what she put out in the world so much they were willing to pay her for it. She'd put away a tidy sum and she was proud of it. For once in her life, the work that made her happy was also paying her way. Perhaps it was that thought which brought her eye to the email she'd been waiting on for weeks now. Her old university advisor had responded to her email. Her finger trembled when she clicked on the icon to open the message.

Reading the message, a tiny bubble of joy bloomed in Olivia's chest. It wasn't much, but it was more emotion than she'd felt in a week. Not only did he remember her, but he was willing to help her get back into school. And, best of all, he said he was excited to have her back in his class. She couldn't believe her luck. He had attached not only the portfolio requirements, but also an application and list of fees. She didn't have to check her bank balance to know she could afford the deposit. Barely. Prices had gone up since she'd left school, but she had been frugal all her life and she could make this work.

I can do this, she thought. I can make a living as an artist.

Most of the portfolio requirements were simple. A still life with shadow. An anatomical sketch. Something in her style. She started with the anatomical sketch. Her hand seemed like the best way to go. After all, she drew people all the time. This one should be easy, even though she needed more realism than she normally employed.

Clearing off a spot on her desk, she aimed her desk lamp at the surface and positioned her hand in the center of the light. Seven minutes of staring at the back of her own hand left her with two thoughts—she was in desperate need of a manicure and she had no idea at all how to begin. It was usually so easy for her. She would decide what to draw and just start with a broad overall sketch, filling in details with clinical precision.

Olivia forced herself to focus, positioning her sketchpad higher on her knee. She swept her pencil across the page in a light line from what would be the tip of her middle finger down to the terminus of her wrist. The line was wobbly, but passable. Everything went downhill from there. The line that was supposed to delineate her metacarpal-phalangeal joints ended up at the center of her palm rather than the top of it. Her thumb line was twice as long as it should've been. Her wrist was wide enough to be her thigh.

Frustration bubbled and that only made her drawing worse. Her artistic style didn't mesh well with stress-locked muscles. She tore the page from her sketchbook and balled it up, tossing it onto the desk, where it landed against her pencil cup.

Her stomach growled and she decided a snack break was in order. In the kitchen she grabbed an apple and shoved it into her mouth. Before returning to her room, she grabbed another apple and a banana. If the anatomical sketch was out, she could give the still life a try. The balled-up paper provided a good textural element for her drawing, and the ridges would provide good shadows, a stated requirement. While she nibbled at the apple she arranged the fruit around her pencil cup, angling the desk lamp to provide the most dramatic shadows she could muster from a forty-watt bulb.

In the first attempt she drew the apple too large. The second attempt had haphazard spacing. The third had poor perspective. Each new failure brought a wave of disappointment that proved harder and harder to ignore. Soon she looked up and from yet another lopsided apple to find the floor strewn with discarded attempts. Her sketchpad was running short of paper and she didn't have the money for this much waste.

She let out a long breath, but it did nothing to dispel the self-doubt gnawing at her. Looking back to the portfolio list for the last requirement, she felt a little better. Something in your own style. She could do that. She knew her own style. She liked her own style.

Her style was fan art and she could kill two birds with one stone by starting a new one right now. Just copying someone else's work. She shook her head to get Riley's voice out of it. This belonged to her, even if Riley didn't believe that. She skipped to the oldest message in her inbox, grabbing her pencils. The subject line made her throat constrict and she dropped her box of pencils. The lid popped off and they scattered across the floor, sliding under the bed and her desk.

The message read, *Looking for some Middies love $$$ for FF and Mind Bender*

The bubble of joy, shrunk by her fruitless attempts at still life, popped and she closed her eyes against the words. Any thought of drawing fled, replaced by a knot of humiliation settling into her chest. She couldn't do it. Not Middies, not fan art. Riley was probably happily ensconced in her fancy apartment in Miami, thrilled to be rid of someone so ridiculous as to think she could get back into art school by drawing TV show fan art.

When Chelsea came back through the front door hours later, Olivia was still curled up on her bed, staring at the ceiling as she hugged her pillow so hard her shoulders ached.

CHAPTER TWENTY-EIGHT

R iley stabbed her thumb into the pause button and tossed the remote control aside. She groaned and let her head fall back against the couch.

"God, this is awful. Why did I think it was a good idea to watch this shit?" she asked.

As usual, she'd received her screener of the *Midtown Avengers* premiere exactly one week before it was set to air. She'd blocked off the whole day for it, knowing it would be an even harder task than usual to watch through the episode. If she was honest with herself, she knew she hated this mostly because of Olivia. It had been two weeks since she'd shown up on Olivia's doorstep to apologize and hadn't been able to see her. Allison had told her not to come back until she knew what to say, and she hadn't gone back. She still didn't know what to say.

"Want a snack, Nic?"

He raised his head, one eye still stuck together with sleep, but he didn't follow her off the couch. She wasn't hungry either, she just wanted to stand up. To walk around. To not look at the frozen mask of joy Flame Fingers wore in this scene where she was showing off the engagement ring she'd acquired at the end of the previous season.

I love you, you big, wild superhero.

The words made Riley's stomach clench. She hadn't eaten well since returning to Miami. Every time she stopped moving for more than a minute, she felt like she might be sick. Every time she stopped moving for more than a minute, she heard those words in her head. She'd hated the line enough when it was in Jodie Gray's voice. Now she heard it in Olivia's voice and she wanted to cry every time. Mostly she wanted to cry because those words in her head always led to the others.

"Don't," she said through clenched teeth. "Don't do this to yourself. Not again."

But how could she not? How could she not remember those horrible words and feel like shit? She deserved to feel like shit. She was a shitty person who said a shitty thing to the person she loved when she was hurt and confused.

"Exactly." She paced the kitchen, snatching a water bottle from the fridge to take on her laps. "I was hurt. Olivia understands that. She should, she was the one who hurt me."

And that started the cycle. The one she'd been in for fourteen days. The one where she felt bad about her actions and then reminded herself how justified they were. It was like a pendulum swinging her helplessly from one extreme of emotion to another. Her moments of angry indignation always made her manic like this.

She didn't mean to hurt Olivia, but Olivia had hurt her first. Didn't that justify what she'd done?

"Of course it does," she said, running her fingers through her hair. "In fact, she should be the one to reach out and apologize. She was the one who started this whole mess."

The more she thought about it, the more she was sure this was all Olivia's fault and so it was up to Olivia to fix it. A little voice in the back of her head reminded her it didn't matter whose fault it was. She was still without the woman she loved. She ignored the voice and pushed back into that sick feeling of rejection when Olivia had quoted the show to her. This time, the stab of pain in her gut came with an icy sense of self-righteousness. It wasn't pleasant, but it made her feel justified in her response. It was better than guilt.

Anger bubbled up at the thought of Olivia, listening to her pronouncement of love and mocking it. Comparing it to that ridiculous show. Comparing it to something fake. Something meaningless.

Because that's what their relationship had been to Olivia. It had been meaningless.

A few days away.

That's what Olivia had called the trip she'd canceled. Not quality time with her girlfriend. Not a chance to reconnect with someone she had romantic feelings for. A getaway. An escape from her real life.

Her empty life.

Riley was angry enough now to swat away her own words. Had they really been wrong? Olivia filled her life with her family's needs so she didn't have to think about her own. Didn't Riley have ample evidence of that? Maybe it was best they'd ended things when they had. Olivia would never put herself first. She'd never put Riley first. It would always be a struggle between the needs of her family and her relationship. Even if Olivia had ever fallen in love with her.

"Which she didn't." Riley said the words out loud because she needed to hear them. "She didn't love you back."

The anger drained out of her and Riley was back to the sick silence of humiliation. Loneliness threatened to swallow her whole. The little voice in the back of her head was quieter now, but it was still there, telling her to be an adult and take responsibility for her actions. Riley ignored it. She grabbed a bag of Cheetos and threw herself back onto the couch. She banged out a few hundred words on her laptop about what she'd seen so far, complete with a sarcastic joke that would no doubt go over the head of all the Middies freaks out there.

Middies freaks like Olivia.

She swallowed her Cheeto with difficulty.

Even a freak couldn't love you.

Before she could get lost in the hurt, Riley buckled down and restarted the show. If she really focused, she'd only have to watch it two or three times.

"If I'm lucky," she said.

She was not lucky. She watched it four times through, fluctuating back and forth between hate-watching and missing major sections because she was crying too hard to hear. She went to bed, exhausted and confused, before the sun went down.

She dreamt of dancing with Olivia in a crowd, other dancers pressing in on them and coming between them so they'd get separated. She kept trying to push through the faceless people keeping them apart, the sound of Olivia's laughter just out of reach. Her dream self knew if they were separated too long, Olivia would find someone else to dance with. Her dream self did not want that to happen, but it did anyway.

She woke with Nicodemus's hot breath on her face and his full, sleeping weight on her chest.

"Geez, buddy." She tried to nudge him so she could take a full breath. "You need a diet."

Nic woke up suddenly and kicked her in the face before streaking under the dresser.

"You're the worst roommate ever, you know that?"

Flopping back on the pillow, Riley thought about her dream. It wasn't the first one she'd had about Olivia since the breakup, but it was the most on the nose. The sound of Olivia's carefree laughter still rang in her ears. She pressed the heel of her hands into her bleary eyes.

She went back to the couch for one last shot at a recap of the Middies premiere. This time, she didn't cry and she didn't get angry. She also didn't take notes or try to come up with sarcastic jokes.

She just watched the show.

How long had it been since she watched a show with queer characters just to watch it? Not to dissect the story or the character development or the plot arc? She couldn't remember. Definitely not since she started writing for Gayntertainment. After all, she needed clicks to keep her gig and nothing brought clicks from lesbians like overanalyzing. The deep dive was her bread and butter.

But she didn't deep dive into Middies this time. Once, after the third commercial break when the pace had started to pick up heading into the big climax, she actually laughed. Not an annoyed laugh, but a real, genuine, "this is funny" laugh. She fought the urge to write down a note and finished the episode.

The credits rolled around the same time Nicodemus strolled into the living room to perform his morning big stretch in front of the TV. After he finished, he sat, his bright eyes fixed on Riley.

She swallowed hard and forced herself to keep eye contact with her judgmental cat. "It didn't suck. It wasn't great, but it didn't suck either."

The thought kept banging around in her head through her shower, breakfast of black coffee, and an impromptu trip to the sandwich shop on the corner for lunch. When she got home, she sat at her computer to write her recap, but the thought of writing something positive about Middies sent her into a spiral of humiliation worse than any she'd experienced yet.

If she'd been wrong about Middies, what else had she been wrong about?

CHAPTER TWENTY-NINE

Sweat had soaked her shirt, dried, soaked it again, and dried again by the time Olivia pushed open her front door. The hinge squealed, but she didn't bother reminding herself to grease it. She wasn't going to do it anyway.

Poppa was napping, and he grumbled when she tapped on his bedroom door and pushed her way in. He took his pills and let her check his blood sugar and blood pressure. The lunch tray on the bedside table was empty, and she did the mental math to determine when he'd finished it. She clicked up his usual afternoon dose and he grimaced but didn't complain as the insulin pen pricked his skin. He wasn't bleeding so freely after his injections these days, and she made sure to note the improved clotting in his medical journal.

"Want to sit on the porch before dinner?" she asked.

"No. I want to finish my nap."

She kissed his forehead and went to the kitchen, pulling vegetables from the fridge. She'd chopped everything and had the oven preheated by five thirty, so she went to collect Chelsea from Lewis's house. Fortunately for all three of them, neither of his parents were home, so they weren't forced into the usual tense small talk. The timer chimed moments after she and Chelsea returned. She added a thin layer of mozzarella and slid the dish back into the oven. The front door opened again, admitting her mother.

"Hi, sweetie." Allison kissed the top of Chelsea's head. "How was your day?"

Chelsea regaled Allison with tales of her exploits with Lewis. Olivia half-listened while she pulled plates from the cabinet. Twice she caught a look pass between Allison and Chelsea, but that was so common these days, she didn't overthink it. She grabbed three glasses and filled them with ice and unsweet tea. Chelsea's voice became a pleasant but unidentifiable hum in the background as she set the table, folding paper napkins into triangles beneath the utensils.

"Smells good," Allison said when Olivia slid the bubbling dish onto a trivet.

"It's just veggie pasta casserole."

"I like veggie pasta casserole."

Olivia shrugged, finding nothing to say worth the effort of opening her mouth. Instead, she searched through the utensil drawer for a serving spoon.

"Why are you still wearing your work uniform?" Allison asked in an overly gentle, almost patronizing voice.

Olivia looked down, plucking at the pungent pale blue polo shirt. She had intended to go to her room after Poppa's, but apparently hadn't made it. There was a smear of dirt on the leg of her khaki shorts and she made a mental note to do laundry before going to bed.

"I didn't realize I was."

"Want me to serve so you can go change?"

There was that voice again, the words low and slow as though she were talking to an angry puppy rather than her grown daughter.

"It's fine." She didn't have the energy to go up to her room. "I'll change after dinner."

She rattled the utensils in the drawer, banging them around until she finally found the serving spoon she wanted. There was a spot of tarnish on the metal surface and a piece of old broccoli crusted to the handle. Chelsea must've done the dishes the last time. She sighed and tossed the spoon in the sink, grabbing a slotted spoon that would be messier. Something else for her to clean up.

"Did you get any drawing done today?" Allison asked.

"No," Olivia said, scooping out a steaming spoonful. Just as she suspected, a dollop of sauce and cheese landed on the counter while she was transferring the scoop to a plate. "I was at work."

"Never stopped you before," Chelsea said. "Why isn't Poppa coming to dinner?"

"He didn't want to." Olivia handed Chelsea the plate. "I'll take him a tray after."

"He never wants to come to dinner, but you always convince him," Allison said.

"Maybe he doesn't want to eat with his sad, obsessed grand-daughter anymore," Olivia snapped. She slapped the spoon on the counter.

The room went deadly silent. Both Chelsea and Allison stared at her. She hated the feel of their eyes on her—judging her. She grabbed the spoon again, noting the little splatters of casserole around it. Olivia spooned out the final serving.

Allison swiveled on her stool to face the dining table. "Chelsea, why don't you go get your grandfather and bring him to dinner."

Chelsea didn't protest for once, just shuffled from the room while Olivia carried the plates to the table. Olivia kept her eyes down, but she heard Allison collecting another place setting. The weight of the day settled into Olivia's bones. She was so tired she could barely stand. She collapsed into the nearest chair, dropping her head into her hands.

Chair legs scraped on the floor as Allison settled into the next chair. She put a hand on Olivia's knee before asking, "Why aren't you drawing anymore?"

Olivia's face burned and the emptiness settled into her chest. She had to swallow hard before she could force the words out. "I get this sick, embarrassed feeling in my gut every time I even think about it."

She didn't tell Allison about the commission she lost because she was taking too long. Or the one she'd refused because it was a Middies piece. Whatever her mom was thinking now, it would be so much worse if she knew about that.

"But it always made you so happy before."

Her voice was soft and sweet. Exactly what anyone would expect from a mother. It should have made her feel something, but it didn't.

Olivia's voice was as hollow as her heart when she said, "A lot of things used to make me happy that don't anymore."

Olivia pressed a napkin into her eyes until little stars popped in her vision. It hurt, but it didn't force out the tears she wanted to cry. Crying would require emotion.

"Have you called Riley?"

"No, and she hasn't called me." Olivia pushed to her feet. She dropped the napkin next to the plate of slightly congealed cheese and vegetables. She stormed past Chelsea and Poppa on the way to her room and neither of them looked at her. They hadn't for weeks. No one had. Not since Riley left.

She took the stairs two at a time and slammed the door behind her. Her whole, tiny room shook with the impact, making her chest swell with pride. It felt more like her to have a temper tantrum and storm off to her room than to mope around the living room. She'd never been the type to let a breakup make her sad. Angry, sure. Relieved, of course. But never sad. But then, she admitted as she dropped face first onto the mattress, no one had ever meant as much to her as Riley had. No one had been able to hurt her because she hadn't really let anyone in. She'd only let Riley see her nerdy side because it was something they shared. Something she thought they'd shared.

Her head was still stuffed in the pillow when the door creaked open. She held the pillow tight around her ears as she called through the foam, "Go away, Allison."

The weight that settled onto the mattress wasn't quite enough to be Allison. She pushed the pillow aside enough to see Chelsea. It was one thing to be a bitch to Allison, but it was something else entirely to be one to Chelsea. She pushed the pillow off and rolled onto her back. Chelsea pulled her knees up to her chest.

"Do you ever miss your dad?" Chelsea asked in a voice that didn't sound like hers. It sounded like the voice of a twelve-year old girl, not the wise-beyond-her-years sister Olivia knew so well.

Olivia nodded because the effort to speak felt too great.

"I don't remember my dad."

Olivia's heart broke at how thin Chelsea's voice was. She wondered how long Chelsea had been wrestling with these thoughts. How long she hadn't seen the torment because she was so wrapped up in her own broken heart.

"You were really young when he died," Olivia said. She rubbed a thumb across Chelsea's clenched fist.

"I don't really miss him because I don't remember him." She was starting to sound more like herself. Logical, thoughtful. "I don't remember what it was like to have a dad so I didn't know what it was like for you when you cried about your dad being gone."

"That's good, Chels. It's better not to be sad."

Not that it was better to feel nothing, she thought.

Chelsea picked at the cuff of her leggings. "I got mad sometimes when you cried."

"I remember," Olivia said.

She didn't just remember. The memories cut into her with mingled embarrassment and rage. Chelsea had been so young, she didn't know any better, but there were times when Olivia felt like she wasn't allowed any feelings in this house between her mother and her sister. Allison's constant apologies made her feel just as guilty as Chelsea's anger.

"I'd yell at you because you were crying and I didn't understand why and I just wanted to play Chutes and Ladders."

The course of the conversation was starting to make sense to Olivia and she shook her head, even managing a laugh.

"It's not the same," Olivia said. She ruffled Chelsea's hair. "You were just a kid."

Chelsea smiled back, her look dangerously smug. "Not the same as what?"

"Not the same as me now, acting like a spoiled brat. You'd lost your dad."

"You lost someone you love."

Olivia's throat tightened, but she couldn't pretend with Chelsea. She nodded and Chelsea watched her, nodding back. "I did love her. Very much."

She didn't tell Chelsea about the pain of that. About arriving home from the hotel that night and sitting in the center of the living room floor, sick with anger and heartbreak. Sick that she'd said that stupid thing instead of telling Riley how very much she loved her. She'd said it out loud to the empty living room and sobbed. Allison had found her like that, crying so hard she gave herself a migraine. If only she could cry like that now.

"I just want you to know that I still don't really understand, but I won't get mad at you for being sad this time. You're allowed to be sad," Chelsea said.

"Maybe you weren't mad then, either. Maybe you were sad but you just didn't understand."

Chelsea shrugged. "I didn't know my dad. You know Riley pretty well."

"I thought I did. Turns out she wasn't the person I thought she was."

"Maybe," Chelsea said. A little crease of concentration formed between her eyebrows. "But you still know who you are, right?"

Olivia looked into Chelsea's eyes for a long time. "I don't know about that either."

"I think you do. I think you can be sad, but still be Olivia. In fact, I think you're sad because you're Olivia. You care about people a whole lot. That's why this is so hard."

Olivia's heart could've burst at the unrestrained sincerity in Chelsea's voice. She prayed to every deity that had ever existed she'd be able to hang onto it as she grew up. She couldn't manage more than a whisper when she said, "You're not as clever as you think you are, kiddo."

Just like that, the teasing, charming Chelsea was fully present. She hopped off the bed and curtsied in her fluffy skirt and leggings. "Yes, I am."

She bolted from the room and Olivia dragged herself off the bed to follow.

CHAPTER THIRTY

T hanks for coming. It really means a lot."
"Dude, you invited me out for beers." Dani dropped onto
the barstool next to Riley. "Why would I say no?"

Riley picked at the coaster under her sweating glass. "Because I
need to talk to you about something."

The pendulum in her brain had swung again and this time she
couldn't get it to go back. Her doubts over the breakup were so
intense, she hadn't slept the night before. She'd stared at the ceiling
of her bedroom for hours, trying not to think of all the nights Olivia
had lain there beside her. Then she stared at a TV screen because it
hurt less. But her brain wouldn't stop accusing her and now she just
had to talk about it.

"It's not even noon, St. James. You can't start conversations like
that. At least let me get a beer first."

Riley didn't respond, she just stared at the sticky woodgrain
beneath her hands while Dani poured herself a beer from the pitcher
between them. Riley had chosen the high top overlooking the beach
for a slice of privacy, but it was just as busy here as at the main bar
behind them. The only thing she hated more than the sick, guilty
feeling in her gut was feeling it while so many people could see and
overhear her. By the time Dani had a beer in hand, Riley was on the
verge of tears.

"Oh, my God, it's not even fun to day drink with you anymore."

Riley scowled at Dani, who was watching the women on the
beach. "Forgive me for letting my broken heart ruin your attempts at
hooking up with half of Miami."

This meet up had been a bad idea. Riley should've known she wouldn't get the answers she wanted from Dani at a bar. Dani had arrived wearing her most obvious cruising outfit yet. Her dock shorts were so short the legs of her boxer briefs showed when she sat down. Which wasn't really an issue since she'd rolled the waistband down until the RodeoH logo was showing. Her loose tank top barely covered more than her sports bra did.

She'd been expecting a sarcastic response, but when she looked over to see why it wasn't forthcoming, she saw why. Dani was unabashedly staring at a bikini-clad brunette walking by.

When Riley scoffed, Dani finally took notice of her. "Oh, don't worry, I'm still getting laid today and you could too if you'd stop crying into your beer like some country music lesbian."

"You're a great friend, Dani."

"I'm exaggerating," Dani said. Her eyes were back on the leggy brunette. "There aren't any country music lesbians."

"You know I interviewed Chely Wright last week, right?"

"Hot blonde."

"Nice." Riley curled her lip in disgust. "First woman to come out in the super religious, homophobic country music world and you reduce her to 'hot blonde'?"

Dani turned back to her, confusion etching a line between her brows. She put down her beer and tipped her chin at an outdoor table. Riley looked where she indicated, spotting an impossibly thin blonde bombshell in a thong bikini.

"No, I meant her. The hot blonde right in front of you. Snap out of it, St. James."

She reinforced the command by snapping her fingers one inch from Riley's eyes.

"That's it." Riley pushed her barstool back. "This was a mistake. I'm leaving."

Before she could slide off the stool, Dani grabbed the front leg and yanked it back under the table. She slung an arm around Riley's shoulder and leaned in close, finally giving Riley her full attention but unfortunately also giving her a face full of beer-breath.

"Don't be dramatic. Tell me what you want to talk about."

"You aren't even listening to me. What's the point?"

"Hey." Dani put her beer down and turned to face Riley. "Shit, this is important, isn't it? I thought you were just looking for an excuse to go out. My bad. Talk to me."

Before she could lose her nerve, Riley blurted, "Am I the asshole?"

"Yes."

"You don't even know what I'm referring to."

Dani scoffed and turned back to her beer. "Of course, I do. This is about your breakup with Olivia. The answer is yes, you're the asshole."

When Dani didn't say more, Riley asked, "That's it? Just yes? Care to elaborate?"

"What more is there to say? You already knew the answer or you wouldn't have asked."

Dani took a swig of beer and Riley bit back the urge to describe her brand of friendship with a few choice words. Instead, she said through gritted teeth, "Walk me through it anyway?"

"Your girl screwed up, but you screwed up worse."

Riley was back to wanting to cry. How had she thought this would work? Dani didn't understand emotions because she didn't really have any. She just fucked and forgot. But Olivia wasn't the kind of woman you could forget. Riley fought the tears stinging her eyes.

"Look, I'm sorry that thing happened to you. It sucks. But it did happen and crying about a shitty thing won't fix it," Dani said. It almost sounded like a nice thing someone's best friend would say when they were fresh off a breakup. Almost.

"Fix it? What the hell is that supposed to mean?"

"It means you can either apologize to your girl and make it up to her, or you can try to work your way into that thong."

"Make it up to her? I already tried to apologize to her, where's her apology to me?" Riley asked.

"You're kidding, right?"

"Do you remember how she responded when I said 'I love you'? Want me to remind you?"

"You're deflecting," Dani said. Riley sputtered as much at the pseudo-psychoanalytic tone as the ridiculous words. Dani continued in the same world-wise manner, "Remember how you were dissing Olivia's art from the start of your relationship?"

"I mean it's just fan art."

"It's really fucking important to her." Dani's eyes bored into her. They were blazing like Riley had hurt someone Dani cared about rather than someone she'd never even met. "You never respected her or the things that mattered to her. It was inevitable Olivia would find out sooner or later. Better for both of you it was sooner."

"That's really shitty of you to say."

Dani sighed and set her beer down on the bar with inordinate care. "Okay. Looks like it's finally time to drop some truth on you. You ready?"

"You obviously are," Riley said. Her hackles were raising higher by the minute.

"You've turned into an elitist snob ever since you sniffed the tiniest bit of success. You used to feel things. Be passionate about things." Dani leaned in toward Riley, who leaned away instinctively. "Now you pretend everything is ironic and you make fun of other people's passions because you don't have any of your own."

The words stung, but a part of her heard the ring of truth in them. She couldn't think about that now, though. She couldn't process anything other than how the only other person she cared about was betraying her the same way Olivia had.

"Fuck you."

"No, seriously." Dani grabbed her shoulder with a firm, biting grip. Riley tried to shake it off, but Dani had always been stronger than her. "I say this because I love you, fuck you. Fuck you so much. You were an asshole to that girl behind her back before you broke her heart."

The words rung in Riley's ears and she refused to hear them. Dani let her shoulder go and filled Riley's glass. Riley wanted to throw it in her face and storm out, but she drank it instead.

"That's the worst part of this. You're moping around like the victim when you took everything from that girl," Dani said. "You know she hasn't posted any new art in the month since y'all broke up, right?"

Riley didn't know that. In fact, she had never looked at Olivia's social media unless it was to drool over selfies. That realization made the beer bitter on her tongue. All those careful weeks of building up her own pain as a shield, and it crumbled away in an instant.

"You broke her heart, her passion, and her livelihood all at once," Dani said.

"Enough," Riley said, but she couldn't look at Dani. Not now that she knew her best friend had known more about her girlfriend's work than she had. "I get it. I'm the asshole."

"No, you don't get it because you are a much bigger asshole than you're admitting to." Dani filled her own glass, emptying the pitcher. "Don't you remember how you made me watch crusty ass *Buffy the Vampire Slayer* when we were kids? Buying the DVDs with God knows what money? I kept saying *South of Nowhere* was where it was at, but you had to watch *Buffy*."

"*Buffy* was better," Riley said.

"Hell yeah it was. And I never would've known that without you."

Riley gave a startled laugh as the images flashed into her mind. "We watched them all the way through. One episode a day after school."

"You would not stop talking about it. I would've watched the dumb stuff on TV at the time instead of devouring the classics," Dani said.

Riley picked at the peeling varnish on the bar. "I forgot about that."

"No shit you forgot." Dani took a long pull from her beer and her eyes wandered to their waitress, busy at the main bar. "You forgot everything about who you were because you're trying to reinvent yourself into someone cool."

"Hey, fuck you. I was cool."

Dani laughed. "No, champ. You were never cool. Neither was I. We were weird and gay. Now being weird and gay is cool, but you haven't figured that shit out. You're a nerd about stuff and you pretend you're not so people don't make fun of you. Then you go around and make fun of other fans. It's a sick circle."

"I don't make fun of fans," Riley said, but she knew it was a lie. She thought back over some of the things she thought, and even said, when she was at QueerCon. She hadn't exactly had the kindest thoughts.

"Not to their faces, just behind their backs. Don't deny it, you make fun of them to me," Dani said.

Riley couldn't hold her head up anymore and it had nothing to do with the beer. While Dani catalogued her faults, all she could think of was Lewis. He was just a kid and he was an effeminate kid. She hadn't needed Allison to tell her he was bullied at school. She hadn't been able to embrace her masc style until she got out of school herself. He was brave for being himself. Middies was all he had. Apart from Chelsea. Apart from another wonderful kid who didn't deserve a jaded asshole like her coming in and making them feel like shit for the thing they loved. Lewis had looked so devastated when he'd thrown that rose at her feet, and he hadn't even heard her say the words. Olivia had. Olivia had taken those words in and she wasn't drawing anymore.

"Do you really think I took that away from her?" Riley swallowed hard. In a voice she was sure Dani wouldn't be able to hear in the crowded bar she asked, "You think she stopped watching the show?"

"You want the truth or you want me to be nice to you 'cause I'm your friend?"

Riley's heart sank at the answer in that nonanswer. She felt Dani move beside her, but she couldn't bring herself to look. She had been obsessed with *Buffy* and *Xena* and everything old-school queer when she was a teenager, but so had Dani. Did Riley's words hurt Dani as much as they had Olivia? How many people had she managed to hurt with her wounded pride?

A pair of tanned legs with ridiculously short shorts and an apron appeared in Riley's line of sight. They seemed to be much closer to Dani than was necessary to take an order.

"I need another pitcher of beer," Dani said. "And your phone number."

It was so wonderfully Dani, Riley couldn't help but laugh. The waitress laughed, too, and trotted back to the bar. Dani patted Riley awkwardly on the back, her eyes most likely still on the retreating waitress's ass.

"Hey, Dani?" Riley squeezed her eyes shut so she didn't have to see the look on Dani's face. "When I make fun of fans and stuff. Do you think I'm making fun of you, too?"

Dani hesitated a beat too long. "Nah. It doesn't mean what it used to for me."

"But it did mean something to you." Another piece clicked into place and Riley said, "You knew about Olivia as an artist before I did. You were following her online, right?"

"She's hella good."

Riley felt ten times worse now than she had the night before. "You follow fan artists. 'Cause you're still a fan."

Dani turned to meet her eyes and there wasn't the usual glee in them. "I told you before. We all want to see ourselves on TV."

"Fuck, Dani. I'm so sorry," Riley said. Dani shrugged. Riley put a hand on her shoulder. "I wasn't thinking and I hurt you, too. I'm sorry. I truly never meant to hurt you."

"See. You're actually really good at apologies." Dani smiled and winked at her. "Accepted, by the way."

A half-baked plan formed in Riley's mind. An apology. A real, meaningful apology.

"I have to fix this," Riley said.

But how? While she thought, Riley was only vaguely aware of the world around her. Forms moved in and out of focus as she thought about Olivia. What kind of apology did she need? What could make up for what she'd done?

The waitress stepped back between Riley and Dani. "Your pitcher," she said, a mischievous half-smile on her lips. After she set down the pitcher, she stepped closer, so close Dani's thigh slid between hers. She pulled a slip of paper out of a ridiculously tiny pocket over her left breast and slipped it into the equally tiny pocket in Dani's shorts. "And the rest of your order."

Dani followed her with her eyes as she walked back to the bar. Riley wasn't sure she was breathing.

"How do I fix this?" Riley asked again.

"No idea." The waitress was looking back at them now, and Dani grabbed the pitcher without breaking eye contact. "Drink this."

Riley lurched forward, getting her glass beneath the stream of beer just in time. She had to move the glass a few times, following the pitcher as Dani poured without looking. She stopped when the glass was only three-quarters full, but it didn't matter. Riley needed to think. She needed to do something big. Like the wild, huge gestures Olivia liked so much. Those were her favorite scenes in all the shows they'd talked about, after all. If Riley could manage one of those gestures, maybe it could make up for what she'd said.

"I think I've got it," Riley said.

"Cool." Dani dug the paper out of her pocket. She seemed incapable of looking away from the waitress.

"What I need is a big gesture. A big, nerdy gesture to win her back. But what can I do?"

"You'll figure it out."

"Will I?"

Dani focused back on her. "Spill it."

"I don't feel that passion anymore about anything," Riley said. It felt good to admit her fear, but also terrifying. "I used to watch crusty shows and now I feel like I'm the crusty one."

"You were until you started fucking that girl," Dani said.

"Hey."

"It's true. She reminded you that you have a soul. Glad someone did."

Tears burned Riley's eyes, but they wouldn't fall. "Do I? I don't really feel it anymore."

Dani turned Riley by the shoulder, forcing her into eye contact that made Riley dizzy. "Listen to me. You are Riley Motherfucking St. James. The best person I know." Dani filled her glass the rest of the way. "Now act like it."

Riley tipped back her beer, wondering if she could find the answers at the bottom of this glass. She tried to think back to what it felt like to be a kid desperate for school to finish so she could watch another episode of a decades old TV show. She couldn't rustle up the memory anymore, though. All she could feel was the way Olivia's laughter made her heart pound harder in her chest. If Dani still thought she was a good person when Riley had been unintentionally hurting her for years, maybe Olivia could, too.

"Hey," Riley said. When Dani stared at the waitress instead of her, Riley grabbed her chin and turned it to face her. "I've been a bad friend. I'm sorry."

Dani's lips were puckered like a fish and it took too long for Riley to realize it was because she was holding her face too tight. She loosened her grip so Dani could speak. "It's cool."

"No, it's not. You've always been a good friend to me. Okay, you've usually been a good friend to me," Riley said.

"Accurate but unkind."

"You've been a good friend and I should have been a good friend."

"You can be a good friend by letting go of my face."

"Only if you accept my apology."

"Done."

"No." Riley shook her head and sighed, releasing Dani. "Coerced forgiveness doesn't count."

"Chill, St. James. Not coerced. I already told you I forgive you. Just remember this, okay?"

Riley's heart lightened to hear Dani's words. She nodded vigorously and told herself to remember how good this felt. It would feel a thousand times better to hear it from Olivia.

Dani tapped out a text message with one hand while she emptied the pitcher into Riley's glass.

"Aren't you drinking any of this?" Riley asked, following Dani's line of sight.

The waitress slid her phone back into her apron pocket and looked at them again. Looked at Dani. She looked vaguely familiar. Had Dani flirted with her before? It was impossible. Dani didn't flirt with the same woman twice. Did she?

"Oh, no," Dani said. "I need to be sober for this, but someone needed to drink that pitcher."

CHAPTER THIRTY-ONE

Olivia was running late, so she barely got the door shut behind her as she rushed into the house. Every single light in the living room and kitchen were blazing, but she didn't have time to be annoyed with Chelsea for leaving all the lights on. Poppa's doctor's appointment was in less than an hour and they'd be late if the traffic was as bad leaving as it was getting home. She burst into Poppa's room.

"Hey, Liv," Poppa said. "What're you doing home so early?"

Allison was there, too, looking just as shocked as Poppa. She was standing beside him, across from the wheelchair on his left side. Olivia bustled into the room, bending down by the wheelchair and checking the brakes were locked.

"I'm taking you to the doctor, Poppa. You know you have an appointment today."

Allison made a little impatient tut. "I'm here and, yes, I already locked the wheelchair. You didn't have to rush home. I told you I'd take him."

"And I told you I'd help. You're supposed to lift the footrests before you move him."

Olivia yanked on the stubborn right footrest and it popped loose.

"I was going to do that next. I can handle this," Allison said, a chill in her voice.

"Of course, you can." Olivia adjusted the angle of the chair so Poppa could transfer more easily. "But I help him into his chair all the time. I can do it." She bent down in front of him.

"You don't have to," Poppa said.

"I don't have the belt on him yet." Allison took a step forward. "On the count of three, okay Poppa?"

"Wait a minute. I'm not quite ready."

"One, two," Olivia said.

"Olivia."

Allison and Poppa shouted at the same time. Poppa's shout came with a small groan. Olivia released him and wrenched back, noticing she had twisted his knee awkwardly since his back foot wasn't in the right position.

"Oh, God, Poppa. I'm so sorry."

"It's okay, dear," he said. The words were strained and he kept rubbing his knee.

"Why don't you sit down and I'll help Poppa into his chair?" Allison's tone didn't leave room for refusal.

Olivia could barely feel her body as she shuffled to the armchair in the corner. She knew how to transfer Poppa into his chair. They'd done the stand pivot transfer a thousand times. She knew where to position his feet and how to ensure she didn't trap his knee when she moved him. She knew she had to make sure he was ready before she did anything.

What had she been thinking? Why had she been so insistent on barging in and taking over? That wasn't like her. None of this was like her. Not her bossiness today or her sulkiness for the last few weeks or the lifelessness that had settled into her soul. She didn't recognize herself anymore.

Olivia watched numbly as Allison wrapped her arms around Poppa and helped him stand. They turned together with perfect precision and Allison effortlessly assisted him down into the chair. He swatted her hand away so he could position his own footrests. As soon as he was secure, he spun himself around and transferred a hard stare between Olivia and Allison.

"Now listen here, you two, I'd like to know why everyone around here treats me like I'm this useless thing," Poppa said.

"You?" Allison asked, her angry stare fixed on Olivia. "I want to know why everyone treats me like I'm useless."

"No one treats either of you like you're useless." Olivia popped up out of the armchair and leveled a finger at both of them in turn. "You both keep acting like I'm going to break any minute. Well, I'm not. I can take care of everything around here if you'd just let me."

Olivia was gearing up for a fight, excitement coursing through her like it hadn't in ages, but, to her surprise, Allison and Poppa just looked at her. Then they looked at each other. Then back at her.

Poppa rolled over close to her and said in his normal, quiet tones, "Liv, angel, why on earth do you think you have to take care of everything?"

"Because you need me. You both do," she said.

They looked at each other again, but there wasn't confusion in their faces this time. They looked sad. Like her words hadn't been obviously true.

Allison walked over and took Olivia's hand in both of hers. Then she reached up and tucked a loose lock of hair behind Olivia's ear. "You don't have to be everything to everyone all the time."

Olivia just blinked. Allison looked at her with an overwhelming tenderness. Olivia looked down at Poppa, and his big, soft eyes were bulging with unshed tears. He looked like a man so full of love he could never hope to contain it all.

Olivia dropped back into the chair, her arm at an awkward angle where Allison held it.

"My silly daughter can take care of me sometimes," Poppa said. He patted Olivia's knee. "She even took a note about that Coumadin dosage change. You remember?"

"I lost the note, but I still remember the change." Allison sat on the arm of the chair, still holding her hand. "Sweetie, we love you so much. We're just worried." Allison looked over at Poppa before continuing, "We're worried you think we need you more than we do. We want you around, Olivia. We don't need you around."

A single, fat tear fell from Poppa's eye when he nodded, still patting her knee.

That tear did it. For the first time in a month, Olivia cried. She didn't just cry. Her heart burst and she sobbed. She cried for all the times she felt like she had to hold the family together. She cried for all the times she'd used her vacation days to take Poppa to appointments instead of going to the beach with her friends, even when Allison was available. She cried for the late nights and early mornings and she cried for her broken heart. She thought of Riley and she cried so hard she thought her throat would tear open and her eyes would swell shut. She cried because she was relieved to discover she was still capable of crying.

When she cried her fill and the world came back to life around her, she found her mother and her grandfather still there with her. Poppa held out his handkerchief and she did her best to dry her eyes, but that had not been a pretty, polite cry. It would take far more than a single, well-worn handkerchief to clean herself up. Still, the fabric was warm from his pocket and it smelled like home.

"I'm sorry for hurting your feelings, my sweet Liv," Poppa said.

"Me too." Allison rubbed her back. "We do need you, just not like you think we do. Does that make sense?"

Olivia nodded and blew her nose. "You didn't hurt my feelings. Either of you."

The crying started again and Allison ran off for a box of tissues from the bathroom. Olivia made her way through a good many of them before she could finish.

"I'm crying because Riley said that to me once. When I canceled plans. Maybe she was right." Olivia smiled up at them. "Maybe you're all right. Maybe I want you to need me."

"It's okay to love as big as you do," Poppa said. "We just don't want you to—"

"I know." Olivia cut him off because she knew she had to say this, not let someone else explain it. "I've been afraid. I've used all of you as an excuse. I've been hiding here in Tampa when I should be going back to school."

"I didn't know you wanted to go back to school." Allison's voice was soft and soothing. "Why haven't you?"

"Because this is easier."

"Taking care of me is easy?" Poppa scoffed. "Now that's not true and you know it."

"It is though." Olivia looked at him and smiled. "Because I'm always enough with you." She transferred her smile to Allison. "And you. And Chelsea."

"You're more than enough," Allison said.

"But out there." Olivia bit back another round of tears and whispered, "What if I'm not enough out there?"

Olivia couldn't quite keep her tears in while she thought about all the times she'd held back. All the times she'd kept Riley at arm's length. Just in case. So she didn't have to fall too hard or too fast. So she didn't end up loving a woman who couldn't possibly think she was enough. Maybe if she'd figured it out sooner, she wouldn't have screwed up Riley's admission of love. Maybe she'd have had the courage to admit her own feelings. Maybe Riley had some right to be hurt. To feel like Olivia had never committed to their relationship. Because maybe she hadn't?

"Now you listen to me, Olivia Duran." Poppa sat straighter in his wheelchair and squinted at her. "You are more than enough. And you're too darn talented and too full of love to waste your life on a cranky old man, a ditzy mother, and a precocious little sister. The world deserves all you have to offer it, and you deserve all it has to offer you."

"While I object to the ditzy mother part," Allison said with a smile. "I agree with the rest of it. Don't you dare hold yourself back, daughter of mine."

Whatever had jarred those buried emotions loose had brought every single one into Olivia at once. She'd never felt so loved, so proud, and so ridiculous at the same moment. She took in all the joy from her family's faces and really let the feelings touch her. She reveled in them. Basked in the glow. She knew with absolute certainty she was worth it. Her only regret was she hadn't figured this out two months ago. How much different would her life have been if she'd had the courage to tell Riley she loved her before it was too late?

Allison gave her hand one last tap and bounced to her feet. "I'm going to take this cranky old man to his doctor's appointment. Why don't you go upstairs and work on a college application?"

To her surprise, given the source, Olivia thought it was good advice, so she followed it. After a quick shower and change of clothes, she settled down at her desk and flipped open her sketchbook.

Chapter Thirty-two

Riley hoped the drive back from the bar would give her time to plan her big gesture. Unfortunately, she had one too many pours from the pitcher and needed a completely sober Dani to drive her home. Even more unfortunately, the two of them were not alone on that drive. The waitress had spent the entire ride back to Riley's place practically in Dani's lap, and Riley was treated to the sounds of them sloppily kissing at every red light. Her annoyance mixed with two and a half beers created the perfect environment for some brooding.

Riley was good at brooding. She had tested the waters as a teenager and practiced often in her twenties, but she had not truly mastered the art until these last few weeks following her breakup with Olivia. Whenever she wasn't working, she was lying on the couch, staring at the ceiling, awash in the peculiar mixture of anger, sadness, and frustration that was the lesbian brood.

Nicodemus was a big fan of her brooding. Lying still for hours, staring darkly at the middle distance was, after all, a cat's greatest skill. Plus, she provided a warm place to curl up and sleep while she wallowed.

She'd chosen to lay face first in the couch this time, arms tucked beneath her like she had when she was a kid falling asleep. Nicodemus leapt onto her back, pacing across her shoulder blades and grinding the air out of her lungs with each pass. He eventually settled down right at the base of her skull and swatted her head.

"Stop that, Nic."

The words were muffled by cushions, but he understood the implications, because he jumped back down. Like most cats, Nicodemus did not live up to his reputation for gracefulness. His overweighted backside smacked into the coffee table, sending a crash through the apartment.

"What the hell, buddy?" Riley groaned, pulling her face off the cushion in time to see him streak under the couch in fear.

With a monumental effort, she peeled herself off the couch and circled the coffee table. He had knocked over one of the DVD box sets she displayed on the coffee table's lower shelves. Seeing what it was, Riley laughed.

"Must be a sign." She hefted the massive box set of all seven seasons of *Buffy the Vampire Slayer*.

She'd purchased the set, stored in a gray box with red blood dripping down the sides, for a ridiculously high price several years ago. Of course, it was available for download now, but she didn't regret the purchase. There were some things—and *Buffy the Vampire Slayer: The Chosen Collection* was one of them—that she just had to own, no matter how rarely she opened it.

With a contented sigh, she lifted the lid, letting the front flap fall open. She'd intended to watch one of her favorite episodes. Maybe "Anne" or the musical episode, "Once More With Feeling." That was the closest Willow and Tara ever got to a sex scene. She'd bought the soundtrack and used to listen on long, broody teenage drives through the rural county where she grew up.

"I bet I still have the CD." She pushed herself off the floor.

The day bed in her office had a trio of big, bulky drawers beneath that Riley used for storage. Apart from the one where she stored her printer paper and manila folders, she hadn't opened them in ages. One of them would surely hold the collection of CDs she couldn't bring herself to trash.

She rocked back onto her heels and stared at the bed. Most of the time, she thought of it as Nic's bed, but right now all she could remember was that this was the first place she and Olivia had made love.

"Except it was just sex." Her throat constricted. "Because she didn't love you."

Riley shook her head and fought back the tears waiting to fall. Even in this state, she didn't believe that. Dani said Riley had broken Olivia's heart. That she'd stopped drawing. She wouldn't have been affected like that if she didn't love Riley back.

"She loved me and I fucked it up. I can show her I'm worth loving again."

The thought brought Riley back to her big gesture, but she still hadn't figured out what it should be. She blew out a breath and spread out on her back on the carpet, arms and legs spread wide.

"What can I do to win her back?"

She'd counted on Dani to help her with a plan, but, after getting the waitress's number, she had been single-minded. Not that she should need help with this big gesture. She knew Olivia best. She should know how to make this gesture work, right? But she'd counted on Dani as a sounding board and that was out the window.

"Stupid Dani. Always trying to get laid."

That uncharitable thought only made her feel worse. She'd been a jerk to Dani for years. When had that started? Why hadn't she noticed?

"Because you got internet famous and you stopped caring about anyone else," she mumbled to the ceiling.

How many relationships had she either ruined or avoided over the last decade in favor of her career? Avoided more than ruined, for sure. After failing a few times, she just stopped trying. Until Olivia. She couldn't help herself. She had been drawn to Olivia from the start. Falling in love with her felt inevitable.

She couldn't get caught in an Olivia whirlpool now. She would drown.

"Why did I come in here?"

Riley looked around, searching for the answer between the feet of her office chair, then the curtains over the tiny window, and finally on the day bed. Nicodemus's head was hanging over the edge of the mattress, watching her with a half-concerned, half-amused stare.

"Soundtrack," she shouted.

Her shout made Nic flinch back, but he bravely held his ground as she scrambled back to her knees and wrenched open the first of the drawers under the bed.

"Why do I have so many sweaters?" Pushing them aside to see what was beneath, she caught the stale scent of wool packed away too long. "I should really go through my stuff more often."

The sweaters were not hiding her CD collection, just a stack of unread novels she couldn't remember buying. The next drawer was even more of a mess. It mostly held knickknacks from vacations she barely remembered taking. In the back corner, she found a box wrapped in Christmas paper with her mom's name on it. Apparently, she'd forgotten to mail home gifts one year.

Beneath the gift, she found paydirt. A stack of cracked jewel cases from the gayest bands in history. At the bottom of the pile, she finally found what she was looking for. A CD with a pale blue insert featuring Sarah Michelle Gellar's face.

Having found what she was looking for, Riley found that she wasn't actually interested in listening to the album anymore. She tossed the CD aside and continued to sort through the drawer. There wasn't much left. A jumble of old concert tickets, some Mardi Gras beads, and, at the very bottom, a three-ring binder in a very familiar shade of vivid purple.

"Holy fucking shit."

Riley snatched the binder out of the drawer, but the moment it was in her hands, she touched it gently, with the respect it deserved.

"This is a really big deal, Nic," she said. She clambered onto the bed next to him. "This is where it all started."

Riley balanced the binder's spine on her lap and let the covers fall open. Notebook paper, overloaded sheet protectors, and creased poster-board flopped apart. Riley stared down at a collage of photographs, cut and pasted onto a page so thickly they bulged and overlapped.

Most of the pictures featured teenage Riley's braces-clad smile, her cheek smooshed against a ridiculously freckly Dani. Riley's bangs were pinned back while the rest of her hair was inexpertly flat-ironed to frame her face. Dani's hair was pulled back into a far less embarrassing simple ponytail. They both wore an assortment of ill-fitting, vintage clothing that was supposed to be cool.

"Dani had a thing against smiling back then," Riley explained to Nicodemus. "She was too hipster for that."

After the collage, there were a few pages of pictures pasted to colorful paper with captions scribbled beneath in a messy, immature version of her handwriting. Then came page after page of her teenage crushes. Mandy Musgrave candid shots and Jennifer Garner from the *13 Going on 30* poster. Lindsay Lohan, Reese Witherspoon, and just about every woman who graced *People Magazine* in her teenage years. As soon as the celebrity pictures appeared, there wasn't a single photograph of anyone Riley actually knew, including herself. It was like when she discovered the celebrity world, everything else in her life vanished.

The smiles and embarrassed laughter the collage had elicited melted into sadness. She jumped off the bed and wandered around her apartment, looking at every bookshelf, every flat surface. As she suspected, she did not find a single photo album. The only two framed photos were from her college graduation and her thirtieth birthday party. Standing back, she tried to look at her life from the outside. From the perspective of someone who came here to get to know her. If she dropped dead tomorrow, what would she leave behind?

Bitterness swelled in her. "It's almost like you're the one with the empty life."

But that wasn't true, was it? She had Dani. Dani liked her. And there had been something about her Olivia liked. She went back to her office and the collage, staring at teenage Riley to identify the differences between present day Riley and the one smiling up at her from the cutout photos. There was far too much to catalogue and hideous hair was only the start.

Riley flipped back to the front of the binder and settled in to read, scratching Nicodemus's chin. Maybe in these assorted pages she could find the person she used to be. Maybe she could retrace the journey from those tragic pinned-back bangs to the lonely asshole she was today. Maybe she could figure out where she went wrong and maybe—just maybe—she could find the way to win Olivia back inside this binder.

CHAPTER THIRTY-THREE

She wasn't getting the curve of Piper Perabo's jawline quite right, but Olivia was really happy with the sketch she was making. It wasn't for a commission. In her bag she had a half-finished drawing of the Catadora kiss and she had some ideas for a Swanqueen piece. The *Imagine Me and You* sketch was for her. She hadn't taken the time to draw something for herself since QueerCon and she was ready to be selfish with her work for an afternoon. After not working for so long, she needed this to feel normal.

She'd chosen *Imagine Me and You* specifically because of the lilies Riley had given her. She thought if she could reclaim this film that she liked but didn't treasure, she could conceive of reclaiming the rest of it. To her surprise, it was working. She'd only had to close her eyes and breathe slowly through one stab of panic and pain.

The day was overcast, swollen rain clouds hung over the harbor, chasing the crowds away and giving her booth a murky light. Since there were so few cars pulling in, she was able to devote a full half hour to the sketch, taking it from blank paper to recognizable ghosts of Rachel and Luce.

Satisfied with her progress, she swapped her sketchbook for the *She-Ra* commission. She didn't have quite the right color pencil for Catra's right eye and she thought, not for the first time, that she would eventually have to start using a digital sketchpad. Not that she could afford it any time soon.

She was lost in the sweep of a stray lock across Adora's cheek when movement outside the booth caught her eye. Annie was approaching, clutching her locked cash drawer to her chest.

"Hey there," Olivia called through the open door.

"Hey." Annie's smile looked forced and she had a telltale shiftiness to her gaze.

"What's wrong? Did you and CeCe have a fight?"

"No. Nothing like that." Annie waited until Olivia had packed her sketchpad away. "Have you been on Gayntertainment today?"

A truck pulled up to the exit side of her booth, the driver already holding out a ticket and a few crumpled bills. Olivia made change. "Not today."

Annie didn't need to know she hadn't been on their favorite website since her breakup. The thought of seeing Riley's byline on an article made her ill.

"There's an article I think you'll want to read," Annie said.

Olivia froze as the new customer handed her a sun-bleached parking ticket. "Middies?"

"No," Annie said softly. "Not Middies."

"Okay," Olivia said. She locked her own cash drawer. "I'll check it out when I have time."

"You should read it when you get home."

"I have to finish this drawing tonight. I'll read it later this week."

When she went to leave the booth, Annie put her hand on Olivia's arm. "Olivia, you should read it tonight." Her voice was calm and low.

Olivia felt the loose stitches she put around her tattered heart snap. Her stomach turned to ice and she tried hard to swallow, but couldn't manage. "It's her, isn't it?"

She couldn't say Riley's name. Every time she did—every time she even thought it—she could see Riley's face. See it smiling and laughing. See it go serious as she brushed hair away from Olivia's face. See it utterly peaceful in sleep.

That was the cruel joke her heart and mind had conspired to play on her over the last few days. Ever since she'd realized how she'd pushed Riley away, pushed her into the anger that flared white-hot that night. She didn't see the Riley from that night anymore. She saw the Riley who was kind and loving. The one who looked at her like she was the only woman in the world. The Riley she had loved so deeply that Olivia was stuck in a black pit of loneliness now that she was gone. She didn't want to see that Riley, not when Olivia wasn't sure she had ever existed.

"Yeah, it is. And trust me, you'll be glad you read it," Annie said.

Olivia slid her iPad onto her desk and dropped her arms into her lap. Tears left a wet trail down her neck and soaked into the collar of her shirt. She'd started crying when Riley first alluded to her in the article, the tears leaking out in a smooth, steady stream. This wasn't the sobbing she'd done with Allison and Poppa a few days ago. Her emotions weren't that raw anymore. She wasn't even that sad. There was a bittersweet edge to her crying now, but it felt like healing. Like letting go.

That didn't mean she could stop crying, though. Tears poured silently down her cheeks as the sun set through her bedroom window.

For the first few days after the fight with Riley, all she wanted was to forget her. Forget the pain and the humiliation. Forget the cruelty and the misunderstandings that had run like a bass line through that whole day. By the end of that week, when it had been clear she could not forget her, she just missed her. Missed her so badly it felt like a piece of her own body had been scooped out and tossed away. She'd waited for that feeling of loss to go away. It always had before. Everyone she'd ever dated had disappeared—usually less dramatically than Riley had, but disappeared nonetheless.

It hadn't gone away. The hole inside her that Riley used to fill had grown every day—every hour—since she'd left. The worst of the pain had been knowing Riley hadn't tried. She hadn't fought for them. She hadn't even apologized. Deep down Olivia had known she wouldn't. It wasn't Riley's style. She was too composed for that. Too cool.

But now. Riley's article had spoken to the deepest parts of Olivia. Had described with near pinpoint accuracy the way she felt about

Middies. The way she had felt about *The L Word* and *Grey's Anatomy* and *Glee* and a dozen other shows that had been her lifeline when the world that made her feel small and insignificant closed in. The world that Middies had saved her from. Riley had always celebrated those shows while remaining aloof. That article was anything but aloof. That article threw her right down into the nerdy depths of fandom and shattered her carefully crafted persona. Olivia had read everything Riley had written over the last few years. Never had she written anything so personal. So honest. So raw.

On its surface, the article had been a recap, but not of a show or a movie. It had been a recap of Riley's life and her willing descent into the nerdiness that defined her life. Her discovery of *Buffy* and the way she'd been embraced by that fandom online. How her queerness and the fandoms had intersected to bring her community and career. How fragile internet fame had felt and how she'd worked so hard to preserve celebrity that she'd lost the joy of the work.

The article was confessional and apology and commitment to growth all wrapped into one. And she had written it for Olivia. As an apology to Olivia. Riley had never used her name, but it was clear who she'd meant. And she'd called Olivia the love of her life. She had told the whole world she'd ruined the best thing that had ever happened to her. Was this even real? Was it possible?

Her crying tapered off to exhausted, slow running tears but she didn't have the energy to do more than mop her cheeks with tissues from her desk. She was contemplating lying down for an early night when the front doorbell interrupted her thoughts. Olivia raised her head, looking toward the stairs to see if Chelsea or Allison would answer the door. But the house was silent. The doorbell rang a second time and Olivia hurried downstairs, jogging across the dark living room.

She guessed Chelsea had forgotten her key or maybe Lewis's parents were angry again. She knew she should have checked her makeup and probably her hair before going to the door, but she didn't have the energy for vanity. All she wanted was to get whoever it was either in her house or out of it so she could go back to her room and decide what to do about Riley. What to do about herself.

The door creaked when it opened, but, for once, she didn't think about the long-neglected bottle of WD-40 in the utility closet. The sun was setting, bathing the stoop in the orange and salmon glow of evening.

Bathing Riley in the orange and salmon glow of evening. Her eyes shined powder-blue in the low light.

"Before you slam the door in my face, I just want to say I'm sorry," Riley said. "I know that doesn't fix it. I know I was terrible. I'm just asking for five minutes. Five minutes to try to prove to you I want to be the woman you deserve. If I can't convince you to give me another chance after five minutes, I'll go and you never have to think about me again. Can I just have five minutes? Please?"

She'd blurted out the words in such a rush, Olivia was having a hard time processing them. In fact, seeing Riley again, even after all the anger and sadness, wasn't doing much for her comprehension either. Riley was still stunning. Still the sexiest woman she'd ever seen. Olivia didn't want to think about how gorgeous she was, but her emotions were all over the place. Between the article, her soul-searching conversation with Poppa and Allison the other day, and finally letting herself cry, she didn't have the energy to use her head. She listened to her heart and her body instead.

"Okay."

Riley looked like she'd been slapped. She'd clearly been gearing up for an impassioned plea, and Olivia's acceptance had surprised her.

"Great. I didn't think you'd want to listen. Thank you."

Riley shuffled her feet and stared into Olivia's eyes. The barest hint of a curve pulled up the corner of her lips. Her shell-shocked stare would've had Olivia dragging her into a kiss two months ago, but too much had happened since.

"Your five minutes is ticking away, Riley." Olivia could've cursed herself. The taste of Riley's name on her tongue was still too sweet. Riley might've apologized to the world, but she owed Olivia a much more personal explanation.

"I brought this." Riley held out a bulging, battered purple three-ring binder. When Olivia crossed her arms rather than take the binder, Riley's smile faltered. "It was mine in high school."

Riley finally wrenched her eyes away from Olivia's and not a moment too soon. Olivia took a slow, steadying breath. She noticed the slightest stiffening of Riley's frame. She'd always been so attuned to this woman. The way she moved. The way every inch of her body reflected her slightest emotion. Riley was nervous now. She shifted her weight from foot to foot, and her free hand, hanging by her hip, shook against her leg.

"It started out as my geometry binder." Riley touched a faded Jonas Brothers sticker across the spine. "That was the only class Dani and I had together freshman year. Once we started watching *Buffy* together after school, we wrote notes back and forth about the episodes in geometry class. Mostly I wrote the notes. Dani actually really likes math."

Riley seemed to recognize she was rambling and hurried on. "One day, Mrs. Sharpe caught us passing notes and we got detention. They called our parents in and showed them my binder full of notes gushing about Willow and Tara rather than geometry. Somehow the whole school found out and the teasing started. By the end of the week, everyone was calling me Lezzie St. James."

"That's awful."

"And not even creative, right?" Riley tried to laugh, but it wasn't genuine. Behind the brief flash of teeth and the strangled sound, there was still pain clear enough for Olivia to see. "The early aughts weren't a great time to be young and queer. Everyone thought they were Perez Hilton with their mean names and shit talking. Even the people trying to be nice made me feel terrible. My English teacher held me after class one day and told me it would get better. She called me an old soul. She thought she was helping probably, but she said it like it was sad."

"You mentioned that in your article."

Hope flashed in Riley's eyes. "You read it?"

"Yeah." How could she possibly describe the emotions she'd felt when reading it? The hope and the sadness. But that article hadn't been for her. It hadn't been an apology to Olivia. She needed more than that. "It was really good. I'm glad you're being thoughtful about your career."

"I am. I've been thinking about my career a lot. This is actually where it started." Riley pulled back the cover of the binder, the plastic and cardboard creaking as it moved. "I hid away all that enthusiasm for fandom after the geometry incident, but I couldn't keep it all inside. I went online. Found some subreddits. Read everything on AfterEllen before it turned into a TERF wasp nest. Eventually I started posting, but I changed my screenname once a month so no one found me. I didn't want to get teased online the way I was in school."

Riley flipped past page after page of notebook paper covered in messy handwriting. She stopped on a sheet with two neatly arranged lists. Her teenage self hadn't been too worried about security, obviously, because one list was screennames like Tara4Eva and KennedySux and the other was passwords like 050702Blue.

"I didn't get teased though." Riley looked down at the list with a fond smile. "People upvoted my comments and told me I was clever. There was such a thriving fandom for *Buffy*. I was probably lucky. If I'd been watching the same shows as everyone else, there wouldn't have been such a big online community for me to fall back on."

"Fandoms can save lives." Olivia didn't bother hiding the bitterness in her voice.

"They can." Riley met her eyes. "I forgot that. I forgot all of this. I didn't want to remember."

"Why not?"

"Because there was pain there, too." Riley flipped a few more pages, stopping on a faded printout. "I had my first girlfriend the summer before junior year. That was also the summer I started writing fanfic."

"You write fanfic?"

"Not anymore." Riley blushed hard, dropping her eyes to the page. "I told her about my favorite one and she encouraged me to post it on FanFiction.net."

Olivia smiled at fond memories. "I spent a whole lot of time there when I was a kid."

"Me too. I was so excited to put my story up and have people read it. Problem was, well, it wasn't great. I got no love for it. Maybe three favorites and not a single review."

Olivia cringed, remembering some of her early attempts at fan art and the lackluster reception they received. It hadn't dimmed her, but she had a different personality than Riley. And she hadn't been teased in school because she hadn't come out yet.

"I was devastated," Riley said. "When I first posted it, my girlfriend was so excited and she told me when I got my first favorite. Then she stopped mentioning it. I couldn't look her in the eye anymore. I broke up with her a few weeks later." Riley's eyes shone in the darkening light and she shook her head like she was trying to shake the memories out of her head.

"It's not easy putting your heart into something and not having it well-received. Some of my early art was legitimately terrible. But you're an amazing writer now," Olivia said.

"Thanks." The rings on the binder snapped open and Riley slid the printout free. She held the paper out to Olivia. "I want you to have this. You don't have to read it if you don't want. I just want you to have it."

"You don't have to give me this. The cringey things we do when we're young don't have to live with us forever."

"But this already has." Riley met her eyes and took a deep breath. "I'm sorry I didn't tell you about *Vanity Fair* or Ashton Case. I was ashamed. I was embarrassed about failing and I didn't want you to know. I wanted you to think I was perfect."

"I don't want perfect, Riley."

"I know that now. And I know it doesn't give me a pass for being an asshole and saying those things. In fact, it makes me more of an asshole because I haven't learned anything from the idiot sixteen-year-old I was."

"Old habits are hard to break," Olivia said, thinking about her conversation with Allison.

"That's why I want you to have this. It takes bravery to have the passion you have. I wasn't brave when I met you. I was a coward," Riley said.

"You're not a coward."

"I am. Or I was. I was so afraid, but I'm not afraid for you to have this. Because I know I can trust you with my failures. I'm not going to keep making the same mistakes, Olivia. I want to be brave. With you. If you'll have me. I love you and I want to be a better partner. Like you are for me."

"I'm not sure that's true." Now it was time for Olivia to be brave. She took her own deep breath and met Riley's confused gaze. "I love you, Riley. I should've said it that night, but I didn't and I'm afraid."

"I swear I won't hurt you like that again," Riley said.

"I'm not afraid of you hurting me. I'm afraid you were right. I'm afraid part of the reason I didn't say it to you then was self-sabotage."

Riley tucked the binder under her arm and took Olivia's hand. The feel of Riley's strong, soft hand in hers brought tears back to her eyes. She squeezed them shut to block out her own embarrassment.

"It's okay, Liv."

"I don't think it is." Olivia gripped Riley's hand. "I've spent so long holding myself back. I've used my sick grandfather and my flighty mother as an excuse not to try."

"Not to try love?"

"Not to try anything. What if I had gone back to art school and couldn't graduate? The classes were so intense and I was so worried I couldn't hack it. I probably didn't need to leave the second time. Allison could've handled it. But what if I wasn't good enough? Instead of finding out, I just hid behind my family obligations and fan art."

"Hey, your fan art is really, really good." At Riley's words, Olivia opened her eyes and was surprised to see Riley glowing. "I've been all over your Instagram and you're fucking awesome, Olivia. Like next level good. It's not something you're hiding behind, it's something you're thriving at. I was an idiot not to notice it before."

Olivia tried not to let that glow transfer from Riley's smile to her heart, but it was a losing battle. Better than when Jodie had said it. Better than the likes and the comments and the emailed compliments.

"Most fan artists also create original characters. I've never done that." Olivia straightened her back. "But I am now. I applied to art school again. Sent in my portfolio last week. I don't know if they'll accept me."

"They will," Riley practically shouted. "You're the best artist I've ever seen."

"That's a little much, but thank you. And I hope they do because I've made a decision. I want more. I'm not going to hold myself back anymore."

"That's great."

"I'm not doing this for you or for us. I'm doing it for me," Olivia said.

"You deserve it." Sadness returned to Riley's eyes and she squeezed Olivia's hand. "But it was never a case of you needing to be more. I was projecting. I need to be more. I need to let people in."

"You deserve that, too."

"Can you give me another chance? Give us another chance? I know I have a lot of growing to do. Life with me won't be perfect, but I'm ready to really try."

"I have growing to do, too." Olivia could barely hear herself over the thudding of blood in her ears. "But, if you're willing to settle for almost perfect, I'll try anything with you."

Riley's hand cupped Olivia's damp cheek. Her smile lit the night sky as she leaned to kiss Olivia. Their kiss was soft and steady, full of apologies and forgiveness. Full of their shared hopes and fears. Full of all the love they'd shared while being frightened to name it.

"Almost perfect is exactly what I want," Riley said.

Epilogue

This is going to be the best day of our lives."

"You said that last year, Chelsea," Lewis said.

"I was right last year." Chelsea stuck her tongue out at Lewis. "And I'm even righter this year."

"The comparative form is more right," Lewis said.

"Are you sure? I'm pretty sure righter is a word."

"It is, but it isn't the right word in this situation."

"Lewis. Chelsea." Allison panted as she hurried down the sidewalk. "I'm late. I'm so sorry."

"It's okay, Mrs. Duran-Spencer." Lewis shared an eye roll with Chelsea and adjusted his backpack straps. "We have time."

"Are you sure? When does the conference start?" Allison asked.

"It isn't a conference, Mom. It's a convention," Chelsea said.

Rather than sharing yet another eye roll with Lewis, she smiled up at Olivia. The smile warmed Olivia's heart. When she first moved out of the family house to go back to school, Chelsea had been sad and quiet. Even when Olivia came home one weekend a month, it wasn't quite the same. But a few months ago, Olivia had found a set of bunk beds at a thrift store and installed them into her tiny guest room. Now Chelsea and Lewis got to come stay with her sometimes and the old camaraderie had come back in spades.

"Sorry. It's my first con." Allison looked nearly as excited as the kids.

Olivia looked over her shoulder. "Lewis, I think the coast is clear," she said.

"You sure?" He picked nervously at his oversized hoodie. "What if they see?"

Allison yanked on Olivia's sleeve, pulling her over so they stood shoulder-to-shoulder, the row of townhouses behind them. "Go ahead, sweetie. Even if they're looking, they won't be able to see," Allison said.

Still Lewis hesitated. After a minute of looking around he said, "Maybe I shouldn't."

"What's wrong?" Allison asked.

"What if people don't like it?" His fidgeting became more erratic. "What if it's not good enough?"

Chelsea turned to him. "What would Riley say if she were here?"

"Nothing. She'd just make googly eyes at your sister and probably trip over the curb." He pointed at Olivia.

"Hey, that's not true," Olivia said. Chelsea and Lewis both gave her a look. "She hasn't tripped over anything in ages."

"Anyway." Chelsea put her hand on Lewis's shoulder and said, solemnly, "What would she say after she made a fool of herself over Olivia?"

"That it takes bravery to be passionate about something," he said quietly. "And I'm the bravest person she knows."

Allison squeezed Olivia's hand a little too tight, but they both kept quiet.

"Exactly. You don't have to do this if you don't want. But, if you do, don't let fear stop you," Chelsea said.

Lewis nodded and carefully peeled the backpack off his shoulders. He was much less careful with the hoodie. It wasn't his style, as he'd told them a dozen times over the last week. Now that his parents' townhouse was out of sight behind the adults, he ripped it off with relish. Beneath the pilled fabric was a bodysuit in slashes of blue and darker blue, almost black. He tossed the hoodie at Olivia and stepped out of the too-large sweatpants he'd grumbled about even more than the hoodie. The bodysuit ended tucked into shiny black sneakers. He plucked at the fabric to make sure it hadn't twisted while hidden from view.

"There should be room in my pack after I get..." His words trailed off as he stuck his tongue between his teeth. "The rest of my costume." He growled the final words as he yanked the glasses out of his bag.

He pulled the spandex hood up over his head and Chelsea helped him adjust it over his hair. The hood fell higher on his forehead and covered less of his throat than the one Blinker wore in the show, but the glasses were authentic. In fact, they were glasses Matt had worn on camera. He'd given them to Riley during their interview when she confided Lewis was a superfan. He even recorded a video on Riley's phone for Lewis and Chelsea, telling them how much their support meant. Lewis kept the glasses in a shadow box hung on his bedroom wall, only removing them for this, his inaugural cosplay event.

"How do I look?" Lewis asked, one sneaker-clad foot scraping the other.

"Like a superhero." Olivia squeezed his shoulder. "But we need to go now or we'll get stuck in traffic. Everyone ready?"

The drive to the hotel was relatively uneventful, but the traffic did get heavier the closer they got to downtown. Taking her eyes off the road for a minute to check the rearview mirror, Olivia saw exactly what she'd expected to see. Chelsea and Lewis had their heads together, their attention fully on the printout Chelsea had made of the QueerCon main floor map.

With the kids entertaining themselves, Olivia snuck a glance at Allison. She was focused on the road, but there was still the hint of a smile in her eyes. In fact, Allison looked ten years younger.

Allison caught her looking. "What?"

"Nothing." Olivia returned her attention to the road. "Did you see Rick last night? Or this morning?"

"Nope. His daughter's visiting a college somewhere. Ohio? Oklahoma? Ontario? One of the Os." Allison waved her hand. "He's not back until Wednesday. Why?"

"It's nothing."

"Don't you nothing me again, young lady." She shook her finger at Olivia, but her smile was genuine.

"I was just going to say you look great."

"Don't I always?"

"Nope," Lewis called from the back seat. Chelsea giggled.

"Yes." Olivia shot a wink at Lewis. "You always look amazing, but there's just something. I don't know."

"You were expecting me to fall apart when you moved away, weren't you?" Allison leaned close and tapped Olivia on the shoulder playfully. "I can survive without you taking care of me, I'll have you know."

"I know you can," Olivia said.

But she didn't. Not really. When she presented Allison with her acceptance letter to return to SCAD, she'd been absolutely terrified. It was even scarier than when she'd told Riley. But they'd both surprised her. Allison by assuring her she could take care of Poppa and Chelsea alone, and Riley by begging to move in with her. Living with Riley the last nine months had been wonderful, but she hadn't really believed Allison could make it without her. Maybe she'd been wrong after all.

They finally reached the hotel, but when she pulled up to the valet stand, Riley wasn't there to meet them like she'd promised.

"Heather must have her busy with something," Olivia said. She handed her keys over. "I guess we can pick up our badges?"

"No." Lewis squeaked when Chelsea elbowed him in the spandex-clad ribs.

"Why don't you show us around the hotel?" Allison said, turning toward the building. "Didn't you say they have a rooftop pool? I want to see that."

Chelsea cut off Olivia's intended protest with a shouted, "Yeah, let's go to the pool."

"Why would you want to go to the pool?" Olivia asked. "You and Lewis are the only two Floridians alive who don't like to swim."

"But there's a bar there, too," Lewis said.

"You're way too young to drink." Olivia squinted at them, one by one. Allison wouldn't catch her eye. "What's going on?"

"Look," Chelsea said with a sigh. "We didn't get to go to the after party last year. We've been listening to you tell the story of hanging out with Jodie and Matt for a year. We just thought maybe they'd be there or something. It's stupid. I know. Please?"

Olivia melted at the pleading in her sister's eyes. When had she grown up so much? She looked at least fifteen these days. Smiling down at Chelsea, Olivia said, "Yes. Of course, we can go to the pool.

But I told you, we're all VIPs this year. You'll have plenty of time to meet people."

"Great." Chelsea ruined the moment by marching off toward the elevators, Lewis in tow. "Let's go."

Allison finally made eye contact with Olivia, shrugging in a "kids these days" way before following. Olivia chased after them, barely making it inside the overcrowded elevator.

"Sorry." A woman with horn-rimmed glasses and a face full of freckles turned to Olivia. "Aren't you Olivia? LivDraws95?"

"Yeah, I am," Olivia said. Heat spread across her cheeks.

"I thought so," the woman said. Her smile took up most of her face. "That Piltover's Finest piece you posted last week was epic. Any chance you'll have it for sale in your print shop online?"

"Not yet, but I'll be selling prints at my table on the main floor. You should stop by."

The elevator doors opened to a long corridor of rooms. "Awesome. I will." The woman with the freckles hopped out.

When the doors closed, Allison nudged her. "Your first sale. Great job, sweetie."

Chelsea and Lewis each gave her a high five. Olivia was still reeling from the knowledge that she had a table at QueerCon. She'd be selling her work at a real, honest-to-goodness fan convention and it seemed like people might actually be willing to buy it. Thinking back to a year ago, when she was afraid to even admit she was a fan artist, she couldn't believe how far she'd come.

Even better than having the table was that she was sharing it with Riley. Not only had her girlfriend come around, she'd fully embraced Olivia's work. Sure, the change hadn't come overnight, but it had really sunk in when Riley moved to Georgia with her. Once they were sharing living space, Riley saw how Olivia came alive while drawing her fan art. She even surprised Olivia with a really nice tablet for Christmas, complete with the most advanced electronic pen. Now they were even talking about collaborating on a web comic, Riley writing and Olivia drawing. Last week they'd opened a Kickstarter, which they'd be promoting at their shared table.

Allison cooed as the elevator doors opened onto the pool deck. "This is so fancy. You've been up here before?"

"Oh, look." Chelsea pulled on Olivia's hand. "Isn't that the bar where you met Matt? Will you show us?"

"Sure, if you want."

Olivia's breath caught and she lost all coherent thought as they rounded the bar. The line of tables along the railing came into view and, in front of that one special table, Riley bounced on the balls of her feet. She looked nervous, but she also looked sexy as hell in a cream-colored linen suit and dusty rose T-shirt. The table beside her held a massive bouquet of red roses and a bottle of champagne in an ice bucket. Riley was fidgeting with her pocket square and smoothing her jacket every few seconds. When their eyes met, Riley's lips parted in a wide, glowing smile.

"Well," Allison said. "What are you waiting for?"

Chelsea and Lewis added their assistance by pushing Olivia forward so enthusiastically she stumbled. It didn't help that Olivia was having a hard time feeling her feet. Or her hands. Or any part of her body. All she could feel was the insistent thudding of her heart, beating louder with every step she took toward Riley.

"Hey." Riley took her hand, her palm cool and a little damp. It was the sweaty palms that brought Olivia back to herself. Even after a year together, it still made her chest swell to make this gorgeous woman nervous.

"Hey yourself," Olivia said. "The roses are a nice touch."

"Huh?" Riley's eyes, still locked on hers, swam in and out of focus. "Oh, the flowers. Actually, those aren't for you. They're for Lewis."

Olivia laughed as Riley picked up the bouquet and handed them over. As always, Lewis blushed as he accepted the roses, but Olivia missed his stammered thanks as Allison leaned over and whispered into her ear, "He's starting to expect the flowers, you know."

"Good," Olivia whispered back. "I want him to know we think he's special every time we come home."

"These are for you." Riley held out a much smaller bouquet wrapped in brown paper.

At first, she thought they were the same lilies Riley often brought home for her, but they weren't quite the right shape. Touching the petals, she saw they were sheets of printer paper intricately folded into the bloom shapes. Some had unending rows of typed words, the rest had the unmistakable lines of sketches.

"It's some of my fanfic. And some of your drawings. Not assignments or commissions. Ones you threw away," Riley said.

Even with the tablet, she still had to do a lot of drawing on paper, especially for school work. And she still had the habit of tearing pages off her sketchpad and balling them up when she got frustrated. She slid her fingertip along one flower, twisted from a sketch that might've been from her figure drawing class. She thought she could make out the sweep of an arm in the center.

"Riley, they're beautiful."

"It's the fanfic I brought you that night. When I showed up at your door." Riley caught her eye and there were tears rimming her ice-blue irises. "The night you gave me another chance."

Olivia touched her cheek. It was soft and warm and felt like home. "The night we gave each other another chance."

"That's what I was thinking about, with the flowers. We make each other better. When we're together, there's nothing more beautiful in the world," Riley said.

A tear spilled out of Olivia's eye, painting a warm, wet trail down her cheek. She hugged the flowers tighter to her chest.

"So I thought." Riley took a step back, then slowly knelt down on one knee. "You might want to spend the rest of your life with me?"

Olivia couldn't see the ring Riley held out to her. Her eyes were too full of tears and her heart was pounding again, this time making her head spin.

"You didn't say it right," Lewis said.

"Shh, Lewis, let her do it," Chelsea whispered.

"But she didn't say it right. She's supposed to say 'Olivia Duran, will you marry me?'"

Olivia and Riley started laughing at the same moment. Riley was shaking her head, but she was still laughing. Olivia turned to give them a look, only to find Allison standing behind them, one hand over each of their mouths.

"Lewis is absolutely right," Riley said. When Olivia turned back to her, Riley wasn't laughing anymore. Her eyes were serious and full of intensity, pulling Olivia irresistibly into her orbit. "Olivia Duran, will you marry me?"

Then Olivia was nodding and crying and repeating "yes" over and over and Riley was sliding the ring onto her finger and everyone, including the strangers watching, were clapping as Riley pulled her into a sweet kiss. If Olivia had her way, she'd be kissing Riley in a very different way. She'd be giving her one of those kisses full of passion and promises that always left her girlfriend—make that fiancée—breathless.

A waiter popped the champagne and poured glasses for the three adults. Lewis and Chelsea got ginger ale in champagne flutes so they could toast along. They'd barely taken a sip before Lewis declared his intention of heading down to the con.

"Now, Lewis," Allison tried, but he was determined.

"It's okay." Olivia held Riley close. "Y'all go. Riley and I will be down in a bit."

"No, they won't," Chelsea said. "They're going back to their room to—"

The rest of her words were cut off by Allison covering her mouth with her hand again. Olivia could hear them arguing all the way back to the elevator, but she was too busy staring at the new ring on her finger to care.

"Were you surprised?"

Riley's voice held a hint of hope. Olivia was happy to be honest. "Very. I assume you bribed my sister and mother to get me up here?"

"And Lewis, too."

Olivia pressed a soft kiss to her lips. "I love you so much, Riley St. James."

"I love you, too, Olivia Duran." When Olivia went back to holding up her ring so the diamond sparkled in the afternoon sun, Riley asked, "Do you like it?"

"I love it."

"Almost perfect?"

"No," Olivia said. "Absolutely perfect."

About the Author

Tagan Shepard (she/her) is the author of seven books of sapphic fiction, including the 2019 Goldie Winner *Bird on a Wire*. When not writing about extraordinary women loving other extraordinary women, she can be found playing video games, reading, or sitting in DC Metro traffic. She lives in Virginia with her wife and two ridiculous cats.

Books Available from Bold Strokes Books

Almost Perfect by Tagan Shepard. A shared love of queer TV brings Olivia and Riley together, but can they keep their real-life love as picture perfect as their on-screen counterparts? (978-1-63679-322-1)

Corpus Calvin by David Swatling. Cloverkist Inn may be haunted, but a ghost materializes from Jason Dekker's past and Calvin's canine instinct kicks in to protect a young boy from mortal danger. (978-1-62639-428-5)

Craving Cassie by Skye Rowan. Siobhan Carney and Cassie Townsend share an instant attraction, but are they brave enough to give up everything they have ever known to be together? (978-1-63679-062-6)

Drifting by Lyn Hemphill. When Tess jumps into the ocean after Jet, she thinks she's saving her life. Of course, she can't possibly know Jet is actually a mermaid desperate to fix her mistake before she causes her clan's demise. (978-1-63679-242-2)

Enigma by Suzie Clarke. Polly has taken an oath to protect and serve her country, but when the spy she's tasked with hunting becomes the love of her life, will she be the one to betray her country? (978-1-63555-999-6)

Finding Fault by Annie McDonald. Can environmental activist Dr. Evie O'Halloran and government investigator Merritt Shepherd set aside their conflicting ideas about saving the planet and risk their hearts enough to save their love? (978-1-63679-257-6)

Hot Keys by R.E. Ward. In 1920s New York City, Betty May Dewitt and her best friend, Jack Norval, are determined to make their Tin Pan Alley dreams come true and discover they will have to fight—not only for their hearts and dreams, but for their lives. (978-1-63679-259-0)

Securing Ava by Anne Shade. Private investigator Paige Richards takes a case to locate and bring back runaway heiress Ava Prescott. But ignoring her attraction may prove impossible when their hearts and lives are at stake. (978-1-63679-297-2)

The Amaranthine Law by Gun Brooke. Tristan Kelly is being hunted for who she is and her incomprehensible past, and despite her overwhelming feelings for Olivia Bryce, she has to reject her to keep her safe. (978-1-63679-235-4)

The Forever Factor by Melissa Brayden. When Bethany and Reid confront their past, they give new meaning to letting go, forgiveness, and a future worth fighting for. (978-1-63679-357-3)

The Frenemy Zone by Yolanda Wallace. Ollie Smith-Nakamura thinks relocating from San Francisco to her dad's rural hometown is the worst idea in the world, but after she meets her new classmate Ariel Hall, she might have a change of heart. (978-1-63679-249-1)

A Cutting Deceit by Cathy Dunnell. Undercover cop Athena takes a job at Valeria's hair salon to gather evidence to prove her husband's connections to organized crime. What starts as a tentative friendship quickly turns into a dangerous affair. (978-1-63679-208-8)

As Seen on TV! by CF Frizzell. Despite their objections, TV hosts Ronnie Sharp, a laid-back chef; and paranormal investigator Peyton Stanford, have to work together. The public is watching. But joining forces is risky, contemptuous, unnerving, provocative—and ridiculously perfect. (978-1-63679-272-9)

Blood Memory by Sandra Barret. Can vampire Jade Murphy protect her friend from a human stalker and keep her dates with the gorgeous Beth Jenssen without revealing her secrets? (978-1-63679-307-8)

Foolproof by Leigh Hays. For Martine Roberts and Elliot Tillman, friends with benefits isn't a foolproof way to hide from the truth at the heart of an affair. (978-1-63679-184-5)

Glass and Stone by Renee Roman. Jordan must accept that she can't control everything that happens in life, and that includes her wayward heart. (978-1-63679-162-3)

Hard Pressed by Aurora Rey. When rivals Mira Lavigne and Dylan Miller are tapped to co-chair Finger Lakes Cider Week, competition gives way to compromise. But will their sexual chemistry lead to love? (978-1-63679-210-1)

The Laws of Magic by M. Ullrich. Nothing is ever what it seems, especially not in the small town of Bender, Massachusetts, where a witch lives to save lives and avoid love. (978-1-63679-222-4)

The Lonely Hearts Rescue by Morgan Lee Miller, Nell Stark, Missouri Vaun. In this novella collection, a hurricane hits the Gulf Coast, and the animals at the Lonely Hearts Rescue Shelter need love, and so do the humans who adopt them. (978-1-63679-231-6)

The Mage and the Monster by Barbara Ann Wright. Two powerful mages, one committed to magic and one controlled by it, strive to free each other and be together while the countries they serve descend into war. (978-1-63679-190-6)

Truly Wanted by J.J. Hale. Sam must decide if she's willing to risk losing her found family to find her happily ever after. (978-1-63679-333-7)

A Good Chance by Ali Vali. Harry, Desi, and Desi's sister Rachel are so close to getting everything they've ever wanted, but Desi's ex-husband is coming back to get his revenge and rip apart their chance at happiness. (978-1-63679-023-7)

A Perfect Fifth by Jaycie Morrison. Streetwise pianist Zara Keller and Lady Jillian Stansfield couldn't be more different; yet their connection brings a new awareness of who they are and what they truly want in their lives—including each other. (978-1-63679-132-6)

Catching Feelings by Ana Hartnett Reichardt. Andrea Foster expected to catch a lot of pitches from the Alder Lion's star pitcher, Maya, but she didn't expect to catch feelings. (978-1-63679-227-9)

Defiant Hearts by Lee Lynch. In these stories, you'll find your lovers, friends, and lesbians you wish you knew—maybe even yourself. (978-1-63679-237-8)

Love and Duty by Catherine Young. All Princess Roseli wants is to marry her three lovers, but with war looming, she must instead marry Princess Lucia to establish a military alliance between their planets. (978-1-63679-256-9)

Murder at Union Station by David S. Pederson. Private Detective Mason Adler struggles to determine who killed a woman found in a trunk without getting himself killed in the process. (978-1-63679-269-9)

Serendipity by Kris Bryant. Serendipity brings jingle writer Annie Foster and celebrity pop star Bristol Baines together, and their undeniable attraction keeps them close, but will their different paths drive them apart? (978-1-63679-224-8)

The Haunted Heart by Jane Kolven. A ghost, a ring, and a quest to find a missing psychic—it's a spell for love. (978-1-63679-245-3)

The Rules of Forever by Nan Campbell. After reconnecting at their high school reunion, Cara and Lauren agree to embark on a textbook definition friends-with-benefits relationship, but trying to keep it uncomplicated is harder than it seems. (978-1-63679-248-4)

Vision of Virtue by Brey Willows. When virtue and desire come together, be prepared for sparks in this next installment of the Memory's Muses series. (978-1-63679-118-0)

Cherry on Top by Georgia Beers. A chance meeting leaves Cherry and Ellis longing for a different life, but when Ellis's search for truth crashes into Cherry's insta-filter world, do they have any hope at all of a happily ever after? (978-1-63679-158-6)

Love and Other Rare Birds by Angie Williams. Ornithologist Dr. Jamie Martin and park ranger Rowan Fleming are searching the Alaskan wilderness for a bird thought to be extinct and they're about to discover opposites really do attract. (978-1-63679-108-1)

Parallel Paradise by Mayapee Chowdhury. When their love affair is put to the test by the homophobia of their family, community, and culture, Bindi and Rimli will need to fight for a chance at love. (978-1-63679-204-0)

Perfectly Matched by Toni Logan. A beautiful Cupid named Hannah, a runaway arrow, and just seventy-two hours to fix a mishap that could be the best mistake she has ever made. (978-1-63679-120-3)

Royal Exposé by Jenny Frame. When they're grouped together for a class assignment, Poppy's enthusiasm for life and love may just save Casey's soul, but will she ever forgive Casey for using her to expose royal secrets? (978-1-63679-165-4)

Slow Burn by Missouri Vaun. A wounded wildland firefighter from California and a struggling artist find solace and love in a small southern town. (978-1-63679-098-5)

The Artist by Sheri Lewis Wohl. Detective Casey Wilson and reclusive artist Tula Crane are drawn together in a web of passion, intrigue, and art that might just hold the key to stopping a killer. (978-1-63679-150-0)

The Inconvenient Heiress by Jane Walsh. An unlikely heiress and a spinster evade the Marriage Mart only to discover true love together. (978-1-63679-173-9)

A Champion for Tinker Creek by D.C. Robeline. Lyle James has rescued his dad's auto repair business, but when city hall condemns his neighborhood, Lyle learns only trusting will save his life and help him find love. (978-1-63679-213-2)

Closed-Door Policy by Erin Zak. Going back to college is never easy, but Caroline Stevens is prepared to work hard and change her life for the better. What she's not prepared for is Dr. Atlanta Morris, her gorgeous new professor. (978-1-63679-181-4)

Homeworld by Gun Brooke. Headed by Captain Holly Crowe, the spaceship Velocity's crew journeys towards their alien ancestors' homeworld, and what they find is completely unexpected—and they're not safe. (978-1-63679-177-7)

Outland by Kristin Keppler & Allisa Bahney. Danielle Clark and Katelyn Turner can't seem to stay away from one another even as the war for the wastelands tests their loyalty to each other and to their people. (978-1-63679-154-8)

Secret Sanctuary by Nance Sparks. US Deputy Marshal Alex Trenton specializes in protecting those awaiting trial, but when danger threatens the woman she's falling for, Alex is in for the fight of her life. (978-1-63679-148-7)

Stranded Hearts by Kris Bryant, Amanda Radley, Emily Smith. In these novellas from award winning authors, fate intervenes on behalf of love when characters are unexpectedly stuck together. With too much time and an irresistible attraction, anything could happen. (978-1-63679-182-1)

The Last Lavender Sister by Melissa Brayden. Aster Lavender sells her gourmet doughnuts and keeps a low profile; she never plans on the town's temporary veterinarian swooping in and making her feel like anything but a wallflower. (978-1-63679-130-2)

The Probability of Love by Dena Blake. As Blair and Rachel keep ending up in the same place despite the odds, can a one-night stand turn into forever? Or will the bet Blair never intended to make ruin their happily ever after? (978-1-63679-188-3)

Worth a Fortune by Sam Ledel. After placing a want ad for a personal secretary, a New York heiress is surprised when the woman who got away is the one interested in the position. (978-1-63679-175-3)